# Goblin Heart

Fae Loxley

Cover by BRoseDesignz (https://www.brosedesignz-bookcovers.com)

Edited by Ana Hansen (https://sparkseditorial.com)

# Acknowledgements

Thank you to my beta readers: Sarah, the Professor, and Dusty, as well as to my fabulous editor Ana Hansen. A big shout-out to my wife for listening to me babble about goblins at ungodly hours of the morning.

*Dedicated to the goblins of my disreputable youth: We're here, we're Queer, and somehow, we made it out all right.*

# Author's Note

This book is a work of fiction. Content advisories include: Claustrophobia, past and present abuse, slight body horror, magical manipulation, strong disassociation, violence, death of peripheral characters, insects, misogynistic/transphobic villains, oral sex, and penetrative vaginal sex.

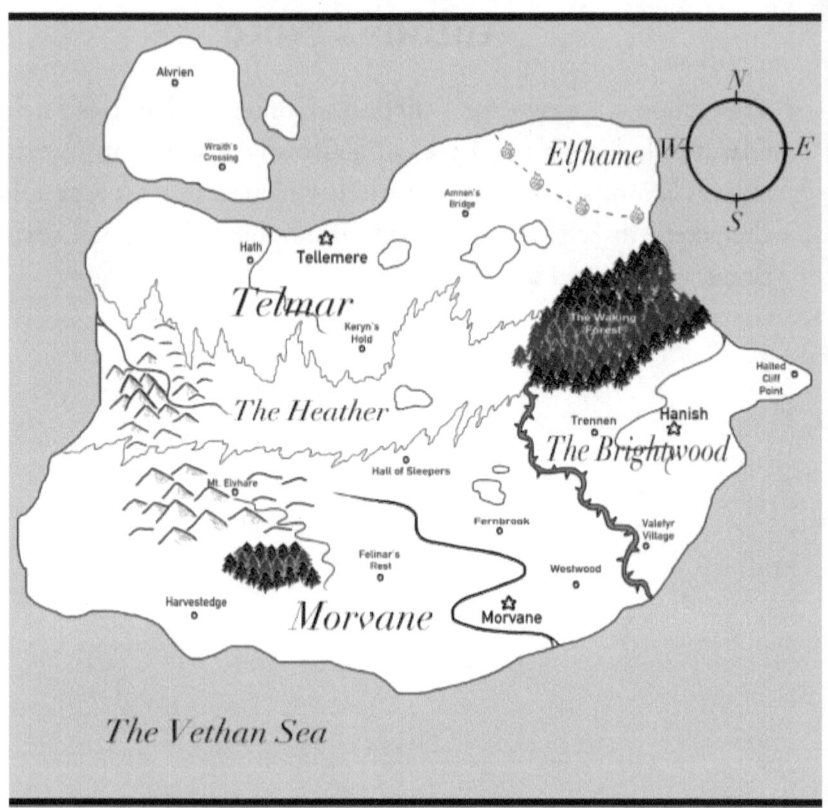
Alvrien
Wraith's Crossing
N
W
E
S
Elfhame
Amnen's Bridge
Hath
Tellemere
Telmar
Keryn's Hold
The Waking Forest
Halted Cliff Point
The Heather
Trennen
Hanish
The Brightwood
Hall of Sleepers
Mt. Elyhare
Fernbrook
Valefyr Village
Felinar's Rest
Westwood
Harvestedge
Morvane
Morvane
The Vethan Sea

# Chapter One

Spring came to the village of Westwood with all the subtlety of a runaway carriage. It tore through the barley fields, sprouts bursting through the loamy earth before the farmhands could finish planting. Toothwort bloomed aggressively in the footpaths, peonies struggled to breathe through the weeds, and dandelions choked the untended festival grounds. Birds nested in every available nook and cranny while goslings learned how to honk and hiss at passersby. Not to be outdone by this display, local barn cats had kittens by the dozens, and every child in Westwood learned to sob pitifully until their parents agreed to adopt another mouser.

Despite the fact that his mother had no children under twenty years old, Will Fletcher's family was not immune.

"Absolutely not." Halpernia Westwood, who'd given up the name Fletcher to marry Murtagh Westwood in a crumbling estate in the middle of nowhere, swept out of the drawing room with her enormous skirts clenched in her hands. "You are to give it to the girl to be done away with."

"But he's an orphan, mother!" Louisa Westwood, who'd *also* discarded the Fletcher name as soon as possible, stumbled out with a tiny orange kitten in her arms. Her golden hair was piled fashionably in whorls over thick netting to give it a domed look, but she was only half-dressed in a nightgown and a robe. The kitten looked entirely nonplussed to be carried around like a doll. "His mother must have abandoned him, or she was eaten by a hawk, or *killed* by one of those horrible goblins in the Brightwood."

"Goblins don't kill kittens," Will said, but Louisa wasn't listening. She went howling after their mother through the cramped, dark halls of their country home, trembling as though *she* were a kitten left out in the grass.

"If Papa were still around, he would help me," Louisa cried. "He'd be the first to save the dear little thing."

Will's stomach lurched, and he set down the book he'd been trying to read. Louisa was too young for *Papa* to be anyone but their stepfather, the man whose face smiled warmly down from the family portrait in the drawing room. She was also right. He probably would have rescued the kitten for her, but invoking him was a sure way to put their mother on edge.

"I said absolutely not!" Will could still hear his mother's imperious voice over Louisa's wailing, loud as a general barking orders at war. The din gradually faded as they marched through the house, leaving Will alone in a rare bubble of silence.

Will looked up at the painting over the mantel. Lord Murtagh Westwood smiled back at him as though he'd been listening to it all, too amused for his own good. He'd been painted in the robes marking him as the king's wizard, and while he was shown laying one hand on Will's shoulder, Will hadn't been there for the sitting. He'd been in a sickbed at the time, the air bright with spells to check his heartbeat and breathing, unable to do more than listen to the voices echoing downstairs. The artist had painted Will with Louisa's face and his mother's hair, a strange creature who'd never existed, smiling in a drawing room with warped wallpaper and a sagging roof.

The estate had been swimming with magic, once. The wallpaper had been carefully etched with runes to make it change color to suit his stepfather's moods. The set of bells gathering dust in the corner had once sung with clear, high voices. Books had unfolded on their own and flapped across the room like birds, following lines that Murtagh had marked on the ceiling with little brass studs. To visitors, Murtagh's magic had been a novelty, a once-in-a-generation power that had pushed him up the ranks of the king's wizards. To his family, it had been a deliberate, calculated act made with runes and complex steps, a puppet show with the strings visible to their eyes alone.

To Will's sisters, knowing the steps of a spell hadn't taken away the charm, but all Will saw were the bones of magic laid bare over every room of the house. Murtagh's influence draped over everything like a miasma, the ghost of old spells etched into walls and doorways, windows and tea kettles. Without his magic to keep the spells running, they were simply more signs of the Westwood home's quiet decay.

Lord Westwood wasn't around to see what had become of his estate, and Lady Westwood was hardly prepared to care for a kitten, let alone a household. Will had no recourse but to do something himself.

Carefully, he made his way to the servants' entrance. There were no servants to report him to his mother after the cook had resigned, and with Louisa making a fuss over the kitten, what was left of the estate would be thrown into chaos. His mother would cave to Louisa eventually, and his stepsister was probably already finding milk for the creature. She was as softhearted as Louisa, but sensible enough not to make a fuss about it. Regardless, Louisa and their mother could make enough noise for half the village. No one would notice that Will had left for at least a few hours.

The path to the woods at the edge of the village was woefully overgrown. It had been bare all winter, the grass encased in a thin layer of ice from the nearby creek. Now, weeds reached Will's knees as he trudged through the mud. Few people had a reason to come to the woods, and if they did want to cross into the Brightwood on the other side, the main entrance was only a few leagues to the east.

It was also heavily guarded. While the goblin court of the Brightwood and the kingdom of Morvane lived under an uneasy peace, the truce wasn't more than twenty years old. The king wanted a registry of everyone who walked in and out of the border, and the last thing Will needed was someone asking why the oldest child of Halpernia Westwood was crossing into goblin country.

The woods were quiet, dappled with pale afternoon light that slid over soft grass and clover. It was hard to believe that people had died for this patch of ground. To Will, it was an hour's walk through the trees, but to some king hundreds of years ago, it had been important enough to lose half a generation to war. Then another, and another, an endless stretch of fighting for a border that looked like any forest in Morvane.

Westwood itself had switched hands a few times, and the woods had been part of the village until Will was a boy, when King Tomas had turned it over in exchange for... something. A trinket from the goblin queen, perhaps. Will hadn't paid much attention to his stepfather's history lessons. It didn't seem like a sensible exchange, but land clearly meant more to kings and queens than it did to everyone else.

The path through the woods brought him to the edge of Valefyr, a small village. The houses all looked roughly the same, but there were a few touches that showed that goblins lived there. Goblins painted their fences blue for good luck, and they kept their paths and gardens tidier than the humans in Westwood.

The streets were clean and cobbled, an expense that Will's mother couldn't afford to maintain, and the bridges were sturdy and free of toll collectors. Magic shimmered in the corner of his eyes, spells to ward off evil or fire, little runes to prevent rot in a garden or summon butterflies. Trees grew closer to the street, giving Will the impression of being under the eaves of the forest, and little pinpricks of light nestled in the branches like distant stars.

"Will!" For the first time that day, Will smiled. An older goblin leaned on a fence at the end of the street. He was at least two heads taller than Will, with a hint of grey to his skin, talons instead of fingers, and the head of a barn owl. When he wanted to smile, his beak clicked and the feathers at his neck fluffed slightly.

"Hello, Olven." Will clasped Olven's arm. "I'm sorry that I couldn't come for the last few days. My mother was hovering."

"Ah, yes," Olven opened the gate for him, leading him toward the smithy tucked behind a comfortable little garden. "My parents were the same. It's in their nature to love us."

Will hesitated, his stomach twisting uncomfortably. "I suppose so."

"Follow me," Olven said. His eyes sparkled with amusement. "I have work for you. All winter, you've begged for this chance. *Olven,* you said, *gracious, kind-hearted Olven. If only you could find it in your power to let me make horseshoes for the rest of my life!* And behold, I grant your wish."

Will groaned. "I thought you had a commission for a sword. Don't you think I'm ready for something new? Something meaningful?" Olven had promised him that he would teach Will sword-making, but all he'd managed so far were more kitchen knives and nails.

"A horseshoe is about as reliable as a sword," Olven said, "except we need it more. Wars and swords come and go, but we will always need horses, my friend. It is a truth of goblinkind."

"We have horses at home, too," Will said.

"Good. Then you know not to complain." Olven slapped Will on the shoulder. "Go, my lad. Help supply the Brightwood."

"You could just tell me to get to work," Will said under his breath.

Olven was, quite possibly, more dramatic than all of Will's family combined. He wept over ruined metal, gave long-winded monologues about the nature of a beetle's soul, and laughed with his entire body, pressing his knees together as though he could barely stand. When he'd first met Will years ago, he'd nearly collapsed with excitement. *A human boy? And you aren't covered in blood or frothing at the mouth? A miracle!*

Will's mother would be horrified to learn that Will was making horseshoes for a goblin smith, but it wasn't as though Will could apply for a position in their village. His mother took her new title seriously. Members of the gentry didn't work for a living. They waited for *other* people to work and took wages from them. If his mother had it her way, they would have nobly starved to death years ago. Will's late stepfather had a pension from the king, but it wasn't nearly enough to survive, so Will worked for Olven as often as he could, and Olven sent Will home with sacks of grain for his trouble. His mother didn't need to know where the grain came from.

Making horseshoes was dull as dishwater, but at least it was familiar work. Will's father had been a smith, and while he barely remembered the big, quiet man who cast a shadow in his early life, he felt at home in the heat and noise of a smithy.

This wasn't magic. It didn't rely on a wizard pumping power into a rune or a gesture. There were no tricks to it. It didn't twist something out of its true purpose; it *gave* metal its purpose. It was simple. Every horseshoe drew Will further from the shadow of magic in Murtagh's house and into the dim, warm memory of his father's forge. The metal gave agreeably beneath Will, and he set quietly to his tasks, stopping now and then to wipe his thick glasses.

"Spring!" Olven cried, his feathers rising gently in the hot air from the forge. "The cool breezes! The flowers blooming! The bugs in the earth! Don't you feel it, boy? It makes you want to go outside and roll in the grass."

"Not particularly," Will said.

"You are too worldly for a boy who hasn't reached thirty yet," Olven said. "Not to worry, you'll learn. Don't forget to drink your water, now. I knew a boy like you, wouldn't drink his water, and he shriveled up like a husk. His father threw himself into the river the next day, you know. He swam out of it again, of course, but we were all quite shocked."

"I... I don't..." Will couldn't find the words to respond.

"Speechless?" Olven nodded sagely. "I know. Many are."

Will drank his water and stayed in the back of the forge, away from the side that faced the street. Visitors tended to stare and whisper when they caught sight of him. The war hadn't been long ago for the goblins either, and while Will remembered watchtowers burning and farms being raided, he'd overheard goblins whispering of desecrated temples and empty villages. They also might inquire with the guards at the border, and Will was wary enough of being spotted, but Olven kept him too busy to be of much notice.

Finally, when the sun sank below the rooftops and the lights pulsed in the trees, Olven called Will over.

"I suppose I am done with you," he said cheerfully, handing Will a bag of flour. "Come back tomorrow and you can do it again."

Will smiled. "Thank you, Olven."

"You are a good boy." Olven patted Will's cheek. "Short and dour, perhaps, but we cannot all be like me."

"Maybe one day," Will said.

Olven clicked his beak. "If you're lucky!"

Will left the woods in considerably better spirits than before. The sack of flour weighed him down, but he didn't mind, and a few hours of peace and quiet was worth the telling-off when he returned home. He cut through an unused field and wondered what Louisa had done with the kitten. That would be one more belly to account for until it could start chasing mice, and kittens were weak, fragile things. Her attempt at altruism could still lead to heartbreak.

He was walking in a daze, working out how to manage the milk budget, when a figure stepped directly in front of him. He stumbled, nearly dropping the flour, and a firm hand gripped his arm.

"I thought I'd find you here."

Will's smile died. Ella, his stepsister, frowned down at him with her father's big brown eyes and the mass of yellow hair, a grim specter of disapproval in an otherwise pleasant day.

"You thought you'd find me in a field?" Will asked.

"I thought you'd be walking out of the Brightwood," Ella said, nodding to the trees at the edge of the cabbage fields. "Is that where you're getting the flour? What are you doing there? How did you even get through the border?"

Familiar resentment bubbled up like steam. No amount of quiet in Olven's garden could prepare him for Ella's sanctimonious lectures. "I'm not *doing* anything. I was at the market and stopped to visit a friend." The old nastiness that only came out at home crawled to the surface. "I know you're too noble to make any, but some people like to talk to each other without trying to form the king's inquisition."

Ella's nostrils flared, and she dug her nails slightly into Will's skin. "Why are you always so horrible? I'm worried about you. You can't walk into goblin country alone. It isn't done."

"Then I didn't," Will said. "Mystery solved."

"And you can't trust what they give you. They could poison you. You can't afford to get sick again, Will."

"How wonderful that you're here to watch my every move," Will said. "Some of us are trying to keep this family alive."

"And I'm not?" Ella raised her lovely voice as sharp and vicious as Will. "Do you think taking food from goblins will save us when we're dying of whatever poison they've laced in that bag? My father isn't around to guard your sickbed, Will!"

Will's breath hitched uncomfortably in his chest.

"I suppose you can starve, then," he said, "if you're so damn set on it!"

"I'm looking after you, you wretched—"

"Oh, good job," Will spat, trying to move around her. "Very gracious."

"Spoiled—" Ella grabbed his arm again, but Will shook her off.

"Says the wizard's little princess!"

"*Ungrateful—*"

"Yes, that's right," Will shouted. "Maybe his pension would be bigger if we'd only thanked him enough! Maybe he'd be alive if I'd gotten to my knees in gratitude when I was vomiting my lungs out! What a novel idea!"

Ella's eyes went wide. At first, Will thought he'd finally gone too far. Murtagh had been her father, after all. She'd been so eager to become Will's older sister when her father had married Will's mother, and Will couldn't seem to stop throwing her good intentions back in her face.

With a surprising burst of strength, Ella grabbed him by the waist and threw him to the ground. They rolled in the grass, the flour sack splitting between them and rising like a miserable white cloud. Will opened his mouth to shout at her, but his voice faltered as a roan gelding thundered through the grass where he'd been standing. Its rider had long white hair that swayed over an expensive riding jacket, and he seemed utterly uninterested in the people he had nearly trampled to death.

"We were standing in the middle of a field," Will shouted, shaking flour out of his hair. He fumbled for his glasses in the grass and shoved them on, blinking hard.

"I think something's wrong with him," Ella said.

Will was about to argue on principle, but unfortunately, Ella was right. The rider was barely hanging on to the reins, and his horse seemed spooked and nervy.

"I'm so sorry!" That voice came from behind Will and Ella, a young man on a black horse, his pale hair hanging in his eyes. "He won't stop! I can't catch up with him!"

Will got to his feet, sighed, and extended a hand to help his stepsister. Ella ignored it, standing on her own. The roan horse was trying to buck its rider, who swayed and gripped the saddle horn with a shaking hand. His hair was longer than his friend's, and it hung over his face as he bowed over the horse's neck and slid to the ground. Will's lingering outrage vanished. A fall from a horse could be deadly, and the man on the ground was eerily still.

"No!" The other man urged his horse toward his fallen friend. Will followed numbly, trailing flour like dust while the gelding trotted off down the field. "Is he dead?" Ella's voice was strangely small. hadn't been there when her father died, but Ella had seen it all—a sudden fall from the saddle, two hearts broken before he hit the ground. Despite the fact that they could barely look at each other without hissing like fighting cats, he felt the impulse to comfort her.

"He's breathing," he said. Ella pressed a hand to her chest as though she'd forgotten to breathe herself.

The other rider clambered off his own horse. "I don't know what happened. It might be his heart."

Ella gasped faintly.

Will approached the body in the grass. The man lying there was long-limbed, dressed in expensive riding clothes and polished boots. Rings glinted on his clawed fingers, and his lips were twisted in a pained scowl, revealing sharp teeth. His skin was a dusky gray-green.

"He's a goblin," Will said. While some humans crossed to the Brightwood, no one ever came the other way. Most goblins didn't look so human, either. Many were animalistic, like Olven, or had features that reminded Will of trees or bushes twisted together in the shape of a face.

"What does that have to do with anything?" the goblin's friend snapped. He knelt at the goblin's side and started unbuttoning his shirt for him. "I know we startled you, but I don't know what I'll do if he's dead."

"He's breathing," Ella repeated, and the man flashed her a nervous smile. Ella's cheeks went a furious pink. "Or I think so. Can I see him? My father was something of a doctor."

"He was a wizard," Will said. "That's not the same."

Ella gave Will a look sharp enough to cut him to pieces. "He was a doctor to *you.*"

"He may need a wizard," the man said, too distracted to realize that Ella seemed two seconds away from murdering Will. He pulled the goblin's shirt open, and Will froze in horror.

Someone had hollowed out the goblin's chest. It was cunningly done, with a smoky glass panel magically woven into his skin to reveal what moved beneath—a complex working of gears, magic, and blood, all centered around a mechanical heart. The brass heart was coated in the runes of a spell, and a magic webbing did the work of the muscles, veins, and flesh that had been removed to place the heart there.

"Who did this to him?" Ella whispered. Her hands trembled over her mouth, and she sank to her knees next to the goblin's friend, her face dangerously pale.

"Whatever did this is weakening," Will took a knee on the man's other side. It had to have been a powerful and layered spell, but Will could see the magic that had made it starting to fade. Before long, the spell would die just like the spells in the Westwood estate, turning the goblin's body into yet another cold, dead husk. The mechanical heart would drop through his body, too heavy without the spell to keep it aloft, and the goblin would die.

This wasn't something a blacksmith could fix. It wasn't a hinge, a gate, or a horseshoe in need of shaping. This needed magic, and the truth of it filled Will's chest with a fear that threatened to choke him.

"You should take him to a wizard," he said.

"How do you know it's weakening?" the man asked, a note of panic in his voice. "I thought that only wizards could detect magic."

Ella glanced at Will, her brows furrowed. Will looked away. "I'm not a wizard. I have enough magic to see it, but this is too complicated."

Will didn't do magic. He hadn't cast a spell once in his life, and he wasn't about to start. He'd managed to keep what little magic he had a secret from his sisters, because he knew they'd want him to reopen the study if they found out. That would inevitably lead to someone from the palace noticing him, possibly even recruiting him to study under a proper wizard. Inquiries would be made, exams given, questions asked. Will's life would be pried apart, and there would be no more quiet mornings in Olven's smithy. "If you can find someone with enough power, they can strengthen the spell for you," Will said, still refusing to look at Ella.

"Could you try? I wouldn't ask if I weren't desperate," the man said. "I don't know you. For all I know, you could kill him. But he's dying, isn't he? I thought he was complaining because I wanted to ride, but... I'll pay you. Handsomely. Just give him enough to make it to a wizard."

"Will wouldn't kill him," Ella said. Her voice had the same gentle tone she reserved for Louisa and baby birds. "Right, Will? Maybe you don't... don't have enough magic to be a wizard, but it should be enough for this."

Will knew that it had to hurt that he'd hidden his ability to see magic from her. Still, the thought of magic wrapping around him again made Will uneasy.

"Maybe I can strap him to my horse," the man said, when the silence stretched on too long.

"We have a carriage at home," Ella said. "My stepmother won't mind if we explain."

The closest wizard was in the capital, half a day's ride from Westwood. Even with a carriage, they probably wouldn't make it in time. Will looked down at the mechanical heart throbbing beneath the glass, and his stepfather's words came back to him, low and calm.

*"Brass is the best metal for this. It's conducive to magic."*

*His stepfather stood over Will, adjusting a spinning brass sphere hanging over Will's bed. The pain bled through him, fierce and hot like blood draining from a wound, his pulse pounding in his ears.*

*"Just a little more, duck," his stepfather said. "You're safe here."*

*The sphere turned. A river of magic gleamed in the air, flowing up and around the sphere and coating his stepfather's hands like paint.*

*"It's too much." His mother's voice, faint through the roar of pain. "You said it wouldn't hurt. You swore, Murtagh."*

*"Hush. It will pass."*

*The sphere turned. The river surged. Will felt his heart hammer against his chest like a child trapped in the dark, struggling to get out. But there was no stopping the river. So long as the brass sphere turned above him, the magic would strengthen, a maelstrom in the heart of his stepfather's study.*

A lifetime later, Will watched a human man bend over his friend with tears welling in his eyes.

"I'm sorry, Luc," the man whispered. "I didn't know."

Ella reached out and covered the man's hand with hers.

Brass. Will tried to remember what he'd heard as a child, lying under the brass sphere with the world shrinking into a bright spike of pain. Brass was conducive to magic. It was malleable, a sponge for power. Will didn't need to use much to give the goblin a little time.

"You said his name is Luc," Will said. "Is that his full name?"

The man blinked. "I don't... I'm not sure..."

"Names have power when casting magic," Will said. It seemed like common knowledge, but perhaps there were some things that only a person raised in a wizard's house would know. A powerful wizard could work dangerous sympathetic magic with someone's name and a lock of their hair. "Did he trust you with his?"

"I know it," the man said. "But I can't just give it out."

"If his name can help Will with a spell," Ella said, "then it can't hurt to try. We won't misuse his name, we swear." She squeezed the man's hand, and he let out a shivery little sigh.

"It's Lucan."

"Lucan, right." Will felt sweat pricking the back of his neck. He could do this. One spell, and that would be enough. He'd go back to working for Olven, who didn't need Will to use magic to shape metal, and the door to his stepfather's study would remain firmly locked.

He reached for his magic, expecting it to be thin and small, a shimmering speck of what it had once been. Instead, he dipped too easily into what felt like endless depths, and magic shone in his hands like the lights in the trees of the Brightwood. He'd expected pain, but his magic didn't feel like the terrible river from his childhood. It was warm, like sinking into a hot bath on a cold day.

He laid his hands on the glass.

"Lucan," he said. He let his magic sink through the glass and into the spell keeping Luc alive. "Come back, now."

At first, all he felt was the warmth of his magic. An insect buzzed near Luc's head, a dark shape crawling through the high grass. Trees rustled gently in the wind at the edge of the field. It occurred to Will that hundreds of soldiers had died in Westwood, perhaps in that same field, their mortal hearts failing as they bled for a scrap of earth. It seemed like such a lonely way to die.

The heart shifted ever so slightly, and Luc sucked in a rough gasp of breath. His eyelids fluttered. The heart started beating stronger, perhaps a touch too fast, but no longer stuttering to a halt.

"It's working," his friend said. "Luc, Luc, can you hear me?"

"Lucan," Will said again, with one more push of power into the spell.

Luc opened his eyes. They were a pale violet, the color barely visible in a thin ring around wide pupils, and when he looked up at Will with his white hair spilling over the grass and his cheeks flushed, it struck Will that he was the most beautiful man he'd ever seen.

Then, with a low, guttural snarl, Luc threw himself at Will, pinned him to the ground, and wrapped a clawed hand around his throat.

# Chapter Two

Will had never thought that he would die covered in flour in the middle of a cabbage field. As a boy, he hadn't thought he would live past fifteen. He should have been grateful to make it to twenty-five, cabbage field or no, but Ella had been right about one thing. Will *was* an ungrateful brat. While other, more selfless men would roll over and let an injured goblin strangle them to death, Will reacted with the rage of a wild creature and the reckless strength of a man who'd spent years working the bellows of the forge. He grabbed a fistful of Luc's hair and yanked as hard as he could, dragging Luc's lovely face inches from his own. He was dimly aware of Luc's friend and Ella shouting and struggling to drag Luc away, but all Will could hear was his low, rich voice in his ear.

"You *dare,*" Luc said, claws pricking the skin of Will's throat. "Every one of you, *touching* me, saying my *name*, as though it belongs to you."

"He was saving your life," Ella cried. Luc glanced down at his open chest, his heart pulsing blood through his body as magic held together his missing pieces. His grip loosened just enough for Will to suck in a pained breath.

"You're fucking welcome," Will said.

"You think I should *thank* you for putting your hands on me?" Luc practically spat the words. "You're some kind of wizard? One of the king's servile little beetles, crawling in the muck while they play with forces they couldn't possibly understand?"

"Actually, no," Will said, trying unsuccessfully to wriggle loose. "Thanks for asking."

"He isn't normally like this," he heard Luc's friend say. "Luc, see reason. I know you've had a shock, but the fellow did keep your heart beating. And he isn't a wizard, he lives with one. Or lived?"

"My father passed away ten years ago, sir," Ella said, as quietly as a well-bred girl whose stepbrother *wasn't* being throttled by the most attractive goblin in Morvane.

"Oh. I'm terribly sorry."

Will caught Luc making the same disbelieving expression he always made at Ella. A flicker of shame appeared in Luc's eyes, and he released Will's throat.

"Don't touch me again."

"I assure you," Will said, "if this is what happens when I save you, I'll let you die next time."

"I'm sorry about Will," Ella told Luc's friend. "He has a horrid disposition at the best of times. You can call me Ella."

"My friends call me Ramon," Luc's friend said, bowing over Ella's hand.

"I'm fine, thank you," Will said, getting to his feet. Luc gave him a sharp look and strode off toward the gelding, which was happily tearing up dandelions at the edge of the field. Ramon tried to reach for him, but he moved swiftly out of his grasp. "You could have warned me that he'd try to kill me."

"I'm as surprised as you are," Ramon said, watching Luc anxiously. "It must have been the shock. I'll be sure to come round with him to apologize when he's recovered."

"No," Will said, a little too quickly.

"We have guests," Ella said, smoothing out her dress with both hands.

Will caught Ella's eye. With Will disappearing to run off to the Brightwood and most of the servants gone, he knew that Ella was left with the lion's share of the chores. If an attractive, wealthy young man called on the house, Will's mother would probably send Ella off to the kitchen to prepare tea while Louisa grimaced and tried to parrot her etiquette lessons.

"They've taken over most of the house, I'm afraid," Will said, as Ella gave him the stare of someone trying to invent telepathy just to say, *don't you ruin this for me, William Fletcher.*

"Perhaps I'll send a letter, then," Ramon said. He winked at Ella. "To thank the charming young lady who helped rescue my friend."

Ella blushed deeper still and mumbled so softly that Will barely heard her say, "The Westwood estate, my lord."

"Oh!" Ramon's expression brightened. "Wizard Westwood was your father? I met him when I was a boy. He used to make those lovely little illusions of a running horse."

"A unicorn," Ella said, "with stripes on its back."

Ramon beamed. "That's right. He must have made it with you in mind. You have the look of someone who would tame a unicorn."

Will preferred being strangled to listening to Ramon compliment his stepsister for looking like a virgin. He went to check on the fallen bag of flour, but the wind had tossed the rest of it over the field. He stared down at it dispassionately, wondering if Olven would understand if he explained that he'd been run down by a dying goblin on horseback.

"That was yours?" Luc walked toward him with the offending horse, which seemed about as remorseful as his rider.

"No," Will said sarcastically, "it came from the sky. I just happened to be walking under it when you rode me down." He paused, looking at Luc's chest. Luc had done up his buttons again, hiding the glass panel from view. "If I hurt you, it wasn't intentional. I've never used magic before."

"It was fine," Luc said. He stood there for a few seconds, staring at his expensive boots. "It's already fading. I'd forgotten what it felt like."

"Pain?" Will asked, curious. "Is that what your heart does? It removes pain?"

"It isn't my heart," Luc said, and turned to lead his horse back to Ramon.

Will watched them from the mess of spilled flour. The sun was sinking below the horizon, and a cold wind blew over the fields, making Ella's long hair wrap around her face. Ramon raised a hand to push it out of her eyes, and when Luc approached, he smiled with a warmth that made Will's chest ache. They looked like old friends, Ramon snaking an arm around Luc's waist, Luc leaning into his touch as Ramon and Ella fussed over him. If Will could only suppress the sardonic brat that took hold of his tongue every time someone came close, perhaps he could be a part of that. Instead, he stood off to the side, waiting for Luc and Ramon to walk their horses toward the village.

Ella strode over, holding her hair back out of the wind. "Weren't they *noble?*"

A kinder man would have agreed. "When one of them isn't trying to kill me."

"He did apologize," Ella said, which was untrue, unless Luc had apologized to *her.* "Thank you, by the by. I don't think I could bear it if Ramon arrived at the house when I'm up to my arms in soap suds. I know we don't always get along..."

"Ever," Will said, ruining the moment again. He sighed and started off toward the estate. "You did save me from being trampled."

"But Will—" Ella hurried to keep up with him. "You've had magic this whole time? You could have opened Father's study. You know he wouldn't have minded. He adored you."

Will was thankful for the darkness sweeping over Westwood, hiding his face in shadow. "It would be too dangerous, Ella."

"But magic isn't dangerous. It's wonderful."

"You'd think that," Will said. "You're the daughter of a wizard, after all."

"And you're the son of one," Ella insisted.

"Stepson," Will snapped, with too much force. Ella blanched. "And not according to the king, in any case. Women can't practice magic, can they?"

"What does that have to do with..." Ella went silent for a few paces. "Oh. Oh, it's been so long, I'd forgotten."

Will supposed that was a compliment. Ella had only been around eleven or so when Will stopped going by his old name. Ella's father had moved Will into his study to better monitor him, and after fighting him like a polecat every time he came close, Will had agreed on one condition.

"If I'm going to die, I might as well die as a boy," he'd said. His mother had been shocked by the ultimatum, but his stepfather had barely reacted. He'd long since stopped assuring Will that he wasn't about to die, so perhaps he'd been tired of fighting him every step of the way.

"The goblin court allows it," he'd said to Will's mother, once again talking over him as though he weren't in the room. "But I suppose one's gender doesn't matter so much when you look the way they do."

"James." Halpernia's voice had been strained. "The king has views on the gentry obscuring their children's sex."

"Well, he owes me a favor or two if it comes out, and there's no reason for anyone to know. Let the boy do what he likes."

It hadn't taken much to convince Will's mother after that. She may not have understood the intricacies of goblin customs, or even human ones, but she claimed to love her children. Or she loved most of them, Will thought. She'd never warmed up to Will's stepsister, no matter how agreeable Ella tried to be.

Being called *Will* hadn't meant much when he'd been confined to his bed. Afterward, Halpernia told guests that her eldest daughter was still in the sickroom upstairs while Will passed himself off as a distant cousin.

"I never understood the law against witchcraft," Ella said as they cut through a small farm toward the road. "I asked my father what separated a woman's magic from a man's, and he went into this long-winded lecture about soft magic and hard magic and different methods of detecting it. He said that a woman's magic is too intuitive. It doesn't follow the runes you need to channel magic properly, so the spells fail."

"That sounds like him," Will said. "But I didn't use runes back there, and Luc seemed fine."

"But there were already runes in the spell," Ella said. "You were just giving them power. That's what magic is, most of the time, laying a path for magic to take. I don't see why..." she paused delicately, "what lies between one's legs... matters in the slightest."

"Well, aren't you a radical?"

The crickets in the bushes stopped singing as full dark crept over the countryside. Stars spread over the sky, the moon a pale crescent, and the high roof of their home cut a black silhouette against it all. A fat, jewel-toned beetle flicked its wings at them from a moss-covered bench and took off, buzzing softly, toward the house.

"I can get the key to his study," Ella said at last, "if you wanted to look inside. I won't tell anyone."

Will didn't answer.

"It's all right to miss him," Ella said. "You were closer to him than almost anyone. I don't begrudge you that, even if you think I do."

It probably stung that he had spent more time with Ella's father than she had, toward the end. He knew she was holding it out as a peace offering. He just couldn't accept it.

"Mother will probably be furious," he said, keeping his gaze straight ahead. "Let me try and calm her down."

Ella sighed, but thankfully didn't press the subject. Will pushed open the front door, greeting the cold, dark hallways of their family home in time for his mother to come sweeping down the stairs.

"Girl!" She cried, turning her hard gaze to Ella. "Where have you *been?* I've been calling all night for water and—oh!" Her face fell into the pitying, simpering expression she always made when she saw Will. "My darling, what happened to you? You're a mess! Did that wretched girl do something to you? Oh, oh, let me see you..." She grasped Will's face in both hands, and Will glanced at Ella.

She fled wordlessly, leaving Will behind with his frantic mother, a suitable sacrifice in the chaos that was life in the Westwood estate.

***

"Are you certain that you're all right, Luc?"

Lucan leaned back in his chair as Faramond of Gratton, crown prince of Morvane and the most good-natured creature ever made, pretended to swing a sword at invisible adversaries. Ramon was an atrocious duelist, but no one had the heart to tell him that, and he grinned as he stuck ghosts through the heart and spun like an inebriated dancer. His light hair was pushed up in a coif, which bobbed nervously every time he tried to lunge.

"I'm only bruised a bit, that's all," Luc said. Warm sunlight from the window draped his back like a cloak. King Tomas liked to say that goblins preferred the dark, but Luc was drawn to warmth, clinging to the hearth in winter and sunning himself like a cat in the spring. He tipped his head back to let the light fall on his face.

"Yes, you do seem more like yourself now." Ramon flopped into a chair beside him. "That was a nasty shock, I won't deny it."

"Mm." Luc pushed Ramon's hand away without looking, correctly assuming that he would try fussing over his heart. "Leave it, Ramon. That country wizard put enough magic into it to last me a while."

"Strange, though," Ramon said. "You'd think the Westwoods would tell us if they had a wizard in their household. Lady Westwood is always petitioning my father for money these days, and I heard she's been selling their farmland to the Godens. Rather gauche of her."

Luc glanced at Ramon sidelong. The trouble with being a prince, he thought, was that no one cared to teach princes anything practical. Ramon knew how to waltz and do the quadrille. He spoke several languages fluently, had a fascination with a rare variety of finch, could recognize a set of teacups from Telmar by touch, and had a truly dizzying knowledge of every noble household in Morvane. However, he didn't know anything about how the country actually worked. He knew nothing of economics or trade, and while sausages and eggs arrived on his plate like magic every morning, he hadn't a clue how any of it got there.

Admittedly, neither did Luc. But Luc wasn't a prince of anything, not anymore.

That should have bothered him. It *had* bothered him, as he'd lain on his back in a field not three leagues from the Brightwood. That strange wizard's magic had flown into him, searing through his body like a wildfire, and bitter resentment had boiled through his body. It had been like a physical wave of rage, cold and hot at the same time, building in one terrible rush as his false heart pounded and his lungs heaved.

Luc hadn't felt anger like that for almost twenty years.

He tried to call it up again, thinking of the way his claws had pricked that man's skin. Will, Ramon had called him. A small man, with black hair and a round face fixed in a scowl, hands flexing over his heart. *Touching* him. Wizards were always touching him. Opening him up, playing with his guts, calling him a good boy, a patient boy, such a sweet companion to dear Faramond.

Will hadn't considered him good or patient. He'd fought back like a cat in a sack, and every sulky look and sarcastic comment had stoked the fury inside Luc, stirring emotions he hadn't felt since he'd been a boy.

"Who was that man?" Luc asked. "The one who saved me."

"Will? I think he's some relation to that jolly girl," Ramon said. "The pretty one. Gosh, Luc, the way she smiled! I never thought that I cared much about dimples on a woman before, but I do when they're on her. *And* she's the daughter of the wizard who saved you the first time. Lucky chance, isn't it?"

Luc examined Ramon's open, honest face. "Yes," he said. "Lucky."

"She'd make a nice mistress, wouldn't she?" Ramon asked. "But she's noble, so there are rules about arranging something like that. A shame I'll never marry."

Luc sighed. "Ramon. We've been over this."

"Yes, I know, you *and* my father *and* my mother. Even mousy little Felicity won't leave me alone. But why should I plan to have a queen already?" Ramon sunk down in his chair like a sulking child. "I'd like a few more years of freedom before Father shackles me to the throne. You have no idea how blessed you are, Luc, not having to worry about that anymore."

Luc smiled thinly. Inheritance in the goblin court wasn't patrilineal. He'd been the seventh in line for the crown, but King Tomas hadn't considered that a queen might want her eldest daughter to inherit. In the king's mind, Luc had been his mother's last chance at an heir to the throne.

He must have thought Luc's mother was all too desperate to end the war, handing over her only son in exchange for peace. Luc barely remembered the journey to Morvane; it had all been a blur of carriage rides, long hours waiting for diplomats to talk in hushed voices in closed rooms, and finally, the kind, spectacled face of Wizard Westwood.

"You probably shouldn't bother with the Westwood girl," Luc said.

"Now, don't you start lecturing me too," Ramon said with a laugh. "You're supposed to be on *my* side." Someone knocked on the door, and Ramon groaned. "Kick them down the stairs, will you?"

"I already had my fill of violence for the year, thanks." Luc ignored Ramon's playful attempt to trip him and opened the door. A guard stood there in the white and blue colors of the king's wizards, and an unpleasant jolt of fear struck Luc. He resisted the urge to slam the door in the guard's face.

"The king's wizards would like to take a look at your heart, my lord," the guard said.

"Good," Ramon said. "It's about time. We've been home for hours without a peep from you lot. You do know that his heart almost stopped? He could have died."

"Yes, Your Highness." The guard's polite expression didn't waver.

"Make sure he's healthy enough to ride," Ramon added, as the guard gestured for Luc to step into the hall. "The way back to Westwood will be dreadful without you, Luc."

"Spoiled brat," Luc said.

"If I am, you're the one spoiling me." Ramon grinned at him as Luc closed the door. Luc turned to the guard, who waved a hand ahead of him.

"If you'll please, my lord."

Luc's chest felt unnaturally heavy as he made his way down the hall. It wasn't the weight he'd felt the last few days before his fall, when even breathing had been a struggle. This was a different feeling, another old emotion rising to the surface, and it took Luc a few minutes to recognize it as dread. He was familiar with fear, but this was deeper, darker, the same twisting agony he'd felt on the carriage ride out of the Brightwood long ago.

The king's wizards usually worked in the lower levels of the palace, but they always met Luc in a bright, sunny room on the first floor. The scent of jasmine wafted through the open window as

Luc entered, and Aengus, the youngest wizard in the king's employ, turned from his desk with a smile.

"Hallo, Luc! How are we feeling?"

"Quite well, thank you," Luc said, forcing a smile.

"Too stilted." Berenger, Westwood's former assistant, walked in through a connecting door. His dark hair was thinning at the top, and he didn't have Aengus' easy, comfortable manner. "Pay attention to the tone of voice, Aengus. Sit down, Luc."

Luc slowly pulled up a chair and sat. The workroom looked more like a student's study than a place for wizardry, with messy bookshelves, desks piled with papers, and open inkwells everywhere. Berenger nodded to Luc, and Luc's shirt fell open without warning, making him flinch back.

"Nervy," Berenger said. "I suppose you would be. Why didn't you tell us when you started feeling pain?"

"I mentioned it to Ramon once or twice," Luc said. "I don't know. I don't think I wanted to be any trouble."

"We'll need to fix that," Aengus said. "Should I summon it now?"

"Might as well." Berenger pulled a chair in front of Luc and sat, peering at Luc's chest. "I *know* that Westwood told you that going too close to the Brightwood will affect the spell holding your heart up, but I suppose the prince must be obeyed. We'll try to help you there, but it's best to avoid the border entirely."

"I'll remember that," Luc said. It wasn't as though he could pass through the border without breaking the treaty, but he didn't doubt that Westwood had arranged the spell to fall apart if he tried. He couldn't hold back a grimace at the thought.

Aengus shook his head and made a note in his journal, and Berenger sighed as though Luc were a toddler throwing a tantrum on the study floor. "Another thing, Lucan. We know you were in dire straits, but in the future, don't let another wizard touch you. Their intentions can influence their magic, and this is a delicate spell." He pressed a hand on the glass panel. "And it seems as though they have. His highness said that you didn't behave particularly well afterward."

"It was the shock," Luc said.

"You do know that I can see your heart beating faster," Berenger said. "Not to worry. Let me see the phylactery, Aengus."

Luc gripped the arms of his chair as Aengus whispered a spell under his breath, summoning a small, green glass jar. Luc had seen him do it countless times, but he could never tell where it came from. Aengus always summoned it from elsewhere, goosebumps rising on his skin as though the jar were bringing a pocket of cold air from where it had been stored. Something moved inside, obscured by filmy liquid, but its nearness made Luc's brass heart race and his mouth go dry.

It was his heart, his true heart, trapped behind glass for almost twenty years. It spun gently in the phylactery in Aengus' hands.

"Oh, dear," Berenger said, as Luc trembled, gaze fixed on his heart. They shouldn't touch it, he thought, fear and rage twisting as Berenger took the glass. They weren't supposed to touch it. That was his. *His* heart. It had been taken from him, *stolen* by that smiling, false, monstrous wizard with his level voice and steady hands.

"Be still," Berenger said, and Luc sagged in the chair. He tried to drag himself up, but his body wouldn't listen. "No unpleasant thoughts, Lucan. No anger, no resentment. You're glad to be here. You're *grateful.* You want us to help you."

Luc's breath hitched, and he struggled against the magic coursing through his body. If a wizard's magic left impressions on a spell, then that meant Will, with his sullen countenance and cutting words, was still in there somewhere. He could fight it.

"You want to be good," Berenger said. It was the same thing Westwood had said the first time, when Luc had been howling in pain on the lid of a brass box in another workroom, his heart beating in Westwood's right hand. "You've only ever loved Prince Faramond and his family."

Luc felt the dread and terror slipping away as a foreign, overwhelming compassion drowned them out. When Luc had been a boy, new to the capital and unable to fight like his sisters or mother, King Tomas had stared down at Luc with nothing but cold, hard calculation in his eyes.

"Make him loyal," he'd said. "Faramond could use a friend."

Luc clenched his eyes shut. When he opened them again, he was sitting in his chair with the king's wizards, a warm, gentle pleasure settling into his bones. Aengus took the heart, and it disappeared in a swirl of magic.

"There we go," Berenger said, patting Luc's knee. "How do you feel, my boy?"

Luc smiled. "Much better," he said, getting to his feet. "Thank you. If you don't need me anymore, I'd best check on Ramon. He'll start swinging that sword around again if someone doesn't stop him."

"You're a good boy, Luc," Berenger said. "Let us know if that heart of yours gives you any trouble."

"Of course," Luc said, and strolled out the door, breathing in the scent of jasmine from the courtyard. He couldn't imagine why he'd been so unnerved a moment before. The fall had been a fright, of course, and magic could be unsettling at times, but all things considered, Ramon was right. He truly *did* have a blessed life.

# Chapter Three

Luc was almost seven years old when the war ended. He only knew how the fighting was going by the tension in his sisters' eyes and the grim silence that followed his mother like a cloak, and tensions had been running high for months. When his second-oldest sister, Alara, reappeared from a skirmish at the border with a missive from the king of Morvane in her hands, Luc thought that it might finally be over. Later that day, he waited with his sisters in the hall outside his mother's study while Alara, his mother, and Crown Princess Jade spoke in increasingly heated tones on the other side of the door.

"If you do this, the crown goes to Alara," Jade said, and Crys, the second youngest next to Luc, sat up straight. Wren and Mina looked like they wanted to rise, but Lily whispered something and gestured to Luc. Luc obediently scooted off the bench and went to join her. She looked the most like their mother, with a wide-set jaw and dark violet eyes, and she adjusted Luc's collar absently.

"You know that Mother has been working very hard lately, Luc." Luc nodded.

It seemed that all their mother ever did was hide away in meetings with her advisors. Jade had been the one to take over arranging tutors and ensuring that he wasn't forgotten in the nursery. She'd even taught him how to play Whist, a board game with colorful marbles that ran down a slot in the wood whenever someone scored a point. Mothers, in Luc's expert opinion, were too stern and disapproving for ordinary life. Sisters were far more interesting.

"Don't tell me to lower my voice," Jade said from the other side of the wall. "He isn't something you can trade, Mother. He's a child!"

"Mother has just been—" Lily flinched when something thumped in the study. "She's been a little..."

"He is my son, Jade." Luc's mother didn't raise her voice, but it cut through the air like a blade. "I'll ask you to remember that."

"He's *mine,*" Jade said. Luc's sisters went still as a line of well-dressed statues. "He was never yours. He's mine. *I* raised him while *you* sent Alara and Wren off to fight in your war."

Luc felt his throat go tight. He didn't know why, but they were fighting over him. A terrible, stomach-wrenching guilt rose to his chest, and Luc tried unsuccessfully to brush away the tears that pricked at his eyes.

"Let's go to the library," Lily suggested.

"A novel idea," Wren said, grabbing Crys' hand. She held out her other hand for Luc, but before he could take it, the door slammed open.

Jade stood in the doorway, looking like the old paintings of the warrior goddess who'd tricked elven god-kings into falling asleep in a river of heather. Her short white hair curled around her ears, and her eyes blazed with barely restrained rage as she walked up to Luc.

"You'll be good?" she asked. "You'll be grateful?"

But that hadn't been what had happened at all. She'd said something else, hadn't she? Something important. Something he wasn't supposed to forget. But the memory was unpleasant, full of anxiety and rising dread, and Luc wasn't allowed to have unpleasant feelings.

"Did I ever tell you about my sister?" Luc asked. They were in Ramon's carriage, trundling down the quaint, weed-strewn roads of Westwood village. He felt the words trail lazily over his tongue, pushing through the warm, comfortable fog in his mind.

"Of course you did," Ramon said with a chuckle. He was in his finest clothes, no doubt to impress that waifish girl they'd met the week before. Their diversion to the country had clearly been a weak excuse to wander toward Westwood, but Luc could hardly refuse him. "Which one? Don't you have eighteen of them?"

"Six," Luc said, tracing a circle on the seat cushion with a curved nail. They weren't claws, but they were thick and sharp enough to be mistaken for them. Foot soldiers used to file theirs to razor-sharp points in the war, slicing through human bellies to expose their hot, heaving innards. Luc kept his blunted. He didn't want to hurt Ramon by mistake

"I can't imagine having that many sisters," Ramon said. "Felicity stays out of the way, at least, but five more of her and she might actually be loud enough to annoy me. And no brothers, thank you. You're enough for my liking." He peered out the carriage window. "What were they like?"

"I loved one of them," Luc said. "Or I loved all of them, but one was..." He tried to find the words, but they slipped away. No unpleasant thoughts, the wizards had said.

"You've been rather distracted lately," Ramon said. "Do try to focus, Luc. I know your people never leave the Brightwood, but we should invite her to the palace. What's her name?"

Luc gazed out the window. The thought of seeing his eldest sister again made something strange push against the fog, and Luc dimly remembered the heat that had consumed him when he'd held that country wizard down by the throat.

He was meant to be good, but there was one small part of him that remained obstinate, and it was connected to the wizard who'd sunk his magic into the inner workings of Luc's heart.

"Will," he said, and Ramon looked up at him with confusion.

"Your sister's name is Will?"

"No. No, I mean that man. The wizard. He'll be at the Westwood house?"

"I hope so," Ramon said, settling back into his seat. "You owe him an apology, after all."

"Yes," Luc said, as a small, forbidden feeling struggled for air in the depth of his mind. "Yes, I do."

***

Halpernia and Louisa Westwood never did anything by halves. It didn't matter that the house was falling into disrepair, that no one in the village would work for them anymore, or that they'd sold all but two of the horses. They were determined to spend the week with Great Aunt Alberta in the capital, and that meant dredging their closets for anything remotely fashionable. They spent all morning fussing about their clothes and the state of the carriage until Will, thoroughly at his limit, strode outside with a book while Ella ran up and down the stairs with bags and last-minute additions.

"And don't forget to clean the kitchen," Will heard his mother shout from the carriage. "We can't afford to let things go to ruin, girl."

"Maybe she should clean *herself* first," Louisa said. "It looks like she's been sleeping in the fireplace again."

Will guiltily caught Ella's eye. Louisa had a point; Ella was a mess. Her hair was unkempt, her gown was streaked with water from the garden pump, and her knuckles were pink from scrubbing dishes. Will could feel her gaze piercing into him, and he hastily closed his book.

"Try not to overexert yourself, my love," his mother called to him. She rapped the carriage roof, and the hired driver led the horses down the overgrown path into town.

"I should probably get started now," Ella said, smoothing out her dress.

Will hovered a few paces away, awkward and unsure. "You don't *have* to help them."

Ella just sighed. "You wouldn't understand. You're under no obligation to help anyone."

"Neither are you." Will followed Ella inside. "Look, I can make tea, and you can let the kitchen be for a few days while I head to the market."

"You mean sneak into the Brightwood," Ella said. "And I can't simply let it be. Your mother left me with a list of chores I need to finish before she gets back, and I'll barely have time to feed that poor kitten, let alone have tea."

"Don't be ridiculous," Will said. "Mother wouldn't saddle you with everything."

"You wouldn't know," she said. "You're never here even when you're home."

"That's not true," Will protested. He spotted Ella looking pointedly at his book and shoved it under one arm. "You can't blame me for reading."

"I'm sure I can't," Ella said, lofty as an empress. "It's just interesting, isn't it, how often you fall into a book when there's work to be done?"

"Go find the kitten," Will said, "and I'll clean the kitchen. Maybe I'll find a book about it. *One Hundred Ways To Clean A Counter*, by Sir Maybe I Didn't Want To Deal With Mother All Morning!"

"You can't even do someone a favor without being horrid," Ella said. "And if you're not dealing with her, who do you think is?"

"I can't believe I was starting to feel sorry for you," Will said. Ella's cheeks went red.

"Sorry?" Her voice raised dangerously for a girl who thought mumbling made her genteel. "You're *sorry* for me?"

"I clearly got over it!" Will cried.

"Good!" Ella said, stomping up the stairs. "I don't think I like the thought of you being nice. It's so contrary to your character that I'd sooner put you back on bed rest!"

"Oh, an excellent jab," Will said, hanging onto the stair railing to watch her storm away. "Work on it a little and you might be as horrid as the rest of us!"

"Sometimes I want to *bite* you!" Ella shouted.

"Go ahead and bite," Will shouted back. "What kind of tea do you want?"

"The only kind we have!" Ella cried, whirling off down the hall on the second floor.

"And where do we keep it?" Will bellowed.

"Go find out!"

Will descended on the kitchen, which was hardly the disaster his mother made it out to be. There were a few pans lying around and the floor looked a little grubby, but it wasn't foul. Olven would probably make Will scrub it, though. For reasons beyond his comprehension, Will was more amenable to scrubbing Olven's floors than his own.

He tried to pretend that the kitchen belonged to the old, cheerful goblin smith, which worked for about five minutes before the lack of rambling anecdotes broke the illusion. If Will were a wizard, and the concept of using magic at all didn't make his skin crawl, he could have the place sparkling with a snap of his fingers. Louisa used to talk about their stepfather surprising the maids with a magically spotless house, causing them to turn in their notice on the spot. Wizards may have been in need at the capital, but people in the countryside thought it was uncanny.

After an hour of cleaning up and ten minutes of digging through drawers for tea, Will heard footsteps behind him. Ella stood in the doorway, the kitten in her apron pocket.

"See?" Will said. "The kitchen's done, and now you have time."

Ella sighed again. She was always sighing around Will. "It's only half done. And the tea is in the tin. The one with the word *TEA* written on it."

"Oh, look who's literate now," Will said, grabbing the tin. Ella barked out an ugly laugh, and he turned to blink at her.

"Stop!" she said.

"You think I'm funny," Will said. "You're a sarcastic little brat yourself, deep down. Aren't you, Ella?"

"I most certainly am not." Ella walked over to pick up a kettle. "That was a laugh out of pity for your deplorable sense of humor. It was *charity.*"

"Of course it was. Do people usually eat something with tea, by the by?"

"You've had afternoon tea every day of your life, William."

"Not every day. I missed about ten years of it and didn't bother attending the others. Tea makes me sick," he added, when Ella frowned. "It's all I could keep down when I was younger."

Ella looked away. "I'm sorry."

"Not your fault." Will felt like he was stepping into dangerous territory. He didn't talk about his early life with Ella. She was too fond of her father, and while she could be judgmental, she didn't need to have her memory of him muddled. "So... food?"

"Usually. I can throw something together, but the kitten needs feeding first."

Now it was Will's turn to sigh. "All right, then. Tell me what to do. It'll give you a chance to boss me around some more. Just don't lecture me on skipping out of one of Mother's breakfasts with the mayor's wife or something."

"I'll try to restrain myself," Ella said.

Between the two of them, they made a rough semblance of an afternoon tea. The pastries suffered under Will's aggressive kneading, but the custard turned out all right, and the tea itself was passable. The drawing room was still a mess after a panicky Louisa had swept through it, so they leaned over the kitchen counter and ate rubbery tarts together.

"You're almost tolerable when you're not being thoroughly uncouth," Ella said.

"So are you, when you're not acting like a warden."

"I don't *try* to be a warden," Ella said. "It's just that Father asked me to look after you. I feel responsible."

Will struggled to keep his expression from darkening. "Well, I'm not sick anymore, so you shouldn't have to hold yourself to that."

"It doesn't worry you at all?" Ella asked. "You don't think that you'll fall sick again?"

"I sincerely doubt it," Will said, in the glib tone that usually steered Louisa or his mother away from pressing the question.

"But Father said—" Ella squeaked as someone knocked on the door. "Oh, no. I hope they didn't turn around."

Ella scrambled off to the front door while Will tried to shove one last pastry into his mouth. He was still chewing when Ella came running back, her face pale.

"They're here."

"Mother and Louisa?" Will asked. "They must have forgotten something."

"No, it's worse than that," Ella said, clutching her hair as though it were likely to fly off. "It's Ramon and Luc."

"Why is that worse?" Will asked, heading toward the front door. Ella grabbed his arm with both hands, her eyes wild.

"They can't see me!" Will, utterly bewildered, looked from the door to Ella. "My *dress*, Will!"

"Borrow one of Louisa's," Will said. The knocker sounded again. "But I don't see why it matters."

"Oh, you are such a *man*," Ella snapped, but she raced for the stairs regardless.

Will opened the door to find Luc and Ramon dressed like noblemen out on a jaunt, with fine tunics, thick hose, and boots that weren't at all practical for the weeds that choked the grounds. They were also carrying several sacks of flour.

"Hello," Ramon said cheerfully. "We've come with a peace offering."

"I'm afraid the ladies have all left for the capital," Will said. "So we might not be able to have guests. They took most of the staff." Footsteps thumped upstairs, and Ramon glanced up. "Except one or two."

"That's all right," Luc said, as Ramon's expression collapsed into abject despair. "Ramon and I were thinking of going to his uncle's club tonight. Perhaps you could join us."

Will stared at him, too surprised to be discreet. The Luc standing in the doorway was a different man than the one Will had met a week ago, but it wasn't simply his expensive clothes. He had a smile almost as vacuous as Ramon's, with none of the keenness that Will had felt at their first meeting. He even moved differently, smoothly, with less care and tension in his limbs.

"I suppose so," Will said. Luc's smile didn't falter. "I'll bring the flour inside, then."

"I'll help." Luc hefted two of the flour sacks. "Show me the way, Will. Ramon, try not to wander. It isn't your house."

Ramon, who'd been edging toward the door to the drawing room, sighed and looked at his feet.

"Uh, this way," Will said warily, picking up the third sack and heading for the kitchen.

Luc gamely set the sacks down where Will pointed, then dusted off his hands. One of the sacks clanged as it fell, and Will walked over to investigate.

"Well, isn't this provincial," Luc said, as though that were a polite, charming thing to say and not entirely confusing.

"If you say so," Will said. "He opened the strange flour bag, exposing hundreds of silver coins. "What is this?"

"Oh, Ramon was hoping you wouldn't notice at first," Luc said. "It's repayment for your help the other day."

Will sifted through the coins. This could be enough to sustain the estate for a year, if he kept the money out of his mother's hands. Nevertheless, a small, stubborn part of him rebelled.

"Are you paying me to keep silent about whatever's happening to your heart?" he asked. "Because if so, you can take this back."

"What do you mean, whatever's happening to it?" Luc asked. "Ramon isn't paying for your silence. He's grateful." Luc's blank violet eyes scanned the kitchen, but Will couldn't see *Luc* behind them. It was as though he were speaking to a tall, painfully attractive doll. "*I'm* grateful."

Will took a step back. "The man who tried to strangle me didn't seem very grateful."

"And I do apologize. I don't know what came over me."

Will wondered if he should find an excuse to send Luc, Ramon, and their bag of silver on their way. Ella would despise him for it, but Will couldn't shake the disquieting feeling that he was talking to a wax statue.

Before Will could move toward the door, Luc interrupted him.

"It was so good of you to *help me*," Luc said. When he raised a hand to brush a lock of hair out of his face, his fingers trembled. His eyes flashed with an emotion so haunted that Will felt something heavy drop into his stomach.

"Is it your heart?" Will asked. Luc's hand started shaking violently, loose strands of hair falling between his fingers. "Did my magic affect you somehow?"

"All magic does," Luc said. His smile broadened, too wide, too strained. "I'm very grateful."

"You mentioned that," Will said.

"What are you two doing in there?" Ramon called.

"Upset the flour!" Will shouted. "We'll join you in a moment."

"I should help him," Luc said. He grabbed Will by the arms, his claws digging into Will's tunic. "I'm always there to *help* him."

"Maybe I need to look at your heart," Will said. Luc was clearly in trouble, but Will didn't know enough about magic to guess how to fix it. Luc leaned over him, putting more of his weight onto Will, and Will's knees buckled.

"My heart," Luc whispered. "Look at my heart. Not enough will."

They were almost kneeling on the kitchen floor, Luc's head bowed over Will's shoulder, his breath hot on Will's skin. Will eased him to the ground and held him up with an arm around his back.

"I need to ask permission this time," Will said, "so you don't try to kill me again."

Luc laughed softly. "Everyone has permission."

Will doubted that was true, given Luc's reaction the week before. Still, that seemed to be as much permission as he would get.

Luc's tunic had funny little loops stitched on the inside, and Will had pushed it halfway up before he realized that Luc had tied his damn points to the thing. He must not have been gentle enough with the ties, because Luc's hose started to sag, slipping down his muscular legs. Will tried not to think about that as he slid his hand under Luc's tunic. The glass over his chest was warm to the touch, and it moved like flesh when Luc breathed in.

Will spread his fingers over it, trying to think. It had worked when he'd called Luc's name before, but that might have led to the current situation. Unfortunately, it was the only option he could think of.

"Lucan," Will whispered, and summoned just enough of his magic to tickle his fingertips. He didn't let it sink into Luc, but kept it on the glass, an unwelcome visitor hovering at the door. "Can you come back again?"

Luc was shaking harder now, shivering in Will's arms.

"Lucan?"

Luc went still. He slumped against Will, their cheeks pressed together, his hands resting on the floor. Will tried to adjust him, and Luc stirred enough to straighten a little. His expression was no longer blank and affable, and some of the sharpness returned to his eyes.

"Luc?" Ramon called.

Luc grabbed Will's shoulder with one hand and half dragged Will into his lap with the other. They were tangled together, Will's legs sliding against Luc's and bunching his hose.

"Gods," Luc said into Will's neck. "I fucking hate you people." Will stiffened. "Not you. I don't know if I hate you. It's the rest of them."

"Humans?" Will asked.

"Wizards."

Will couldn't help the bitter laugh that burst out of him. "That makes two of us."

"You can't hate wizards. You are one." Luc finally released him, letting Will slip off his lap. "Don't tell anyone I..."

"Hugged me?" Will asked.

"Don't tell them that I let you use magic on me," Luc said. He tried to get to his feet, and Will rose to help him, grasping his arm.

"You should still have someone more skilled look at you," Will said.

"They did, I assure you." Luc paused to adjust his disheveled clothes.

"Did someone else do this, then?" Will asked. "Did they... change you? Make you act like that doe-eyed friend of yours?"

Luc almost smiled, but the expression disappeared as soon as it came. "He isn't so bad. I suppose you're already involved, so you might as well... but no. You're a Westwood."

"Don't call me that," Will said. "I helped you because you needed it, but I'm not a wizard, and I'm not a Westwood. My name's Fletcher."

Luc frowned. He looked more attractive when he was displeased—his eyes cold, his jaw clenched, brows lowered in an expression that made Will feel as though he were pinned to the wall by his gaze alone. "You live in his house."

"And?" Will asked. "He isn't around to stop me, is he?"

Footsteps sounded in the hall, and Luc pushed Will against the wall, out of sight of the doorway. Will tried to push him back, but Luc casually held him there with one hand.

"You aren't loyal to him?" His voice was soft. "Even though you live here, with enough magic to undermine some of the strongest spells in Morvane?"

Will looked away, but Luc grabbed his chin, forcing him to meet his eyes.

"I don't know why it matters," Will said.

"It matters to me." Luc's grip on Will tightened. Something hot and heavy burned in Will's belly, and he shifted his legs to avoid brushing against Luc. Luc's gaze slid down, then back to his face. "I can't tell you unless I know."

"Luc? You won't believe the *lovely* creature who appeared at the stairs after you abandoned me." Ramon came flouncing in like a curly-haired puppy attempting to look coy and debonair. Behind him, Ella hovered in one of Louisa's old dresses, which showed off a truly astonishing amount of skin. She hastily tugged the bodice up while Ramon's back was turned. "Well! Aren't we cozy."

Luc smoothly drew away from Will, leaving him feeling breathless. "I was telling him how terribly sorry I am for my outburst. Wasn't I, Will?"

"Yes," Will said, with barely restrained sarcasm. "We're good friends now."

Ella didn't seem remotely convinced, but Ramon nodded. "That's swell. I was thinking, we could probably let another visitor into the club if Ella wants to come."

"The club?" Luc asked, raising his brows. "For *gentlemen*?"

Will could almost see Ramon's thoughts strain to drag themselves away from Ella to settle on something remotely like self-restraint. "Oh, damn."

"That's right," Luc said. He strode over to Ella and took her hand. He bowed over it, the picture of nobility. "We'd like to borrow Will, if you don't mind."

Ella smiled warmly, and Ramon narrowed his eyes behind Luc's back. "He goes where he likes, I'm sure."

"But you're the lady of the house," Luc said. "It's only fair."

Ella mumbled something Will couldn't hear, a blush rising to her cheeks. When Luc straightened, his eyes flashed with the fierce, lovely glitter of a midwinter frost.

"There," he said, "it's settled. Our new friend is coming with us."

# Chapter Four

"Here now, Luc." Ramon leaned against the counter at the Heron's Repose, only two drinks in and already three sheets to the wind.

The club wasn't one of their usual haunts, too dark and quiet for Ramon and his young, rowdy companions from the capital. A few older men sat in a corner with cards while a group of country nobles hovered near Ramon, too cowed by his title to approach. "There are rules that must be followed. You can't just make eyes at another fellow's girl."

Luc poured Ramon another glass of brandy. "I wasn't making eyes at her, Ramon. I was being polite."

"And she isn't your girl," Will said.

Ramon scoffed into his glass. Usually, Luc would take the opportunity to comfort him, but he felt blissfully free of the impulse after Will's work of magic in the Westwood kitchen. He still cared for Ramon, but he wasn't certain how much of that was magic and how much was the result of growing up with him. Will was the only reason he could consider the possibility in the first place, and Luc felt an odd mix of emotion as he examined the short, irritable wizard pretending to sip fine brandy.

Wizardry was one of the few positions that could push a minor noble into the upper echelons of the court, but Will seemed opposed to the very concept. How could a wizard hate his own profession, particularly one who grew up in Westwood's shadow? Westwood's apprentices adored him; Berenger still spoke of him with an awed reverence reserved for goddesses and priests. Yet there Will was, stubbornly clinging to another name.

Luc touched Ramon's arm, drawing him a step away. "Why don't I work on the wizard? He could be the door to making Ella your girl for more than a season, if you like."

"A season is good enough for me," Ramon said. "I know what you're doing. My father told you to convince me to take a wife again."

"Not quite. It was your mother this time." Ramon rolled his eyes. "Give me an hour. You can see if any of these country nobles are worth knowing in the meantime."

"If they're brave enough to do more than stare," Ramon said. "Fine. Work your goblin wiles on him."

Luc flashed Ramon a toothy smile and turned to snatch Will's drink out of his hand. Will glared up at him, lips parted, but Luc interrupted before he could speak.

"You aren't drinking that. Let's go upstairs, and I can show you a game we play in the capital."

Will tried to match his gait, crowding into him at the base of the stairs. "You're bossy when you aren't acting like *him*."

"Am I?" Luc felt a bubble of elation at the thought. In the palace, Luc had always been unerringly polite to servants and members of the court. That could have been part of the magic keeping him docile and subservient, and the fact that he could show any arrogance at all was a small triumph.

"You roped me into coming here, didn't you?" Will whispered.

"No," Luc said. He opened a door to a small private room, checked for anyone hiding in the corners, and ushered Will inside. "You came because you're curious. Admit it."

"I'm here because Ella likes that man downstairs," Will said. He walked jerkily, as though just the act of walking irritated him, and Luc wondered how that much aggravation could live in one body. He felt drawn to Will, fascinated by the forbidden emotion that came so easily to that strange, scowling wizard.

"No, you didn't." Luc firmly closed the door. "Tell me about your connection to the wizard Westwood, and I'll tell you what's been happening to this heart."

Will turned on a heel with the sulkiest look yet. "He was my stepfather." Luc gestured for him to carry on, and Will groaned. "He married my mother when I was a child. *She* wanted a title and *he* wanted to be a wizard. That's all."

"But he would have been a wizard without her," Luc said. He could sense it now. They were close to whatever made Will's lip curl when Luc called him a wizard, the bitterness that shadowed every word he spoke. Luc moved closer, and Will turned aside, as though looking him in the eye would force out the truth.

"The wizard Westwood took pains to make himself seem affable and kind," Luc said.

"I know." Will's voice was tight and thin, almost breaking.

"He wasn't, though." Luc slowly backed Will toward a chair. Will fell when the back of his knees hit the cushion, and he looked up at Luc with fury in his dark eyes.

"He wasn't even a wizard." Luc froze, half bending over Will. That had been the last thing he'd expected to hear. He'd assumed that Westwood had experimented on his stepson somehow, perhaps even to test the spell he worked on Luc. He'd been prepared for a dozen small horrors that Westwood could have committed behind closed doors, but not this.

"Of course he was a wizard."

"Where did he get the magic?" Will spat the words. He clutched at himself, fingers digging into his belly. "He had enough magic in his body to run the machines he hooked up to *me*. I was six. Six years old, and he'd given me a new room full of toys in a house bigger than anything I'd ever seen before, then he put that fucking *thing* over my bed and he used me like... like kindling. Every time he had to leave for the capital, he took more magic from me, and every time he drained my magic, it felt like I was dying. I couldn't move from that bed until the day he died."

Luc stared at the trembling man beneath him. Using another wizard's magic was profane. It was practically the only thing the human and goblin courts agreed on. Before the fall of Elfhame, the elven god-kings had used wizards as wellsprings for their own magic. They'd drained them until they'd become wretched, broken husks of their former selves, and the discovery of their bodies had been one of the first catalysts for the uprising. The practice had been forbidden when the god-kings fell.

"Did your mother know?" Luc asked. "Could she have told the king? Taking another man's magic is punishable by death."

"He gave her a title," Will said. He dragged his hands over his face, but no tears shone in his eyes. "She knows that I hate her. She tries to fuss over me now, but she sold me. She sold me, and *he* used me, and I was a quiet little tool until his horse did everyone a service and threw him."

A horrible thought came to Luc then, slow as a corpse flower unfolding. "He became a court wizard after he took your magic."

Will sneered into the shadows. "That's when the gold started coming in."

Luc sank to a knee, but he was still so tall that they were almost face to face. "Westwood was the one who did this to me," he said, tapping his chest. Will's expression shifted from derision to dawning horror. "My mother sold me, too. She gave me to the king to end the war, and the king had Westwood remove my heart."

Will looked sick. "He used my magic to rip out your heart? But that makes you the *queen's* son? Queen Lethe?"

Luc hadn't heard anyone refer to his mother by name in years, but perhaps people who lived on the border knew her better than those in the capital. "You didn't recognize Ramon? Prince Faramond?"

"That's the crown prince?" Will asked. Luc felt the instinct to defend him, but held his tongue. "Gods. But why? Why take your heart? What was the point of it?"

"The king wanted to control me," Luc said. "I was troublesome at first."

"You were a kid who was given to the enemy," Will said. "The humans everyone says drink blood and worship the bones of the old gods."

Luc vaguely recalled his sisters talking about those rumors when he'd been a boy, but it was surprising to hear them repeated by a human. How many echoes of the Brightwood remained in Will's village?

"The king was not so understanding," Luc said, "and the queen was afraid for Ramon's safety. They took my heart, gave me this one, and now, wizards who hold my heart can tell me to be... good."

"To be grateful," Will said, repeating what Luc had told him earlier that day. He ducked his head, black hair hanging in his eyes. "And they used my magic for that. I want to drag that piece of shit out of his grave and kill him again."

"Inventive," Luc said. He couldn't resist drinking in Will's rage. He still felt too removed from his own, as though it were straining through a thin cloth, not quite whole. "That's why I was acting strangely. The king's wizards wanted to reinforce the spell, and they were a little heavy-handed this time. But something about your magic changed me enough to resist them. I can feel again; not fully, but enough to know what I've been missing. It must be because your magic created this spell."

"How do I fix it?" When Will looked up, he was weeping. Not for himself, Luc realized. He was ill-tempered, but he wasn't unkind, and Luc felt a sudden swell of affection that was nothing like the love he held for Ramon. "It was my magic that hurt you. I'm responsible."

"*Westwood* hurt me." Luc brushed Will's cheek with the side of his hand.

Will stared past Luc, his gaze distant. "I have to fix this."

Luc chose his words carefully. He didn't want to pin all his hopes on one person, but there was no one else who seemed to understand the enormity of what had been done to him. "I know you say you aren't a wizard, but there has to be something we can do. If I could bring you my heart, perhaps you could put it back."

Will raised his hand to the spot that Luc had touched. "But I don't know how. I never learned magic. I was barely aware of what Westwood was doing when he was working magic on *me.*"

"There has to be something," Luc said. "Books, papers, a study."

Will went pale. "There is."

Luc remembered lying on the cold slab in Westwood's workroom in the palace, and the strange, shivery feeling of Westwood drawing out his heart. He could only imagine what happened in a study with no king to oversee his work.

"Can you try for me?" Luc took Will's hands in his, and Will turned away again, a pink flush running up his neck. "I know you barely know me. You have no reason to help. Your stepfather did this without your consent."

"That makes it worse," Will said. He bit his lower lip. "You know that if we find your heart again, this could mean war."

"It might not," Luc said. "If we can do it quietly enough, I can return to the Brightwood, and the king won't want to admit that he lost his bargaining tool against my mother."

"It's still dangerous," Will said. For a breath, Luc thought he might refuse. Then his brows lowered, and Luc saw that what he'd taken for brattiness was a resolve as hard as iron. "But he should have never taken your heart."

"Thank you." Luc squeezed his hands. "I'm sorry that—"

The door swung open behind him, and Ramon slouched through the doorway, looking miserable. "They're all a terrible bunch of bores, Luc." He came to a stop in the middle of the room, and Luc quickly released Will.

"We were just..." Will started to say, but Ramon interrupted him with a bright laugh.

"So you *weren't* making eyes at that girl after all," he said. "I should have known. I've heard that goblins can be a little backward in their affections."

Luc bristled, caught between the warmth he always felt for Ramon and the obvious insult. *Morvane* was the backward one; while love wasn't restricted to one sex or gender in the goblin court, Morvane had carried over the elven god-kings' obsession with a rigid hierarchy. Men had ruled Morvane since the god-kings fell, and to maintain that rule, they forbade any deviation that could threaten their delicate balance. The goblin court had long since moved on from such nonsense.

It was better for Ramon to think they were lovers than that they were plotting to steal back his heart, but Luc wasn't certain how Will would feel. He met Will's eyes, and something flickered deep down, an expression Luc hadn't seen on his face before.

"Please, Your Highness," Will said. "Don't tell my mother."

"Oh, gods, don't start with *your highness*," Ramon said, flopping into a chair. "I don't mind, so long as you don't take him from me. Not that you can, of course, but you're welcome to visit the palace so long as you tell your pretty sister how gracious I am."

Will nodded and got to his feet. "I... I should go."

"Cute," Ramon said, looking far too amused.

Luc rose to help Will to the door.

"I'll send for you," he said.

"Or I will," Ramon added, propping his chin on his hand. "I've never smuggled someone *else's* mistress into the palace before. Except you wouldn't call him a mistress. What *do* you call him?"

"Will," Luc said, giving Ramon a warning look.

"Don't be dull. I'll find a name for it. This *is* fun," Ramon added, grinning at Will. "Remember me to your sister."

Will fled, and Luc closed the door with a sigh. "You didn't have to scare him off."

"I wasn't scaring anyone," Ramon said, with the faintest tone of outrage. "I'm only surprised that your type is short, grim, and country bumpkin."

Luc collapsed on a chair next to Ramon. "He has hidden depths."

Ramon snickered. "Does he?"

Luc hadn't given much thought to lovers before. He'd helped ferry plenty of Ramon's in and out of the royal apartments, but he'd kept a piece of himself in reserve when pretty girls dared to flirt with the imposing goblin prince. He'd always been too busy for love.

He thought of Will's dark eyes gleaming with rage at the thought of Westwood holding his heart. He couldn't see himself lying with any of the gentle, earnest courtiers who treated him like a curiosity, but someone like Will...

"I don't mind you discovering his hidden depths," Ramon said, as Luc turned the new, small feeling over in his mind. "Just remember who's still there when he's gone."

"Oh, Ramon," Luc said, laying a hand over his false heart, "I'm the last man who needs reminding."

***

Will only left the study once before his stepfather died.

The ride to the capital was a blur of sharp, stinging pain and the heavy jolt of carriage wheels, and even though Will hadn't seen his old home in the capital since he'd moved to the Westwood estate, he was in too much pain to do more than curl around his belly.

"Stop being so dramatic," Murtagh said. He sat on the opposite bench in the carriage, dressed in dark blue wizards' robes. "I haven't made use of you in days." He nudged Will's leg with a polished boot. "Sit up. You'll need to walk into the palace."

Will slowly uncurled and pushed himself up on shaking limbs, trying to suppress the knot in his heaving stomach. Murtagh wasn't paying attention to him, too focused on the palace approaching through the carriage window. He was pretty like Ella, his large eyes holding a warmth that never seemed to fade, even when he was burning through Will like a consuming fire. Will used to like fire. It reminded him of the glow of the forge in his father's home in the capital. Now, he felt too much like kindling to make room for anything other than pure, seething hatred.

Will pitched forward and vomited bile all over Murtagh's polished shoes.

Murtagh cried out in disgust and pushed Will back onto the bench. "You disgusting little guttersnipe! You did that deliberately."

"Fuck your boots," Will said, relishing the words even as a cold shiver ran through his body.

Murtagh wiped his boots clean with a sneer. "That's your father speaking."

"Good. *Fuck* your boots," Will repeated.

Murtagh struck Will across the face, but the sting of his palm was nothing to the pain that racked Will's body.

"You're far too young to speak like a smith," Murtagh said. "You're the child of a wizard now. You should act like one."

"Mother's marrying a wizard?" Will asked. "What'll happen to you?"

Murtagh struck him again, and Will laughed. He was beyond tears. He'd lost them all when his father had died, and the last thin protection against men like Murtagh had crumbled to dust.

He didn't know how Murtagh assumed he would be able to walk into the palace on his own. He only managed three steps before he fell, crumpling in his ugly gray skirts that fell like heavy curtains around his legs. Murtagh groaned and gestured sharply with his hand, and Will felt the magic pulling out of him as a spell settled over his shoulders.

"I didn't want to use magic before the ritual," Murtagh said, picking Will up like a sack of grain, "but you leave me no choice. Now be silent, or people will know you're here."

Will raised his voice. "I hope you die. I hope I die and I drag you down with me. I hope you die and my father finds you and kills you again so your soul can't come back."

"Your father," Murtagh hissed, shaking Will so hard that his teeth rattled, "was an illiterate fool who squandered his life making *horseshoes*."

"At least horses are interesting," Will said.

"You would have been *wasted* with him," Murtagh muttered, and strode off toward the yawning doors to the palace.

He must have cast a silencing spell over Will, because no matter how loudly Will shouted at servants and courtiers passing by, no one turned his way. The halls became a dizzying maze of stairs and corridors leading down, and Will lost track of his bearings, jostled by Murtagh's heavy stride.

They finally stopped in a small, dark room that looked like a replica of Murtagh's study, down to the spinning brass instruments and shelves packed tightly with books and jars. The only difference was a narrow brass box in the middle of the room. It gleamed dully in the dim light, and Will was dragged back to the memory of his father's body stuffed in a coffin that shouldn't have fit his bulky frame, swallowed by the earth.

"It's a lovely piece of spellwork, isn't it?" Murtagh said. He set Will down on the floor and rapped his knuckles on the lid. "My people found it in an elven king's barrow. Imagine it. A god-king built this, *used* this. With a wizard powering the box, it made the god-king strong enough to rule half of Morvane."

Will tried to crawl away from it. Something was wrong with that box. It *felt* wrong, as though the air itself were buzzing like a hive of bees.

"I had to modify it for you, of course," Murtagh said. "The elves weren't clever enough to find their wizards young."

"You're going to put me in there," Will said. He dragged himself toward the door, arms shaking.

"Only for a moment," Murtagh said. "I'm not an elf, after all. I just need you for something important."

Will was nearly at the door before Murtagh turned around. He tried to fight back, but he was too weak to do more than struggle helplessly as Murtagh lifted him into the air again. Murtagh spoke a word, and the lid of the box opened. A brass sphere was attached to the inside of the lid, so broad and heavy that it couldn't possibly leave enough room in the box for a body.

"Don't," Will begged. "Please, don't. Please take me back. I'm sorry I insulted you. I'm sorry. I didn't mean it."

"Of course you meant it," Murtagh said pleasantly. He laid Will in the box. When Will tried to grip the edges to pull himself out, Murtagh shoved him down again. "You're an uncouth, disgusting little commoner. You can't help it. It's in your nature, like a stray dog picking up fleas. But at least you can be useful."

He closed the lid over Will, trapping him in the dark. The brass sphere pinned him down by the chest, and Will struggled to breathe around the weight on his lungs. He couldn't move without injuring himself, and the sphere was too firmly lodged for him to wriggle around it. He was trapped in the dark, held down by a device made by the old god-kings long ago.

Voices spoke above him, muffled through the brass box. Will tried to beat his fists against the side of the box, but he barely made an impact. Finally, the brass sphere started to glow like the one that hung above Will's bed, and Will felt the sudden pull of his magic being summoned out of him.

He screamed. Above him, through the fog of pain that threatened to consume him, he could vaguely hear another boy shouting, but it must have been his own voice echoing in the box. Then the pain pushed him past the hoarse, breathless rattle beyond screaming, and Will fell into a cold, hard blackness.

*This must have been what my father felt like when they buried him,* Will thought, clenching his fingers as a lingering cry of pain rang in the air.

Then he thought nothing at all.

***

The study door was a dark stain against the graying wallpaper of the Westwood house.

The goblin court had a saying for the dead. Olven had repeated it a few times, when speaking of old friends who'd died in the war. *They've joined the revelry.* In the old days, when the goblin folk lived on the edges of the world, hiding from the elves who hunted them down for sport, the chorus had been a comforting dream. Goblins who'd been struck down by elven arrows would rise to join a long, wild parade of dancing spirits, and their singing kept the world turning and the trees of the Brightwood growing strong.

"One day," Olven used to say, when he was teaching Will in the forge, "when I join the revelry, I would like to know that my knowledge passes on."

Will didn't like to think of Murtagh Westwood's ghost dancing with a crowd of gleeful spirits. He preferred him still, decomposing in the family plot behind the abandoned garden. Someone who would rip the magic from one boy and the heart out of another didn't deserve to dance.

Will had been there the day the ritual had happened. He'd known it the moment Luc told him that Murtagh Westwood had taken his heart. Luc must have been above him, lying on the box while it siphoned Will's magic, his heart beating in Murtagh's hands.

Will touched the door handle. His stomach lurched, bile rising to his throat.

Ella had the key, but Will had crept in well after midnight, and she hadn't stirred when he'd passed her room. The key was the one piece of Ella's inheritance that Halpernia hadn't frittered away or locked in the cellar for safekeeping. Ella probably kept the door locked to keep Halpernia from selling the devices inside, but Will knew that Halpernia wouldn't have touched them even if she could.

"The door stays closed," he'd told her, the one time his mother had suggested it. "You owe me that much."

Halpernia had clasped Will's face in her hands, fluttering about him like an injured moth. "Oh, what you must think of me. You cannot understand what brought us here, darling. We were destitute after your father left us. Hate me if you must, my love, but it was all for you."

Will thought of the god-king's box and shuddered.

The money hadn't done much for him when he'd been too ill to move, shivering on his sickbed for weeks after he'd been locked in the box. He'd barely been able to speak for months, let alone eat or drink. What good had money ever done for him?

Will grabbed the door handle. It was just a bit of metal, nothing more. Murtagh wasn't waiting behind the door for him, the brass sphere turning, his bespectacled face looking down at him with his warm, quiet smile. He was dead. Bones and rot and creeping insects. He wasn't there.

Will touched a tendril of his magic, drawing it to his fingers. He didn't know the spell for unlocking a door, if there was one. Westwood had simply waved a hand to open it, showing off how casually he could use Will's magic, but he hadn't explained it.

"I need you to open," Will whispered. "I need you to *open.*"

Nothing happened.

"Open, you worthless piece of garbage," Will snapped.

Warmth bloomed in Will's fingers, and he felt something thunk softly inside the door. He turned the handle, and the door pushed open slowly, revealing a dark, gaping maw.

"Light," he ordered. He'd seen Murtagh call balls of light in his palm before, but this time, nothing happened. Will pointed toward a candle sitting on the desk, just visible through the doorway. "*Light.*"

Nothing happened. The metal devices in the study lay dull and shadowed within: the lenses Westwood had used to examine the flow of his magic, the bottles he'd tried to fill with reserves for long visits to the capital, the desk he'd worked at while Will tried not to moan too loudly, and the small bed with a brass sphere hanging over it by a chain.

Will staggered toward it. The sphere turned slightly, moved by a draft, and Will reeled back as though he'd been struck. He slammed the door shut and clamped his hands over it.

"Lock again," he told it. "Lock, damn you, *lock.*"

The mechanism clicked again, and Will threw himself against the opposite wall, chest heaving. He couldn't do this. He had to find another way.

Ella's door opened down the hall, and she stepped halfway out of her room. "Will? Are you all right?"

"Go back to bed," Will said. He pushed away from the wall and strode toward his own room. As he passed Ella, looking sad and small in her threadbare nightgown, Will paused to add, "He called you pretty, by the way. If that means anything."

He stalked off, trying to ignore Ella's soft voice behind him. "Did he say anything else?"

"I'm no one's messenger," Will said, and fled into his own room, where the darkness held no horrors.

***

"Magic?"

Olven leaned against his counter with a cup of tea in his talons, neck feathers fluffed like an irate cat. Will had set off for the Brightwood before dawn, mostly to avoid Ella's pressing questions about the night before, and had arrived to find Olven's smithy closed for a holiday. Instead of his worn apron and heavy linen clothes, Olven wore a thick sweater with a glorious rainbow scarf, and the door to his home was open.

"You have not given me the impression of one who trusts magic enough to ask about it," Olven said, and he spoke with such a slow, careful cadence that Will was certain he already knew the truth.

"You know I have it," he said.

"I suspected. But it isn't my concern, is it? You do good work, and it helps to have another person in the smithy. Magic is neither here nor there."

"It might be a concern now," Will said. "I was hoping... I don't have anyone I can ask about it at home. I thought you might know more."

Olven gave him another keen look, and Will wondered how much of his life Olven had already guessed. He didn't speak much about his home in Westwood when he visited the forge, and Olven didn't pry, but little details had a way of slipping out.

"I don't use magic," Olven said at last. "I have friends who have it, but my magic lies in the work of my talons. I might be able to answer a few questions, I suppose."

"Would any of your friends want to talk about it?" Will asked. It was odd seeing Olven in his ordinary clothes, quite comfortable in a warm, cramped kitchen. "Though human magic might be different."

"All magic is different," Olven said. "It's like art. You can mimic another person's style, but the hand that holds the brush is yours. I have a friend, Fern, her magic comes out in her carvings. She makes a new one for every spell, like this." He picked up a small wooden carving of an apple. "It keeps my food fresh. Can you see it?"

Will took the wooden apple and adjusted his glasses. He could just see the glimmer of magic inside of the apple, woven into the wood itself. "I think so."

Olven picked up a string of beads. "And this. It's a charm for repelling insects, made by an old lover. They're happily married now, made a beaded dress for one of the princesses, quite successful."

Will examined the charm. "But the magic isn't in the beads," he said. "It's in the string."

"Very good!" Olven set his cup down and dug through one of his drawers. He pulled out a mask shaped like a cat's face and placed it over his eyes. "And what do you see here? Guess!"

The cat mask was practically swallowed by Olven's feathers, but magic shone on its surface. "A magical cat mask? But I don't know what it does."

"You see nothing else?" Olven sounded delighted. He set the mask down. "That should have made me look like a little black cat, smaller than my tea kettle. Nothing?"

"No, you're still the same size," Will said.

Olven nodded. "I thought so. I didn't want to press, but you're always looking up when there's magic in the room, as though you can see it."

"All wizards can see magic, though," Will said.

"Not the ones I know. They can sense it, but not always *see* it." Olven gave Will a long, considering look, his usually excitable nature dimming. "I know that you do not come here from the main road. You come through the woods. Have you wondered why no one else comes that way? Why even goblin folk did not enter the woods during the war?"

Will didn't understand. "It's just a patch of forest."

"To you it is. To me, I see thorns. Thick, impenetrable thorns." Olven gestured as though he could summon them from the air. "Our ancestors enchanted the border long ago, to hide us from the elves. Illusion magic is dangerous. If the mind thinks it is real, a thorn will sting."

"But there *aren't* any thorns," Will said.

"That's because you see what's truly there." Olven put his cat mask in the drawer. "I've never heard of it myself, but I assume your magic has something to do with the truth. Perhaps you could break illusions, or speed the growth of a garden, or..."

"Call someone back," Will said, thinking of Luc, "if they're dying or lost."

Olven clicked his beak together, but it wasn't in the chittering way that signified laughter. "Careful. Necromancy is taboo for a reason."

"Not that!" Will assured him, mortified that Olven would consider it. Most of the old god-kings had been necromancers. Goblins and humans might have gone back to fighting each other after the elves were killed, but at least they agreed not to raise any undead rulers to shamble around the countryside. "The dead should stay buried."

"As you say," Olven said, still sounding too wary for comfort. "What brought this change? You haven't spoken of magic before, and you've never been pleased when I've used my charms around the smithy."

"I'm trying to help someone. A friend."

"Good intentions mean nothing without the skill to do the job," Olven said. "It's good that you came to me. I will ask my friends if they have heard of magic like yours. I will ask *discreetly,*" he added, when Will blanched at the thought of someone talking about his magic in the goblin court.

"Thank you," Will said. "I know that you don't have to go out of your way for me."

Olven shook his head. "You're a good boy, Will. You listen to my stories when others would find a reason to excuse themselves. Most humans who come through the border still see us as servants of the elves, not descendants of those who overthrew them."

"More than a few goblins would see humans as frothing barbarians," Will pointed out.

Olven's expression went distant. "Some memories persist longer than others. But no matter. The next time you visit, perhaps I will have learned something. In the meantime, do not rush things. You cannot weave a tapestry if you cannot first spin thread."

"Well, technically..."

"No!" Some of Olven's usual humor crept back into his voice. "Do not question it! Now, since you are here, I will introduce you to a proper goblin breakfast. Eggs and toast first, yes, and little tomatoes from the garden."

He started a passionate lecture on the nature of his neighbor's chickens as Will leaned on the counter, letting the chatter wash over him. He wondered if this was what life had been like for Luc. He probably had servants to look after him as a boy, but had he grown up listening to gossip about magical eggs and night markets with fruit that could make people speak in other languages? Had he walked under the lights of the Brightwood and asked what made them settle in the trees? It felt wrong that Will could so easily cross the border into the Brightwood while Luc was left behind, trapped with the people holding his heart.

"Olven," he said, cutting through a story about a chicken that had gotten onto the roof of a magistrate's house, "does anyone ever talk about Queen Lethe's son? He's living in the capital only a few days away, isn't he?"

Olven fell silent. His back was turned to Will at the stove, but his feathers betrayed his emotion, flattening against the back of his neck.

"It's best not to mention the prince," Olven said in a quiet voice.

"But—"

"No." Olven's tone was firm. "Some things we do not speak of to outsiders. This is one of them."

Will tried to suppress the sting of Olven's words. *Outsiders*. He knew he didn't truly belong here, in this warm, comfortable home that wasn't haunted by the specter of Westwood's influence, but being told outright hurt more than he expected.

He thought of Luc sprawled on the grass not two leagues from the forest, his brass heart sinking into his chest. It seemed as though his absence had left a chasm too deep for Will to broach, but *someone* in the Brightwood had to care enough to want him to come home.

"Olven," he said warily.

Olven moved closer, his voice low. "Is it about the prince again?"

Will kept his gaze lowered. A black beetle crawled along the wall near the floor, its iridescent shell gleaming. He focused on it instead of Olven, not wanting to see distrust in his face.

"I met someone in Morvane," Will said. "A goblin."

Olven was silent for a long minute. The beetle tested the slick kitchen tiles one leg at a time, its approach hesitant and slow.

"Is he well?" It was as though Olven couldn't even say Luc's name or title. Perhaps saying it made it real, and that meant Olven had to think about his prince living in Morvane, cut off from his family.

"No," Will said at last. "No, he isn't well at all."

The beetle paused, its shell splitting, wings momentarily sliding out before snapping back in again.

"And your sudden interest in magic?" Olven asked. "Does it have something to do with him?"

"Maybe I can help," Will whispered.

"Dangerous," Olven said. "Very dangerous, Will." He touched Will's shoulder, and Will looked up into eyes filled with deep pain. "I would not see you put yourself at undue risk, boy."

"I'll be careful," Will said. "You can't tell me to sit back and do nothing."

The eggs were starting to burn, so Olven turned to set the pan off the heat. "You're a human," Olven said. "Your memories are not as long as ours. There are some goblin folk whose grandsires remember the elves." He scraped the eggs off the pan and put the burned pieces on his plate before putting the rest on Will's.

"What does that—" Will started to say, but Olven interrupted him, his voice soft.

"At that time, there were some goblin villages that tried to make deals with Elfhame. They gave their children to them. One or two in a generation, hardy goblins, tall and elf-like. They thought that if they gave the elves something to hunt, they wouldn't turn on goblin villages when the fey mood took them. It was a necessary sacrifice, they said."

"They gave their children to the elves to be *hunted?*" Will asked.

"And some of your people gave the elves their wizards. Necessary sacrifices, yes? But the elves burned the villages regardless. They drained the wizards of their magic, slaughtered our children, and then killed the parents who gave their children so readily to the elves for a few years of peace."

Olven dropped thick slices of bread on their plates. "With no elves to hate, we mimicked them. We became the raiders, the hunters, humans and goblins. And when the time came, we made an offering. A boy. I saw his carriage pass when he went through the gate. The queen said that it had to be done for the sake of peace. He was lost to us." He looked away, his eyes dark. "I cannot speak against the queen, but goblins remember. There are no necessary sacrifices."

# Chapter Five

Luc was sparring with one of Ramon's personal guards when the queen summoned him to her chambers.

Queen Imogen was not fond of Luc. He'd always known it, even before Will's influence had drawn some of his true self to the surface. She'd disapproved of Luc spending too much time with Faramond, claiming he was a poor influence. Luc had spent years trying to earn her favor before she'd finally stopped trying to separate them.

"I wish I had your problems, Luc," Alistair said, sheathing his sword. "Imagine getting an interruption from the queen herself."

The instructor was an older man with dark hair and a vicious scar down one side of his face, which Ramon and Luc had long speculated was a souvenir from the war. Even with that mark of a goblin claws on his skin, he'd always treated Luc as an equal, with none of the wariness or distrust of some of his fellow former soldiers. Despite the fact that he'd only attained a post as the prince's guard a few years before, it felt as though Alistair had always been there, quietly following him and Ramon as they navigated the palace.

"Don't tell me you've never been formally presented to their majesties," Luc said, putting his sword away. He wasn't allowed to wear one on his person unless he was acting as an unofficial guard for Ramon.

"Only to receive orders." Alistair helped Luc out of his padded fencing vest. "I doubt they know my name, and I prefer it that way. It's a quiet life for me, Prince Luc."

Luc gave him a true smile. Alistair was also one of the few people in the palace who called him by his old title. "A quiet life can't be that terrible."

"There are worse things," Alistair said. "Mind your shadow."

Luc knew his meaning without needing to turn around. Felicity, Faramond's quiet, nervy little sister, was always hanging around the training grounds when Luc took his lessons there. She was there now, her yellow hair tucked under a veil, clasping her hands so fiercely that the skin stretched under her nails. Luc approached her with a bow, and she shrank further into the shadows.

"Your parents have summoned me," Luc said. "Do you want to follow me there? What happened to your ladies?"

"Left them," Felicity said tightly. She gave him the impression of a wound spring ready to snap, speaking in short bursts and forever grabbing her arms. She'd been born around the time Luc had come to Morvane, but she'd spent so much time hiding or locked away in her room that he couldn't quite see her as a sister.

She hunched her shoulders and stumped up the stairs next to Luc. "I have a question."

"Go right ahead," Luc said. They passed a line of old paintings depicting different angles of the royal garden.

"Do you *like* Faramond?"

He gave her a curious look. "We practically grew up together. I suppose that engenders affection, don't you think?"

Felicity didn't answer. She seemed pensive, her mouth pinched tight, eyes dark.

"Are you wondering if I like you, too?" Luc asked.

"I'm not a child," Felicity said. "I'm nineteen. I know you don't like me. I don't mind that. I just don't know why you like *him*."

"But I *do* like you," Luc said.

Felicity shook her head, her hair falling out of her veil. "Never mind. I knew this was pointless."

She turned around and stomped back down the stairs, looking like an irritable heron with its neck tucked down to its chest.

Felicity could probably do something to let out all that nervous energy, but Morvane didn't allow women to wield bows or swords, and she was a deplorable horsewoman. His sisters would have pulled her out of her shell quickly enough.

He was remembering more about them now. He wondered if suppressing his memory had been part of Westwood's spell, or if the bitterness of being wrested from his sisters had turned their memory into something unpleasant. It was another sin to be laid at Westwood's grave, wherever it was in the weed-choked grounds of his country home.

The queen's chambers were next to the king's, but the connecting door rarely stayed closed. Luc found them both sitting on her daybed when he entered, the king in crimson robes, the queen in a delicate gray and red gown. The queen's smile didn't reach her eyes, but she gestured for Luc to sit in a low chair near the daybed. He bowed before he moved across the room, and some of the ice melted in the queen's manner.

"We wanted to speak to you," the king said.

Luc kept his expression calm and polite. Will's magic slowly faded by the day, not powerful enough to fight the spells that clung to Luc's true heart, but Luc still had trouble hiding his trepidation. "Yes, Your Majesties?"

"You and Faramond have been spending a great deal of time close to the Brightwood," Queen Imogen said.

Luc let himself show surprise at that. "Our business kept us close to Westwood. We would never try to violate the treaty by approaching the gate."

"What business, exactly?" the king asked.

In the past, Luc had always answered honestly. He tried to keep to the truth as much as possible, while carefully omitting Will's involvement. "We met a young lady there. A noblewoman," Luc added, when the queen raised her brows, "gently raised. Faramond has taken a liking to her."

"Has he?" The king's mood seemed to lift considerably. "Is she from good stock? A big family, many sons?"

"I don't recall any prominent families coming from Westwood," the queen said.

"Her father was the king's wizard when I was a boy," Luc said, and the queen and king gave each other a sharp look. He knew what they had to be thinking. The only king's wizard from that region was Murtagh Westwood himself.

"Unacceptable, I'm afraid," the queen said. "We can't have magic in our bloodline."

"But if he cares enough about this girl to drag our Luc to the border, perhaps that's a sign that Ramon is finally considering his responsibilities." The king didn't seem to share his wife's reservations. "I was starting to think that he was like the king of Telmar."

Luc drew back, confused. Telmar had built itself around the bones of the old elven empire, staying out of Morvane's war to instead herd sheep by the sea, and no diplomats from Telmar had visited Morvane since Luc was taken. The journey involved crossing a hazardous river of heather filled with old elven magic, and few Telmarians considered it worth the risk.

King Tomas smiled at Luc's expression. "The king of Telmar took up with a man last winter."

"I suppose he's in a position to allow it," Luc said, not pointing out that Morvane was the only country to find the practice unlawful.

"Oh, that nonsense is rampant over there," King Tomas said, clearly warming up to the scandal of it all. "They let their women make war, they pay no heed to the ancient customs, and they're far too... elvish in their inclinations."

"But the elves were the first to forbid women from fighting," Luc said. "And marriage—"

"I don't think this is an appropriate conversation," Queen Imogen said. She got to her feet, prompting Luc and the king to rise out of politeness. "I suppose we can allow Faramond his diversions, Lucan, but please remind him of his duty to the realm."

"Yes, Your Majesty." Luc bowed, flinching a little as King Tomas slapped a hand on his back.

"Don't trouble yourself with the concerns of women, boy. And ensure that Faramond doesn't get this girl with child, will you? I love him, but between the two of you, you're the only one with a good head on your shoulders." He laughed and smacked Luc's arm. "We've made sure of *that*!"

Unable to trust himself to speak, Luc bowed and followed the king out of the queen's chambers. He didn't allow himself to breathe again until he'd hurried down the opposite stairs, where he tucked himself into an alcove, covered his face with his hands, and let out a ragged sigh.

"What were they on to *you* about?" Felicity appeared in the shadow of a statue on the other side of the stairwell, sitting with her knees tucked to her chest. Luc jumped, nearly slamming his head against the top of the alcove.

"Your Highness," he said, trying not to let his irritation show. "What are you doing there?"

"Hiding from my ladies-in-waiting," Felicity said. "What'd my mother say? Was it about Faramond finding a wife, or me finding a husband?"

"The first part," Luc said. "Why *are* you hiding from your ladies-in-waiting, Felicity?"

"Hate them," Felicity said shortly. She shuffled back behind the statue. "Tell them where I am and I'll put shit in your boots for the rest of your life."

"That's reasonable." Something had clearly gone wrong in the king and queen's choice of nannies and governesses. Ramon was too flighty to sit still for more than a minute, and it was hard to say what *wasn't* strange about Felicity.

"Faramond's been looking for you, by the way," Felicity said, now little more than a pair of embroidered slippers poking out from behind the statue. "He says he has a letter for you. He was smiling in that frustrating way of his."

That had to be a letter from Will. Ramon had been teasing Luc constantly for finding a lover, so he'd most likely read the letter himself. Luc could only hope that Will had the sense not to write anything incriminating.

"You didn't see me," Felicity said, as Luc raced down the steps.

As he had suspected, Luc found Ramon reading Will's letter on a bench in the courtyard. He smiled brightly at Luc as he approached, folding the letter carelessly in his hands.

"Your sister threatened me again," Luc said, snatching the letter from him.

"She'll never go through with it, whatever it was." Ramon patted the bench, and when Luc sat down, he swung his legs onto Luc's lap. "Is she hiding from her ladies?"

"Yes, but I've been ordered not to tell you where. Is this from Will?" Luc opened the letter.

Thankfully, Will knew better than to write anything that might arouse suspicion. The trouble was, he'd gone too far in the opposite direction, writing only two lines on the thick parchment.

*Luc. Need to see you soonest. -W*

"What a romantic," Ramon drawled. "I like the bit about how his heart beats for you alone. A true poet, isn't he?"

"Hush." Luc glanced around them, eyeing a pair of courtiers talking under an apple tree. "Discretion, Ramon."

"Oh, right. It's still terribly dry, isn't it?" Ramon lowered his voice. "I hope his hidden depths are worth it. Have you seen his tool yet? Is that why this letter has you all aflutter?"

"I'm not aflutter," Luc said. Hopefully, Will had found Westwood's old notes. It was hard to tell by his handwriting whether the letter was a good sign or not. He tucked it in his jacket pocket and paused, anticipating the gleeful display he was about to witness. "How soon do you think we could go back to Westwood?"

"If we say that we're hunting at Michel's estate, I expect we can divert our path long enough for you to... do whatever it is you fellows do." Ramon idly clicked his heels together. "We can make it official by actually hunting the next day. Michel will be good for it, and you know he likes any excuse to avoid talking about crops with his steward. Aren't I the best friend a goblin could have, Luc? Tell me I'm the best friend a goblin could have, go on."

"You're the best friend I have in this courtyard," Luc said. Ramon scoffed and pushed him. "Don't make me fan the flames of your ego, Ramon. It burns hot enough already."

"See, this is why you have me," Ramon said, flopping back so that his hair hung down off the end of the bench. With the apple blossoms blooming and the sun falling soft over the courtyard, Ramon looked beatific. "If I weren't around, you'd be a no-nonsense homebody with nothing of importance to do. How fortunate it is that you have me to look after you."

***

Will was one minute away from stuffing Ella in the cellar and leaving her there.

"Louisa's lonely," she'd said that morning, when she'd found Will hunched in a corner with a book on the history of theoretical magic. Will had glowered at her, but Ella hadn't moved. Louisa and Halpernia had been home for several days, remarking on the mysterious increase in Murtagh's pension. Will had been slipping a few extra silver coins in the sachets from the capital, just enough to warrant hiring people from the market to deliver milk and cheese again. Even that had been too much, apparently, because Halpernia had already depleted the extra funds by ordering new cloth at the tailor's. The resulting chaos had kept Will from sneaking off to the

Brightwood. He'd finally found somewhere to hide, but Ella had known him well enough to spot him immediately.

"She has a dozen friends," Will had said, holding the book to his chest like a protective talisman.

Ella had been unmoved. "Yes, but she only has one brother. Do you want to prove that you're a part of this family? Then take her for a walk while I finish clearing out the hearth."

"You just want her to stop following you around," Will had said. Ella had only glared at him. "Oh, all right. If you insist, *Mother.*"

So there Will was, trudging through the garden while Louisa babbled at his side, her brown ringlets bouncing with every step.

"And Genessa said that no one respectable marries a soldier, because you don't know what they got up to when they were fighting in the goblin court," Louisa was saying, halfway through recounting the past five years of her life.

The unfortunate truth was that Ella was right. Will didn't know half of these people, but he probably should have. He'd spent so long hiding from Halpernia, and therefore Louisa by association, that he'd missed great swathes of her life. He struggled to keep up, making noncommittal noises every time Louisa referred to someone she assumed he knew about.

"Louisa," he said at last, jumping into a rare gap in her story, "I think I may have done you a disservice."

"How?" Louisa asked.

"By not being around more," Will said. He watched her face, looking for a flicker of resentment, but Louisa only tilted her head like Olven inspecting his work.

"What do you mean? I never noticed you going away. Now, Therese was found with a glove that wasn't hers, but Ylissa says—"

"I'm away all the time," Will said. "I disappear for hours. You never caught on?"

"Don't be silly, Will," Louisa said. "Where would you go? There's just the village, the capital, and the Brightwood, and no one's interested in a bunch of thorny old trees. So Ylissa says..."

Will wondered if Louisa would even notice if he slipped away now. If it weren't for his mother constantly attempting to patch up a childhood of being trapped in his stepfather's study, Will could probably put a hat and coat on a broom and get away with living in the back of Olven's smithy.

"Louisa," Will said, trying yet again to break through her long tale about Ylissa and the disreputable soldier, "if you're upset, you can always say something."

"For goodness' sake!" Louisa cried. "I'll just tell *Mother* about it, then!"

Will turned to watch her as she marched back to the house, entirely at a loss.

"Look," he said helplessly, "I'm trying."

"You certainly are," Louisa said, and picked up her skirts to step over a dandelion. She shrieked as a pair of beetles flew out of the grass at her feet. "I hate this! Leave it to a *man* to let me walk through a bug-infested garden!"

She hadn't made it more than a few paces when the scullery door slammed open. Halpernia rushed out, hands extended, her nicest shawl hanging off her shoulders. Louisa froze.

"Is someone hurt?" she asked, in a tight, small voice. "Is it Ella?"

"The girl? No, why would she...?" Halpernia blinked rapidly, looking like a puppet in an earthquake, strings trembling. "Don't be absurd, Louisa. We have guests. *Important* guests. Prince Faramond is at our doorstep, and here you are with mud on your slippers!"

Louisa gaped, standing stock-still as Halpernia fluttered around her. "But... but why?"

Halpernia glanced at Will. "He and his goblin servant seem to be looking for *you*."

"Luc isn't a servant," Will said. His pulse quickened. Luc must have received his letter. His palms started to sweat, and he brushed them on his trousers.

"I don't care what his name is." Halpernia swung her shawl around Louisa. "Why didn't you tell me that you met the prince? Oh, Louisa, remember to sit up straight. Your older sister is upstairs in bed, remember? And if he asks, Will is your cousin."

Louisa raised a shaking hand to adjust the shawl. "Yes, Mother, I know. He's been Cousin Will my whole life."

"They may also want to see Ella," he said.

"Don't be ridiculous," Halpernia said. "I sent her out of the way so that she doesn't distract the prince from our Louisa. Come, darling, we mustn't keep him waiting."

"Ella's as much of a lady as Louisa," Will said, following his mother as she towed his open-mouthed sister across the lawn. He felt oddly protective of Ella, even if she *was* bossy and tempestuous beneath her gentle facade.

"Ladies don't roll in soot, William."

"If you hired servants," Will started to say, but his mother and sister had already outpaced him. He walked after them slowly, guilt twisting in his stomach. He knew he should press the issue, but he needed to find a moment alone with Luc, and he couldn't do that if his mother was displeased with him.

Halpernia had already descended on the prince when Will entered the house, pushing a terrified Louisa in his direction while Ramon smiled politely. Will bowed when he approached, and Luc somberly inclined his head. He looked sharp in a hunting jacket and high boots, and jeweled pins kept his hair in place behind his pointed ears.

"Perhaps I can show Luc the observatory while you become better acquainted," Will said. Halpernia gave him a look of near-worshipful relief.

"What a lovely idea, dear William," she said. "Your Highness, you must see our garden. We have the loveliest little birds this time of year, don't we, Louisa?"

Ramon perked up like a hunting dog. "Really? What kind of birds?"

"We have these little fat thrushes," Louisa whispered. "I... I paint them sometimes."

"Oh, you don't need to hear about *that*," Halpernia insisted, but Ramon was already making for the back door, Louisa tripping at his heels.

Luc wove his arm around Will's. "That should keep him occupied." He spoke low in Will's ear, causing a shiver to roll down Will's back. "Have you found anything?"

"Upstairs," Will said. Luc kept his shoulder pressed to Will's as they ascended the stairs, his grip on Will's arm a little too snug. "Do you need my magic again?"

"I might," Luc said. "It's fading." They reached the second floor, with the worn rugs, warped wallpaper, and sagging roof. "What have you learned?"

Will felt his face go warm. "I think my magic has something to do with the truth. I opened a lock with it the other day, so that could have been... revealing the truth, somehow? I don't know. Westwood seemed to use it for everything."

"Did you learn this from his notes?" Luc asked, scanning the hallway. "Which room is his study?"

Will felt his face go hotter still. "I couldn't go inside. That's why I asked you here. If I opened the door, could you..." It felt pathetic to ask, but understanding flashed in Luc's eyes.

"I don't mind. You're already helping me more than you should."

Will slipped free of Luc's grasp. The door to the study loomed over him, the closed mouth of a sleeping wolf. He placed his hands on the door handle.

"Open," he ordered. "You want to open. Your *duty* is to open."

The lock thunked, and Luc's brows rose. "So you tell it what the truth is, and it follows suit."

"A friend suggested something like that." Will pushed the door open. Westwood's devices gleamed in the dull sunlight from the hall, and a strip of light shone through a shuttered window by the bed. Will steadied himself with a hand on the frame, but he couldn't force himself to step forward.

Luc touched his arm. "Keep watch for me," he said softly, and walked into the dark study. He leaned over the bed to open the shutters, then paused. The brass ball spun lazily over his right shoulder.

"Would they see the shutters from the garden?" he asked.

"The bird nests are all on the other side of the house." The words came out thin, Will's lungs constricting with fear. "Don't touch that ball next to you."

Luc nodded and pushed the shutters open. Light fell over the bed where Will had lain for half of his life, the air choked with dust. Luc gazed down at it, his blunt claws tracing the wooden frame.

"It's so small," he said. "You must have been very young."

"It stunted my growth." Will dug his nails into the doorframe. "A side effect of draining my magic, I suppose."

Luc turned away from the bed, his brows pressed tight together. He went to the desk, but Will couldn't see what he found there, too busy watching the sphere for any sign of unexpected movement.

"Do you remember where he kept his older notes?" Luc asked. Will barely heard him. The sphere swung with the morning breeze, chain clinking against the hook in the ceiling. "Will?"

Will couldn't move. Deep down, something told him that if he moved, the sphere would take him. It would crush him, just as the other sphere had nearly done when Will had been trapped in the box. Luc crossed in front of the sphere, his body outlined in pale light. He touched Will's face, and the scrape of clawlike nails over Will's cheek broke his trance.

"I need to get rid of it," Will said. He pushed past Luc, crossing the small study too quickly. It was still cramped, a mess of brass and parchment, and Will breathed heavily as he grabbed the sphere in both hands.

Will let his rage build around his magic, his fingers flexing against the sphere, the old terror thick in his throat.

"You're just metal," he told the sphere. "You're not even the right *kind* of metal. Tin and copper and lead, that's what you are."

Luc sucked in a sharp breath, but Will couldn't stop to look for the source of his alarm. He bowed over the sphere, tugging it down on its chain. The metal went hot under his skin, sliding and shifting.

"You're just metal," Will said again. The surface of the sphere wriggled like a nest of snakes, and Will stepped back with a cry of disgust as it fell apart beneath him. Scraps of metal squirmed and writhed until lumps of it lay at his feet, useless and dead.

"What is that?" Luc asked. "What did you do?"

Will nudged one of the lumps with his foot. The chain that had held the sphere swung near his cheek, creaking softly. "Copper, tin, and lead," Will said.

Luc seemed shaken. "That isn't how Westwood used magic."

"He used it however he wanted," Will said, still staring down at the mess on the floor. "That's probably why it hurt so much."

"You changed what it was." Will didn't like the hint of fear in Luc's voice as he bent to examine what he'd made of the sphere. "That's powerful, Will. You're changing the nature of things. The king would conscript you in a second if he knew that you could do this."

"Then it's good that he doesn't know," Will said, kicking the scraps of metal under the bed. He could feel himself shaking. He understood Luc's meaning all too well. This wasn't just opening a lock. It wasn't calling fire or making pretty illusions. It was closer to what Westwood had tried to do to Luc. Will realized that if *he* held Luc's heart in his hands and told him how to feel, it would probably be irreversible. Luc would become whatever Will wanted him to be.

"I'd never use my magic to change you," Will said, turning to face him. "*Never.*"

"I believe you." Luc sounded surprised to say it aloud.

"No." Will didn't know how to say it. "My magic already has been used to hurt you."

"I know."

"You *don't*," Will insisted hotly. Luc drew back in alarm. "I was there, Luc. Murtagh brought me to the palace on the day he took your heart. I was in the box."

"The box?" Luc frowned. It took a moment, but when realization dawned on his face, his green skin went ashen. "The slab. You were *inside* it? Beneath me?"

"He needed to draw on my magic directly," Will said. "It was an elven device. I guess the sphere above my bed was a copy of it. But I was there. So you get why I have to do this. *My* magic was used to hurt you, but it won't hurt you again."

Luc took Will by the shoulders. "You were a child. We were *both* children. You aren't responsible. Murtagh was."

"He's not alive to fix it," Will said, "not that he ever would. At least he didn't know how to use my magic the right way. It was just a tool to him. Maybe that's why I was able to call you back."

"That's what I don't understand," Luc said. He turned back to the desk, rummaging through its contents. "You keep talking about magic as though it's specialized, but the wizards at the palace all use the same texts and instructions."

"I'm still figuring it out." Will ducked down to pull out a drawer by his old bed. Without the sphere to haunt him, moving around the study wasn't as nauseating. His hands were still unsteady, papers slipping out of his fingers and to the floor.

Luc crouched beside him, a warm hand on his shoulder. "You can step outside if you must."

"I know I'm a coward," Will said, grabbing the papers. "Sorry to make you come all this way just to help me open a door."

"You aren't a coward," Luc said. He made Will turn to face him. His white hair fell in tendrils over his face, and his violet eyes glowed in the pale light of the study.

"You're the only one who's cared enough to do anything," Luc said. "All those people in the palace, watching me, touching my heart, letting other people tell me what I am and who I love. They could have done something. My own mother could have refused to send me here. But you didn't hesitate." He stroked Will's cheek again, fingers sliding over the shell of his ear. "That's not cowardice."

Will looked down, unable to meet his eyes.

Luc tilted his chin up. "If your magic deals with the truth, maybe you should start saying it."

Will's lips parted, but he couldn't find the words. He'd been hiding from more than just his mother's flustered attention and the slow decay of the estate. He'd been miserably unhappy, trapped in a home haunted by the ghost of his younger self, hiding from the magic tainted by the man who should have protected him.

"I never wanted to be a wizard," Will said. The words burst out of him in a rush, harsh and rough-edged. "But if I am one, I want to use my magic to do something good. I want to be more than... than this." He gestured to the study, the bed, the detritus that had once been the sphere. "I want to use magic the way they do in the Brightwood."

Luc knelt on the floor in front of him. "How do you know what magic they use in the Brightwood?"

"I've been there." Will tried to look away, afraid that Luc might resent him for it, but Luc held his face in a firm grip. "My magic helps me get through the thorns. There's a smith there, Olven, he showed me some of the magic the goblins have done. It's small, but it's helpful. It doesn't have to hurt people."

"You can navigate the thorns," Luc said. "You've been to the Brightwood." He smiled, but it wasn't the vacant, unsettling grin that came with his magicked heart. His eyes were shining, sharp teeth bared. "What a curious man you are, William Fletcher."

Luc slid his fingers through Will's hair, cupping the back of his head. The heat of him felt like magic, warm and full, a surge of dizzying elation rising through Will's body. It filled him like steam, and he raised a hand to Luc's thigh.

Will had some experience with men. Traveling farmhands passing through Westwood were more than willing to spend time with a young man who wouldn't spread tales. They didn't bother with gentle touches and sidelong glances. There wasn't enough time for that. Will was used to fellows making their intentions known, not having to guess what they meant when they stroked his hair and called him *curious.*

A voice rose from the other side of the house, and Luc pulled away, leaving Will kneeling in the center of the study with shafts of light pooling over the floor.

"We should hurry," Luc said. Will felt adrift, yearning for something he hadn't known he could ask for. He swiped a hand over his mouth. The pressure lingered, the ghost of warm lips that hadn't quite touched him. "We don't have much time before they return."

# Chapter Six

Luc cursed softly to himself as he urged his horse down a path between barley fields. He'd been with Faramond at their friend's estate for two days, but he couldn't get Will out of his mind. He'd been strangely quiet toward the end, gazing awkwardly down at his hands as Luc had busied himself with opening drawers and checking behind books.

It had been all Luc's fault, of course. He hadn't checked if Will was comfortable with Ramon thinking they were lovers. He'd become too familiar too quickly, drowning in false affection and starving for something tangible. They were bound, he and Will, but the binding lay in the tangled mess of pain and terror on that bronze slab in the bowels of the palace. Luc had been so flustered by how close he'd come to ruining their fragile kinship that he hadn't asked Will to strengthen his magic on his heart. He could feel Will's influence becoming so faint that he had to struggle to hold on to his guilt.

At least Ramon agreed to let Luc go back to Westwood on his own. Luc suspected that the king thought that his wizards would keep him docile enough not to run, but there was no telling what they would do if he *did* try to escape. He and Ramon could only evade their guards long enough, and Ramon had to send one with Luc to avoid trouble.

Alistair had volunteered for the journey. He rode a piebald mare next to Luc, his scarred face turned to the distant tree line of the Brightwood. A cool spring breeze rolled over the fields, tousling Alistair's dark brown hair and making Luc shiver in his riding leathers. Alistair didn't try to fill the silence with chatter like Ramon, giving the impression of a man happy simply to be out in the open air.

"Are you from the country, Alistair?" Luc asked.

"I'm from the north, near Telmar." Alistair gestured vaguely behind them. "But I know this place well enough. I fought here in the war. Ran across one of your sisters, in fact."

"You never mentioned that before," Luc said, surprised.

"I figured the king would disapprove." Alistair smiled softly to himself. "She was a terror, that Princess Alara."

"You sound like you almost respect her," Luc said. He had so few memories of Alara that he felt a tight, hard hunger at the sound of her name.

"Of course I respect her. She was a damn good fighter, and a better leader. Most would be content to give orders from their tents and let others do the fighting, but not her." Alistair gazed toward the Brightwood and raised a hand in front of his face. "I came that close to her once."

"She didn't..." Luc eyed the scars over Alistair's cheek and mouth, unsure how to voice his suspicions.

Alistair smiled, his scar tugging at his mouth. "You mean, did she give me my beauty mark? This isn't goblin-made. War can be chaotic, Your Highness. You're more likely to impale yourself on your own sword when you're a lad with a few weeks' training."

"But you must resent us a little," Luc said.

Alistair shrugged. "I've tried resentment, Your Highness. It didn't suit me."

Luc wondered what that must be like. His own resentment and fury had been locked away for so long that it felt foreign now. He struggled to grasp it, but it slipped away, disappearing into a calm, placid haze that felt like falling into a pit full of wool.

Thankfully, they didn't have to call on Will at the front door. Luc spotted him trudging through a wild field less than a league away, his hair tossed in the wind, his long tunic twisting around his legs as he walked. He carried a bulky bag slung over one arm, and he was smiling fiercely to himself. Luc drew his horse to a halt, but Will had already spotted him and Alistair, his smile fading as he raised a hand to shield his eyes from the sun.

"Luc?"

Luc dismounted, and Alistair wordlessly took the reins of his horse. "I'll be at your back, Your Highness," Alistair said. "Nothing here can hurt you, I think, unless they've started breeding carnivorous rabbits while I've been gone."

"Thank you," Luc said. Alistair gave him a lazy salute and clicked his tongue at the horses, guiding them a safe distance away.

Will seemed frozen to the spot, his cheeks gone pink from the cold wind. He raked a hand through his hair, which promptly blew in his face. "Luc. I didn't expect you back so soon. Is it your..." He glanced at Alistair and surreptitiously tapped his chest.

"I'm sorry to alarm you." Luc couldn't risk speaking in the open when the wind was blowing toward Alistair. He was an agreeable man, but he was still in the king's employ. He offered a hand to take Will's bag. "Allow me to escort you home."

Will readjusted his bag rather than give it over. "Mother will be unhappy to see you without the prince."

"I'll express his regrets." Ramon had been utterly entranced by the birds in the overgrown Westwood garden, but had called Will's mother a "meddlesome social climber," which wasn't entirely untrue. He'd been more unkind to Will's poor youngest sister, though. She'd seemed rather nice, if a little prone to anxious babbling, and her face hadn't been as pinched and plain as Ramon implied.

Will seemed on edge, drumming his fingers on his thighs as he walked and avoiding Luc's gaze. He stopped abruptly when they reached the edge of the Westwood estate, turned to look back at Alistair, and grabbed Luc's arm.

"I need to show you something," he said, with a meaningful look at Alistair.

Luc gestured to Alistair, who raised his voice to be heard over the wind. "I'll stable the horses, shall I?"

"Good," Will said, before Luc could reply. He yanked Luc forward, his brows furrowed, pushing through overgrown flower plots and dandelions. He didn't stop until they reached a small, narrow door in the side of the estate, half hidden by a scraggly flower bush. Will dragged Luc through it and into a narrow, unpainted hallway.

"Where are we?" Luc whispered.

"Servants' stair," Will said. Luc had seen the servants' halls in the palace, but they'd been comfortable enough, if not a little plain. This was just a bare hallway with narrow wooden stairs leading up into darkness. He also had yet to see an actual servant at the estate, and the dust clinging to the floorboards suggested that there hadn't been one in a while.

Will hadn't let go of Luc's hand. It felt like they were connected at the palms, heat running up Luc's arm as Will pulled him through another narrow door. This was more familiar ground. They passed Westwood's study, scuttling into another, smaller room. There wasn't much to it, just a narrow bed shoved against the wall and a truly alarming stack of books. A box by the bed overflowed with clothes like an upended wardrobe.

This had to be Will's bedroom.

Will released Luc as though he were on fire and closed the door.

"Will," Luc said, "I should apologize—"

Will shushed him, stalking around the room like an irritable cat. "I need to think. It should be enough. It'll probably work. I don't know."

"Are you... all right?" Luc asked.

"No! Yes. I need to think," Will said again. He went to the door and touched the lock. "Locks keep things from getting out, right?

Well, you'll keep in sound now. Anyone who isn't inside this room won't hear what's being said."

Luc frowned. He knew that wizards could make runes to suppress sound, but that usually involved scrawling sigils on paper. This felt more like Will was throwing a bucket of water on a bush and calling it tea.

"Step outside for a moment," Will said. Luc opened the door and crept into the hallway. Will carefully closed the door after him, then opened it again. "Did you hear that?"

"Hear what?"

"Excellent," Will said, and dragged Luc back inside. He still had a wild, restless energy, but he was smiling again. With his windswept hair falling into his eyes, he looked younger, happier, like the exuberant young man he could have been without Westwood. "How is your heart? Is it giving you trouble? Did they try to make you behave again?"

"Slow down," Luc said, placing a hand on Will's chest. He let go when Will's eyes widened slightly, the pink flush from his walk outside rising to his ears. "It's only been a few days. This is remarkable, Will."

"You should be allowed to say what you want without anyone punishing you for it," Will said. The room wasn't so cramped that they had to press close, but Will was practically underfoot. Luc had to clasp his hands behind his back to avoid touching Will for balance. "Let me see your heart, just in case."

Luc slowly sat on the bed, since it was the only option other than falling to his knees. Will dropped down next to him, boyish in his rough, careless movements. "You seem different. Lighter."

"I was heading back from Olven's," Will said. That meant he'd been to the Brightwood, Luc realized. "He's so talkative that some of it must've rubbed off on me."

Luc started undoing the laces of his riding jacket. "I wanted to apologize for what happened earlier. I was too familiar, and I never asked how you felt about Ramon thinking we're close."

Will looked up at him sharply. Even with him seated, Will was shorter than him. Luc wondered how many pet wizards of the old elven god-kings had been like Will, robbed of pivotal years of growth. "You weren't too familiar."

"But I know how people from Morvane feel about, ah... relations between men, or between women..."

"Goblins don't care," Will said bluntly. "Half the people who come to Olven's smithy aren't women *or* men. What are they supposed to do, stay celibate?"

"*I* know that, but you were raised here."

"And look how that turned out," Will said. "Luc. I favor men. I've *always* favored men. Half the fellows in the countryside favor men, even though they pretend not to, and if you check the houses of every pair of spinsters in Morvane, you'll be hard-pressed to find more than one bedroom."

Luc felt as though he were floundering in a shallow pool. He'd expected some resistance; he hadn't expected Will to trample all over his understanding of Morvane. "I suppose that's... that's possible..."

"There you go," Will said. He rolled his eyes. "Men lay with one another all the time in Telmar, too. I've heard the stories."

"Apparently their king does, too," Luc said. Will raised his brows.

"Really? I wonder if he's looking for a consort who knows his way around the forge." He laid his hands on Luc's chest. "Can I call you out?"

"Wait." Luc shifted uncomfortably. "What do you mean, if the king of Telmar is looking for a consort?" Something odd and unpleasant struggled to make itself known inside him, burning hot as a brand.

"I'm only saying," Will said far too casually, "I wouldn't mind bending a king over the bed." He raised his brows. "Luc?"

"Just... just do the spell," Luc said. He couldn't think of Will bending anyone over a bed, let alone the king of Telmar, without his mind slyly putting himself in the king's place. It was entirely inappropriate. Will was *helping* him. He clearly had no interest in Luc if he was speculating over bedding kings, and Luc had enough on Ramon's social calendar to think of *anyone* bending him over *anything.*

"Lucan," Will said, and Luc could feel his magic now, a warmth to his hands on his chest. "I want you here."

Luc gasped as he felt the fog fade enough for more of his true self to push through. A surge of emotion followed—the fear of discovery, outrage at being taken from a land where loving a man wouldn't be forbidden, and an old, aching bitterness toward his mother and the king. Under it all was a sharp, stinging jealousy at the thought of someone else lying under Will, being touched by him, feeling the heat of his body.

"Oh, *fuck* the king of Telmar," Luc said.

Will let out a startled laugh. "What's that about?"

"If you're found out when this is done, you might as well come to the Brightwood with me," Luc said, feeling the heat rise to his face. "Not run off to some godsforsaken elven ruin."

"Why, Luc," Will said, smiling, "you're possessive *and* bossy when you're not under that scum-sucking wizard's spell."

"I don't mean to be unpleasant," Luc said, resenting even the urge to apologize.

Will laughed again. "No, be unpleasant. Tell me what you hate about the king of Telmar. Is it the thought of me bedding him?" Will slid his hands down Luc's chest. "Or him bedding *me?*"

"No one's bedding you," Luc snapped.

"Not for lack of trying," Will said. "I'm told that I have a talented mouth."

"You're doing this deliberately."

"Doing what?" Will pulled his hands away. "Being *familiar?*"

Luc sighed, leaned over Will's grinning face, and kissed him.

For a brief moment, Will was frozen beneath him. Then his lips parted, deepening the kiss, and Will reached up to clutch Luc's arms.

"You *are* jealous," Will said when he pulled away. He had far too much satisfaction in his voice.

"And you're an insufferable tease."

"Oh, yes, insufferable." Will sat up on his knees, and Luc gasped as he was tipped on his back onto the bed, Will crouching over him. "I hear that often enough."

Will pressed his mouth to Luc's. He parted Luc's lips expertly with his tongue, hungry and hot. It was nothing like the sweet, gentle caresses Luc had imagined in quiet moments alone; there was something primal in it, a need that grasped him like the roots of a tree in dark soil. Luc clutched Will back, gasping for breath between kisses, his cock stirring, an ache low in his belly.

Will bent to kiss Luc's neck, and Luc shuddered at the resulting prickle of pleasure. "I suppose I can tell you that you're unfairly beautiful now."

"Most people wouldn't call a goblin that," Luc said.

"Most people have no sense, then." Will grabbed Luc's hands and moved them to his hips. His brows furrowed, lips pressed tight. "Do you remember how in the goblin court, some goblins move between womanhood and manhood? Some cross over from one to the other?"

Luc hesitated, thrown by Will's suddenly serious tone. "My sister Wren did that."

Will gestured to himself, moving his hands up and down his torso. "So did I. I'm only Cousin William to people like that friend of yours because there are no records of my mother having a son."

"Oh." Luc barely remembered what Jade had told him about Wren, but he'd always understood that asserting her gender was a natural part of her coming of age. King Tomas would probably disapprove, but he didn't even believe that women should be allowed to hold a sword or practice magic.

"Do you have any Morvanish thoughts about that?" Will asked.

"No!" Luc raised his hands in defense against Will's powerful glare. "I thought *you* would!"

"Even people in Telmar don't care, and they build their houses on elven ruins," Will said, "as though they aren't about to be haunted by pissed-off ghost elves until the end of time."

"Elves didn't believe in an afterlife," Luc said, "so there might not *be* ghost elves."

"That's not the point." Will tried to brush his hair back out of his eyes. "I'm well aware of how people here can be about things that should be commonplace. You *are* beautiful. It's frankly offensive how beautiful you are. If someone has told you otherwise, they clearly have no taste in men."

Luc stared up at him, utterly unmoored. Will seemed to move through the world with an unerring confidence, entirely solid in his convictions. He could be irritable and grim at times, but he was still *good.*

Will seemed to notice Luc's hesitation, because he laid his hands over Luc's. "Touch me."

"Where?" Luc felt suddenly young, his lack of experience too stark.

Will's expression softened. "Anywhere you like. I don't usually let people touch me like this. They might find something they're not expecting—or *not* find something they *do* expect."

"What was it you said?" Luc said. "Something about most people having no sense?" He trailed his hands up to Will's waist, and Will writhed in his lap, brushing his ass against Luc's hardening cock. Luc sucked in a sharp breath, and Will leaned down to kiss him again. Something wicked flashed in Will's eyes, and he shifted, adjusting so that his thigh pushed between Luc's thighs. He moved as he kissed Luc, his thigh sliding against Luc's cock, the friction making Luc tense and shudder.

"Do you like this sort of *familiarity* between men?" Will's tone was teasing, but there was still a hint of fondness there. He ran his fingers through Luc's hair and kissed him hard and deep, cutting off Luc's attempt to answer.

"Perhaps," Luc managed to say when he came up for air. "Yes. Yes, I do."

Will kept grinding his thigh into Luc's cock, his dark eyes fixed on Luc's face. "Do you ever think about someone touching you like this, when you're lying on your expensive silk sheets in the palace?"

"It should say something about me," Luc said, feeling a little dizzy with the heat coursing through him, "that I'd be satisfied being taken on the floor at this point."

"Oh, I'm not taking you," Will said, and the way his voice lowered made Luc's cock jump. "Not yet. But thank you for the suggestion. Touch my hair again, I liked that."

"You treat lovemaking the same way you treat magic," Luc said, obliging with a bemused smile. "You're always giving orders."

"*Lovemaking*," Will said. "Of course a prince would be a romantic."

"Is this not what you call it in the country?" Luc asked, and shivered as Will started moving with more purpose, grinding his thigh against him. Luc's hips jerked almost involuntarily.

"We don't really call it much of anything," Will said. "Nobles sometimes say they're *walking out*. Me? I call it sucking a traveling farmhand's cock before he heads north for the harvest."

Luc must have betrayed his shock at that, because Will's smile took on a softness that cut through his usual acerbic tone.

"You've never had someone's mouth on you." He went still, leaning over Luc, somehow a towering presence despite the difference in their heights. His lips were swollen with kisses, soft and slightly parted, his pupils blown wide and dark with desire.

Luc tightened his grip on Will's hair.

"Will?" A woman's voice called out over the catch of their breath and the rush of desire roaring through Luc's body. Her tone was urgent, almost fearful. "William!"

"Ella," Will groaned, and dropped his head to Luc's shoulder. "Maybe she'll give up."

Someone knocked smartly on the door.

"I know you're here. Your friend's horses are in the stable!"

"We should get up before she summons your mother," Luc said reluctantly. Will sighed and got to his feet, then held out a hand to help Luc up. Luc nearly dragged him down again by accident, and they staggered upright together, clasping each other's arms.

Will gave Luc a moment to straighten his jacket before he strode to the door and turned the lock. He raised his voice as it fell open. "For gods' sake, Ella, I was having a moment of privacy!"

"I swear," Ella said. She was wearing a far simpler dress than the ones Luc had seen before, dirt-stained and threadbare at the hem, and she carried a sheaf of paper in one hand. "You'd be happiest underground with nothing but books for company." She stopped short when she saw Luc. It seemed that the meek little mouse Ramon dreamt of was more like Will than she let on. "Oh. My lord, I didn't see you there."

"Don't worry," Will said, "he won't tell Ramon anything untoward about you, like you secretly having a personality."

Ella glared at him. Luc wanted to note that siblings should at least *try* to get along, but he hadn't exactly made any headway between Felicity and Ramon over the years. He could barely remember if any of his sisters had fought.

"Please forgive my cousin, my lord," Ella said. "He was raised by donkeys."

"Because I'm an ass?" Will asked with mock politeness.

"I would never lower myself to use such language." Ella brandished the paper toward Will. "But that's neither here nor there. We just learned the news."

Will turned to Luc, confusion clear across his face. "News? What news?"

"He didn't tell you?" Ella asked, glancing at Luc.

Luc shrugged helplessly. "I'm afraid you have me at a loss, my lady."

"It's a missive from the king," Ella said. She shoved the paper into Will's hands. "They're holding a festival to honor the anniversary of the end of the war. Every eligible maiden in Morvane is to attend."

"Eligible maidens?" Will asked. Luc inched closer to read over Will's shoulder. The missive seemed official, with the thick wax seal of the Morvanish royal family at the top. "Eligible for what? Virgin sacrifices?"

Ella's voice lowered to a horrified hiss. "William!"

"They're the ones asking for maidens," Will said.

"Stop being a beast and listen to me." Ella tapped the paper. "This changes everything. *Everything.* At the end of the festival, Prince Faramond will choose the woman who will be his queen!"

***

"You purposely undermined me!"

Faramond slammed open the door to the king's chambers with a resounding bang, rattling the windows and making the queen jump from her seat against the far wall. He hadn't even bothered to change out of his clothes from the long, tense ride to the capital, and his hair was a bird's nest of yellow tangles. Luc followed at his heels, unsure whether he needed to restrain Ramon before he shoved his father through one of the stained glass windows.

King Tomas rose from his chair. Felicity sat nearby, hunched over a marble chess stand between them. "Faramond, you will compose yourself."

"Compose myself?" Ramon grabbed the king's empty chair and flung it across the room. Felicity flinched, and the queen rushed over to pull her away from Ramon.

Luc could barely move. He'd never seen Ramon fly into a rage like this before. He'd been prone to tantrums as a child, but Luc had learned to spot them as they were coming, smoothing the way before Ramon's temper broke. The man scowling at King Tomas was nearly unrecognizable from Luc's boyish, carefree friend, and Luc edged around the room to put himself between Ramon and his sister and mother.

Luc hadn't been the one to break the news to Ramon. Their friend's estate had received a similar missive by the time Luc and Alistair had returned, and Ramon had already ordered the horses to be readied. He'd been silent and pensive, rebuffing any attempt Luc made to ask his opinion of the festival.

Luc saw now that Ramon's silence hadn't been him processing the news, but a slow, terrible rage.

"I am not a child to be moved about and arranged for," Ramon said. "You had no right to do this. *No* right."

"You had plenty of time to choose a wife." King Tomas' voice was eerily calm. He stood squarely before his son, hands on his belt. "We gave you many allowances. The time has come due, Faramond. You will choose a wife, you will wed her, you will have an heir on her—"

"So that I can be followed around by a bevy of little brats all day?" Ramon practically spat the words. "Haunted by a power-grubbing woman inserting herself into my affairs?"

"That's a bleak view of marriage, my boy," King Tomas said. "If you're so set on having a wife who won't vex you, the festival will give you a chance to find her."

Luc shifted uncomfortably. He'd always known that Ramon had a flippant air toward his relationships with women, preferring brief, surreptitious affairs, but he hadn't heard him speak of them like this.

"Even Luc hates this." Ramon glanced his way. "I can find a wife perfectly well when the time comes to sire an heir."

"That time is now, Ramon, and don't bring Lucan into this. This matter is between you and your duty to the crown."

"You *made* Luc part of this," Ramon snapped, "and I need to ensure that any woman I take into this palace won't try to wrest him from me!"

"He is my ward first, boy." King Tomas' voice lowered dangerously. "He can be taken from you at my pleasure."

Luc felt something unpleasant stir in the pit of his stomach, but before he could react, Felicity flew out of her mother's grasp.

"I can't watch this," she said, and strode out of the room, her veil fluttering in her wake.

"You will make a formal apology to your sister when this is done," the king said, "for your ungentlemanly conduct."

"Perhaps she was more upset by *you* treating Luc like a toy you can take away from us," Ramon said, "instead of a man with his own need for *dignity* and respect."

"Watch your tone, boy." King Tomas' voice was an ominous rumble.

Ramon stepped forward, close enough to lay his hands on his father if he wanted to. Luc caught the queen's nervous gaze and approached him, gently placing a hand on Ramon's arm. Ramon didn't look his way, but some of the tension seemed to drain from his body.

"You can't hold this festival without me," Ramon said. "But if you insist on this, I have my own conditions."

"I will consider them," the king said.

"A long engagement," Ramon said. "Ten years at least."

"Five."

"Eight."

"Very well," the king said.

"And if this farce is to be in honor of peace," Ramon added, a cold, keen gleam in his eyes, "then we'll commit to that promise. I want invitations sent to delegates in the goblin court."

The room fell into a sudden, shocked silence. Luc felt the queen's gaze fixed on the back of his head without having to turn.

"Those are my terms," Ramon said. "The goblin court comes to the festival, or I do not." He jerked his head at Luc. "Let's give my father a moment to *consider* it."

Luc bowed hurriedly to the king and queen as Ramon turned on his heel.

"See that he apologizes to Felicity," the king said, his face grim and wan.

Luc mumbled his assent and fled. He found Ramon already halfway down the hall, walking with a firm, quick stride.

"Ramon," Luc whispered, "what were you thinking?"

"Not here," Ramon said tightly. He pulled Luc into his chambers, locked the door, and collapsed onto a chaise. "Did you see their faces? They'll never allow it."

"That was a dangerous move," Luc said.

"If you're worried about my father separating us, he won't." Ramon groaned softly and started wiggling off his riding boots. "I know that you think you owe him because his wizard saved your life when your heart failed. That's why you always do what he says."

Luc didn't answer. He didn't think he could without betraying the comfortable lie Ramon had grown up believing.

"This will work out either way," Ramon said. He pushed off his boots with a sigh of relief. "Think about it, Luc. If he disagrees, I don't need to choose a wife. If he agrees to it, which is unlikely, *you* can see your family while I can figure out which gently bred maiden won't scream at the sight of a goblin."

Luc was touched, despite Ramon's burst of temper in the king's rooms. He hadn't thought that part of Ramon's reticence had been whether his future bride would balk at sharing a palace with a goblin. "You should still try to give the women a little grace. Marriage may not be as terrible as you think."

"Oh, goblins and your queer ideas about women and men. You'd think we'd have helped you grow out of that by now." Ramon propped his feet up on a pillow. "I'll allow that women aren't the power-hungry harpies I described to my father, but I had to tell him *something.* And you must admit that marriage sounds like an awful chore. Can you imagine spending the rest of your life with that funny little wizard, for instance?"

Luc thought of Will crouching over him, his face flushed, hands warm on his skin. Will excitedly playing with magic, ordering locks around, speaking of the Brightwood with unexpected delight. "I suppose it would be impractical here."

"Exactly."

"But you never considered what love might be like?" Luc asked.

"Love is too precious for marriage." Luc straightened, surprised, and Ramon looked away. "I wouldn't want to tarnish it. Being king involves doing things that might strain the conditions of love. Take you." He gestured widely in Luc's direction. "Mother was furious when Father had his wizard give you that heart. I heard them shouting about it through the door, and they stopped even *trying* for more children after that. They'd been quite fond of each other before, you know."

"They seem fond now," Luc said hesitantly. Had the queen opposed the spell because she hadn't wanted Luc close to Ramon, or had she opposed it on principle? She'd never come across as someone likely to sympathize with a young goblin, but she'd always been so quiet, purposely placing herself in the background unless she was called on to speak.

"They've mended things a bit, yes. But it's not the same." Ramon sighed heavily. "Gods, I don't like talking about this. Things used to be simple. Remember that?"

"Dimly." Luc started undoing his jacket. "Why don't we clean up and see if they've brought that new poet to the library?"

Ramon rolled off the chaise with all the drama of a trained actor. "I was hoping I could hide in my bed until everyone forgets that I nearly shouted the palace down."

"You're the one who wanted the poet in the first place," Luc said, mussing Ramon's hair as he passed.

The poet was indeed in the library when they arrived, cozily tucked away at a writing desk. He was one of Ramon's favorites, a man who favored a new style of poetry without rhyming, and he and Ramon spoke at length about meter and verse while Luc tried not to think about how easily the king could remove him from Ramon's life. He didn't like the thought of being shunted from one person to another, a bought servant with no choice in his affection.

Luc and Will needed to find Luc's true heart before the king used it to make him loyal to someone other than Ramon. Luc felt as though he owed some fealty to the king and queen, but not enough to deter him from going against their wishes to recover it. He was

Ramon's companion first. Ramon didn't know the truth, so Luc was safe, but only so long as Ramon didn't spur the king into turning Luc's attention elsewhere.

He was about to leave Ramon for the training grounds when the queen entered the library, flanked by her ladies-in-waiting. They were dressed in dark green and gray, older women with bright, watchful gazes and families of their own. The queen was guarded and soft-voiced around her husband, but she walked at the head of her ladies with an air of command.

"My son," she said, and Ramon turned from his conversation with the royal poet. She held out a hand, and he reluctantly walked over to take it with a bow. "Have you recovered from your illness enough to speak with me?"

Luc watched Ramon from the shadows. Calling Ramon's temper an illness was certainly one way of hiding that the royal family was in an unstable state.

"Yes, Mother."

"Then you'll be happy to know that your father and I have accepted your offer," the queen said. She looked around the room, and her gaze lit on Luc, holding him in place. "We will be happy to extend an invitation to a delegation from the Brightwood."

Luc didn't see Ramon's reaction. He was trapped by the queen's dark eyes. A complex emotion lay there, not honesty or distrust but something in between, a nebulous wariness framed by long, black lashes and heavy curls.

"You will have one month before the ball," she said. Her voice was low, but Luc had the feeling that she wasn't speaking to Ramon. "See to it that you are suitably prepared."

# Chapter Seven

All it had taken was one afternoon for Will's life to turn on its head.

Nearly all of Morvane was in a state of panic. All the tailors and dressmakers had lines of anxious ladies' maids winding around the street, and every enterprising mama in the country was trying desperately to convince their unmarried daughters to sway the prince.

Poor Louisa probably had the worst of it. She'd been driven weeping into the garden four times already, unable to keep up with her mother's sudden standards. Will was exempt on account of being "far too much of a man by now to pretend for an evening," which was a welcome relief. For a terrifying moment, he'd thought that his mother would try stuffing him into a dress on the off chance that Ramon lost most of his eyesight before the festival.

While Louisa and Halpernia fought over Louisa's new lack of freedom, Ella carried her sewing everywhere to modify Louisa's dress in time. Will took advantage of the chaos to bury himself in Murtagh Westwood's notes. It was a weak distraction from the memory of Luc lying beneath him, his touch light and hesitant, on the edge of release from a few kisses. Will had never been with a man who didn't want something quick and simple before he moved on to the next village. Luc didn't feel simple. They were too tangled up in one another, their paths crossing a thousand different ways.

Murtagh's notes weren't simple either. Much of it was like trying to piece together another language. Murtagh's knowledge of magic had all been through the rote instructions of former wizards, and he seemed to have had trouble making Will's magic behave through brute force. Most of the notes were about channeling Will's magic into something manageable. It had worked better the closer Will had been to Murtagh, which meant that he'd probably built Luc's false heart while Will had laid in the sickbed next to him. The thought of Murtagh carefully making a device to control one child while draining another of his magic made Will sick. He had to stop several times to steady his breathing, but none of the notes said anything about Luc's heart itself.

One night, when Louisa had locked herself into her room after a furious screaming match with Halpernia, Will crept down the hall to the study. He shook out his arms, wary of even touching the handle. It had been easier with Luc there to support him, but on his own, the door seemed to hum with energy like the air before a lightning strike.

He reached for the handle, then paused. A faint line shone at the crack of the door, tickling the edge of Will's slippers. He took the handle and pushed the door open.

Ella sat at the desk, a small lamp burning beside her. Baskets of cloth sat at her feet, and she looked up from a strip of fabric spread over her lap. It shimmered in the candlelight, and Will realized that it was a clever patchwork of tiny cloth diamonds, expertly sewn together to make it look like the fading colors of a sunset.

"Hello, Will," Ella said. She went back to stitching.

"You don't seem surprised to see me here," Will said, closing the door after him. Ella kept her head bowed over her sewing.

"The ball over your old bed is gone. I assumed you'd tell me in your own time." Ella took another diamond of cloth and started attaching it to the others. She moved quickly, confidently, her brows tight in concentration.

"I was curious about my magic," Will said at last.

Ella nodded. "I thought so. You can go through any of his books you like. I won't mind."

Will edged toward one of the bookshelves, thinking of how thoroughly he'd torn through Murtagh's notes before. "Why are *you* here?"

"It's quiet." Ella picked up another diamond. "I come here when I need to think, sometimes. It makes me feel closer to Father, like he's watching over me." Her voice lowered to a whisper. "Keeping me safe."

Will's stomach twisted with guilt and yearning in equal measures. His father had died when Will had been too young to remember much beyond brief, vague memories. For all that he'd done to Will and Luc, Ella's father had loved her. Will couldn't bring himself to shatter her memories of him.

"My father had a smithy," Will said. "He used to come home smelling like soot and iron, and Mother made him wash outside in a bucket before he came inside. I'd sit out there with him and talk about what he'd made that day."

"You never talk about him," Ella said.

"I don't remember enough to talk about." Will pulled out a few books of handwritten notes and sat on the floor near the empty fireplace. It wasn't easy to read in the dim light of the lantern, but he felt too much like an intruder to come closer. "But I know how that feels. Needing a place that's yours. That was mine. A few minutes outside the house, listening to him talk."

Ella moved the lantern slightly, and a shaft of light fell over the books. "Not your mother, though." It wasn't a question.

"No."

"What did she do to you, Will?" Ella put her needle in a pincushion and folded her hands over her lap. "She's the one you're hiding from."

Will couldn't tell her the truth. That, too, would ruin the security of her father's ghost in her mind. But he could come close enough. "She sold me to someone. Someone who hurt me."

Ella set her stitching aside. "Your sickness, Will. It wasn't an ordinary one, was it? Not if my father couldn't cure you. It was a curse of some kind."

"Something like that," Will said.

"And she let them curse you?" Ella asked. "Why?"

"We didn't have any money left after my father died," Will said, looking away. "It had to come from somewhere."

The light on the desk flickered, and Will jolted as Ella knelt on the floor, pulling him into her arms. Her soft hair brushed his cheek, and Will froze, unsure how to respond to the sudden embrace.

"I'm sorry," she whispered. "She shouldn't have done that to you."

Will struggled to swallow. "She was desperate. It's fine now."

"It isn't," Ella said. "You deserved a mother, Will. Someone who loved you."

Will felt like his body was twisting with the force of his guilt. "So did you."

"I had one, for a time." Ella drew back, her eyes shining. "I don't remember much other than her gowns, which were always so lovely and soft. I thought I had a mother again with Halpernia. But she wasn't anyone's mother, really. Even to poor Louisa."

"Louisa might kill her soon enough," Will said, and Ella smiled weakly. He didn't think he could keep talking about his mother with Ella looking so at home in her father's old study. "That doesn't look like her dress."

"Oh, no, it's mine." Ella brought the cloth down for Will to examine. "Halpernia said I could come if I finished Louisa's gown first. I don't have anything of my own fit for a ball, but if I turned these scraps into a gown... You see, there would be petals here, to make it look like a cloud?"

"I don't know much about sewing," Will said, "but it looks complicated." Too complicated to finish in less than two months, but he didn't need to say it. Ella met his gaze briefly before turning aside.

"If I work through the night, perhaps..."

Will stood. He walked over to the desk and took out Ella's sewing needle. "Can I try something?" he asked.

"So long as it isn't sewing," Ella said with a wry smile.

"It's magic," Will said. "I think." He looked at the needle. "Your job is to stitch things together," he told it, calling his magic to his fingers. "That's what you were made for."

"Father never—" Ella started to say, but Will waved a hand at her. She fell silent.

"You'll do what Ella wants," Will said, feeling more than a little foolish. "Ella holds you all the time. You know the way she moves. You can move *faster* if she wants you to. You could even move on your own."

He turned and sheepishly handed the needle to Ella. "Try... try telling it to do something."

"I've never heard of magic working like this," Ella said, but she brought it to her makeshift gown. "Um, can you stitch this diamond to the others, please?"

She yelped as the needle flew out of her hands. It twisted around the sewing thread and darted toward the dress, deftly stitching a diamond in the span of a breath.

Ella whipped around to stare at him, her hands fisted in delight. "Oh, Will. Will, you did *magic.*"

"Let's see what else it can do," Will said.

They had the dress sprawled over the floor in seconds. Ella directed Will, making him lay out diamonds in a pattern that made no sense to him but gradually formed a shape that *could* have been the skirts of a gown. She set the needle on it, and they stepped back to watch as the needle raced up and down over the floor, piecing the diamonds together.

"I can't believe it," Ella said, and turned to kiss Will's cheek. "You don't know what this means to me."

"I don't think the prince will mind if you show up in rags, personally," Will said.

"He doesn't need to choose me," Ella said, sitting down to watch the needle work, "but it's nice to be wanted. Sometimes that's enough."

Will thought of Luc stroking his hair, bright-eyed and smiling, calling him *kind.* "I think I might understand."

"*Do* you?" Ella's smile went sly. "You aren't thinking about that tall goblin fellow, are you?" When Will gaped at her, she covered her mouth to muffle a laugh. "Oh, Will. You think I haven't noticed all those times you ran off with some tall, strapping farmer for a talk? A *talk,* William?"

Will groaned. "Of course you spied on me."

"I didn't have to spy, you were that obvious. You're obvious now," she added. "So is he. He looks at you like a puppy, you know."

"He does not." Something clicked nearby, and Will checked to make sure the needle wasn't thumping into the floorboards. "We just have some things in common, that's all."

"That's better than those farmhands," Ella said. "You didn't have anything in common with them. He does seem rather charming, and so terribly polite."

"He shouldn't have to be charming or polite," Will said. Something clicked again, and he turned around to look for it. "But he's a captive, so he has to be."

"A captive!" Ella made a face. "That sounds so—"

"True," Will said, glancing under the bed. "That's the word you're looking for."

"Oh." Ella leaned against the bookshelf behind her, watching him carefully. "You *do* like him."

"I shouldn't have to like him to think he deserves better." Will skimmed through one of the books, frowning. Murtagh's handwriting was usually clear enough to read, but this was written in a shaky, shortened script, with half the words misspelled.

"I always thought you were cold," Ella said, "but it was just this place that made you that way. It's good to see you happy." She peered over his shoulder. "What *is* that? They can't be my father's notes."

"That's what I was thinking," Will said. Something clicked close by, but he pushed the distraction from his mind, too curious about the book. "But it's still about magic. Look, it says *steel bad fr prutec. silvur. 34g.* Protection, maybe? Silver?"

"It could be his old instructor's notes." Ella sat next to Will. "May I?" He handed her the book, and she flipped through it. "You're right about the magic. This looks like a spell list, here. Oh. Oh, my. It's for finding *bodies*. It must have been written during the war. So it has to be Father's instructor, then."

Will read the list. It was fairly simple, the kind of ingredients Olven would have ready at the smithy, with instructions for making a crude compass. It seemed that whoever used the compass would be able to find remains that had been scattered by battlefire.

"Thank the gods we don't need that anymore," Ella said, skimming to another page. "And here's a spell for a hammer that doesn't break. I suppose that's useful in battle, but the drawing looks like an odd sort of hammer, doesn't it?"

"It's a smith's hammer." Will felt a strange jump in his chest at the sight of the rough sketch. "Two faces, see? One for striking, one for shaping. The handle breaks more than the head, though."

"How odd." Ella skimmed to the beginning. "Maybe he wrote his name."

Ella tensed beside him, and Will looked down at the top of the page, where someone had scratched their name in a thick script.

*Robert Fletcher.* "That's my *father*," Will said. "What is *his* book doing in Murtagh's study?"

"What was he doing writing about magic?" Ella asked.

"I don't know!" Will frantically turned the pages, as though he could summon his father for answers if he looked hard enough.

There were diagrams on mending gates to ward against burglars, shaping horseshoes that never fell off, and even how to make the kind of knives Will was making for Olven. It read more like a blacksmithing guide than a spell book. "No one told me that he had magic. But Murtagh knew. He *knew*. He kept these books in his *study*."

"Maybe he wanted to tell you when you were older," Ella said, but even she didn't look convinced. "How many of these books were his? My father didn't know your father, did he?"

"That's a good fucking question," Will said. He could just about handle his father having magic. It made sense. Magic ran in the family, after all. But his father being friends with Murtagh made his skin crawl. Over the years, his father had become a comfortable specter, too distant and unformed to be capable of harm or duplicity. "But no. They weren't friends. They couldn't have been. Your father always said that I was acting too much like a smith when he was cross with me."

Ella blanched. "He said that?"

Will cursed himself. "He had opinions, Ella. That doesn't mean he didn't love you. But it doesn't explain why these books are here, either."

"Your mother might know." Ella didn't sound particularly pleased at the thought.

"She's embarrassed by him." Will thumbed through a complex diagram that even Olven would have trouble figuring out. "But she wouldn't be if she knew that my father had magic."

"So why did *my* father know if she didn't?" Ella took down another book off the shelf, looked at the front page, and discarded it. She looked over her shoulder at the needle, which was still sewing away, and turned back to the shelf. "Help me look for more."

Will scrambled to his feet. "Thank you," he said, as Ella pointed him toward the shelf next to hers.

"I'd want to know if it was about my father," Ella said. "I'd want to know everything about him."

Will grimaced, familiar guilt stinging his throat. "What if you don't like what you learn?"

Ella cast him a sidelong look. "I didn't know that he thought so poorly of your father's profession. He always told me that working people had their own dignity, but perhaps there was something he didn't like about smithing in particular."

"It's hard to say," Will said, turning again to the bookshelves.

In the end, they found four books with Robert Fletcher's name on the front. They were all scattered and disorganized, with terribly written shorthand and little designs scrawled in the margins. Will's father may have had magic, but he came at it haphazardly, clearly experimenting with each spell like a man fumbling in the dark.

"This magic is altogether strange," Ella said. The needle had long run out of thread and lay sadly in the middle of the floor, but Ella seemed too interested in the books to notice. "Is yours like this?"

"I think so," Will said. "I might not be the only one. They practice magic differently in the Brightwood, too."

"I grew up so frightened of the Brightwood," Ella said. "But you like it there, don't you?"

"I do." Will turned the page of his father's book. "There's a smith called Olven—have I told you about him yet?"

"You haven't told me anything," Ella said, "but I'd like to know."

Will realized that, somehow, Ella was the only member of his family he wanted to talk about the Brightwood with. "All right," he said. "What do you want to—" Something buzzed behind him, and Will whipped around in time to see a fat black beetle land on the bookshelf behind him. Ella exclaimed softly, making the same gentle expression she reserved for Louisa's kitten.

"Oh, look at you." She lifted the beetle in her hands. It was easily half the size of her palm, and its iridescent surface looked oddly familiar. It clicked again, wings appearing and vanishing in a blink, and Ella cooed at it. "You're beautiful."

"It's a bug, Ella." The sight of the insect sitting placidly in Ella's hands made his skin crawl.

"Beetles can be as lovely as a painting if you look at them the right way," Ella said. "I've been seeing quite a few of them lately. Louisa keeps stepping on them, but I don't think they're hurting anyone."

"I've seen them, too," Will said, remembering the beetle in Olven's kitchen. Didn't Olven have a charm to ward off insects? What was one doing in his kitchen? He supposed that insects and animals could pass through the illusions in the woods at the border, which would account for them being in the Brightwood as well, but Will couldn't shake the disquiet building in his stomach. He didn't think he'd *only* seen one at Olven's. "How did that get in here?"

"Oh, probably through the window," Ella said, unlatching the shutters with one hand. "Did you open it the last time you were here?"

"I think so," Will said carefully.

"Then that explains it," Ella said. She tipped the beetle out the window, and Will heard it buzzing as it flew off. Ella leaned against the windowsill, her long hair falling over one shoulder. "I'm glad we could do this, Will. It feels lonely here sometimes, and you're vexing, but—oh, I don't know. Isn't that what having a brother is meant to be like?"

Will leaned on the other side of the window and searched the darkness outside for the flutter of wings. "Maybe. I suppose I should thank you for putting up with me, then?"

Ella lay a hand on his arm. "You're welcome." She closed the shutters again, blocking out the night beyond. "Now, stop trying to distract me and let's see what your father had to say in those journals."

***

"There's a man looking for you."

Luc tried not to impale himself on his own sword as Felicity emerged from the shadows of the training yards, looking like a ghost trying to haunt the palace in broad daylight. Alistair, who'd been running Luc through a series of complicated drills, stepped back with a grin as Felicity scrambled over the railing of the fencing circle. Her veil was askew, revealing yellow hair cropped far too close to her ears. Felicity grimly readjusted it when she caught Luc staring.

"What kind of man?" Luc asked.

"A short one." Felicity glared at Alistair, who took a measured step back. She handed a folded paper to Luc. "I took this from one of Faramond's pages."

"You can't just steal from your brother's servants," Luc said, opening the letter.

"I can if Mother is planning to marry me off," Felicity said.

"Then you should reading *her* correspondence." Luc scanned the letter, recognizing Will's short, careful script immediately. It didn't say much other than that Will would be waiting for him at the Long Shot Inn.

"Which page?" Luc and Felicity both startled at that. Alistair leaned against the railing next to them, his dark gaze fixed on Felicity. "We should know if one of the crown prince's servants is giving away his letters."

Felicity narrowed her eyes at him. "Who's *we?*"

Alistair shrugged. "It's just curious, isn't it? Maybe it was the page I saw scurrying around the other day. He was a new one, a lanky little thing, gold hair in his eyes. Probably cut it himself," he added.

Felicity's scowl darkened. "Why would *I* care what a page looks like?"

"That's a good question," Alistair said. Felicity glared at him for another tense second, then strode off, muttering under her breath.

"Is Felicity masquerading as a page?" Luc asked, keeping his voice low.

Alistair watched Felicity walk out of hearing before he answered. "I can't say, Your Highness. But I have seen a boy in a page uniform with a habit of disappearing in much the same way as the princess."

That could be a dangerous habit, if it were true. The king didn't look kindly on subterfuge—though if Felicity had been successfully stealing correspondence, his spymaster should sharpen up a little.

It could simply be more of Felicity's eccentricities, but if she *preferred* being a page to hiding in the shadows like a gargoyle, there was a chance that she could be like Will. It would explain some of her paranoia and reluctance to embrace the life of a social princess, but it was rude in goblin society to speculate on someone else's gender. If he were at home, Luc would simply ask. Perhaps he could speak to Felicity in private the next time she ambushed him in a dark corner.

If Wren came to the festival, *she* could speak to Felicity herself. Luc tried to suppress the twisting, painful ache in his chest at the thought. He couldn't risk hoping that his family might come, and even if they did, he couldn't say what they'd think of his Morvanish manners. It was easier to focus on other things, like Felicity, or Will, or throwing himself into dueling practice.

"This would be easier to handle in the goblin court." He didn't realize he'd said it aloud until he caught Alistair nodding.

"A second naming *would* be more practical," Alistair said. A second naming was what goblins called it when people like Will or Luc's sister announced their true gender. Luc was surprised to hear it from a human, but he supposed that Morvanish people didn't have a term for the practice. "Is the letter good news, Your Highness?"

"I think so," Luc said. "Would you be amenable to a walk in the city this afternoon?"

"I'll petition their majesties," Alistair said.

Alistair returned to him when Luc had finished preparing for the outing. Luc had decided on a trim vest that made his shoulders appear slightly broader—not that he was *trying* to entice Will. They had work to do, after all. Will was probably there to speak about his heart, not to tear his clothes to pieces and take him on the floor of the inn.

Of course, if he *wanted* to, Luc wouldn't precisely say no.

Alistair bowed shortly when Luc opened the door. "I'm to accompany you to the city, Your Highness. Prince Faramond sends his regards, but he is dealing with matters of state."

That probably meant he'd been roped into planning for the festival again. Luc didn't envy him. Ramon had looked ragged the last few times they'd managed to find a minute alone, and he seemed almost as displeased with the prospect of an impending betrothal as his sibling.

The capital city of Morvane wasn't as structured as Hanish, the capital of the Brightwood. It didn't have a proper name, for one. It was just Morvane, the heart of the country *and* the country itself, built as a trading hub in the times of the elven god-kings. Slaves of the god-kings had been ferried to Elfhame from the river that divided the city, and the burning of the slave ships had been the first catalyst of the rebellion.

The scars of that time showed in the cramped buildings that rebels had rebuilt after their fires burned the docks, and in the jars of ash hanging in doorways and windowsills. Fire had been what had killed the god-kings, so ash was a symbol of protection. Some of the jars were rumored to hold the ashes of one of the god-kings, the elf wizard who'd come to Morvane to suppress the rebellion.

Goblins had their own ways to honor the war, but Luc was more familiar with the Morvanish traditions. The streets were named after famous human warriors of the rebellion, and Morvanish people still paused at certain road markers to make a gesture for luck, an old salute that was now just another superstition. Luc had to pass three markers on his way to the inn.

The Long Shot Inn overlooked the river, which was dotted with boats and bisected by a narrow wooden drawbridge. Spells on the stone walls kept the river clean, so people walking on foot usually swam across rather than take the bridge. A line of swimmers were sprawled out in the sun when Luc reached the inn, their bright, colorful clothing darkened by the water.

Will must have swum across as well, because Luc found him sunning himself on a bench beside the inn, his hair damp and his jacket draped over his knees. He grinned when he saw Luc, and Luc's chest ached again.

"I went across for chocolate," Will said. He opened his bag, which must have been spelled to repel water, retrieving a bag of sugar-dusted truffles. He tossed one to Luc. The chocolate was sharply bitter and sweet, melting softly on his tongue. Luc wondered if Will's mouth tasted the same. "Courtesy of Ramon's sack of silver. I have a room upstairs if you want to talk philosophy again."

Luc almost asked what he meant, but he caught Will looking at Alistair and nodded. "Will is something of a scholar," he told Alistair. "Ramon said he'd die of boredom if we started on again."

"I've never been one for it myself," Alistair admitted. "We should have a few hours before we need to return."

Luc handed Alistair a few coins for a meal at the inn, but Alistair gave them back, positioning himself by the door to the room Will had rented. Luc didn't bother attempting to give Will the money to compensate for the room instead. Will would only scowl and mutter. As it was, he seemed displeased by Alistair's presence at the door. He leaned down to the lock and whispered into it, brows lowered. It must have been a spell, though it was hard to tell without any runes to glow when the magic took hold.

"That should muffle our voices," he said. "I don't want the innkeeper knowing that I cast a spell on her door, so we'll have to be careful."

"You really must speak to our mages," Luc said, examining the lock. "The ones in the Brightwood," he added quickly. "They'd be fascinated by this."

"I wish I could," Will said. "They sound like they aren't as constricted as the wizards here. Luc." He pulled Luc to the bed, but instead of pushing him down like Luc's fanciful fantasies hoped for, he sat them both down. "I don't think my stepfather's notes will help us. They're all about how to control my magic. Apparently it kept fighting him." A smile flickered across his face, but it disappeared as quickly as it came. "There's nothing about your heart, and even if I tried to use his spells to reverse it, I don't think they would work. But I did find something else."

He pulled a heavy leather journal out of his bag. The pages were yellow with age, and when he opened it, the spine creaked alarmingly. Luc leaned over it, curious.

"It's my father's," Will said. He smiled sheepishly, looking younger without the grim, worried expression he usually wore. "I think he had magic like mine. But it doesn't have anything to do with the truth. It's all centered around metalwork."

Luc took the book from Will. The writing inside was shaky and barely legible, but he could just make out what seemed like a spell for enchanting a spoon. "Do you think your magic is connected to metal too?"

"It doesn't explain why I can see through the thorns," Will said, "but the rest of it seems like it fits. But look. Right here, there's a spell he used for soldiers. It's a compass, but it's supposed to help you recover pieces of dead soldiers for burial."

"Rather morbid," Luc said with a grimace.

"Luc." Will rolled his eyes. "Don't you think I could change the spell a little? What if I'm trying to find a missing piece of a *living* person?"

Luc stared into Will's dark eyes. "You could make a compass for my heart."

"It has to be in the palace," Will said. "We just need to find out *where.* If I can make this compass work, I can find it. Do you think you could get away with searching the lower levels of the palace? I think Murtagh brought me downstairs, but there's no telling where he kept your heart."

Luc shook his head. "I would be followed if I tried to look." He thought of Felicity slinking through the palace unseen. If he knew her well enough to trust her, she could probably get into places that a goblin ward of the king could not. It was still too much of a risk. "It can't be in any of the places I'm permitted to go, so it must be beneath the palace. I was forbidden to go there when the spell was made. But that's where the wizards live. You may have raw power, Will, but I don't think you can stand against over a dozen wizards and apprentices."

"That's still one step closer," Will said. "We just need a way to search the dungeons and crypts when the wizards aren't there."

"You can't," Luc said. "There's always someone."

Will stared down at his feet, his jaw working as though he were swallowing words he couldn't say. At last, he asked, "Will the wizards be there during the festival?"

Luc thought about it. "They've invited the goblin court, so the king will want to show off his power. Still, you might not be able to slip away."

"Wait," Will said, face tight with concern. "Your mother's coming?"

"She might not," Luc said.

Will touched Luc's hand, a small, tentative attempt at comfort. "Is that better than if she does come?"

"I don't know." Luc felt strange when he tried to think about it, as though the spell on his heart was trying to grasp his thoughts and drag them down. "I don't think I can say right now. Let's focus on my heart first. I'll figure out how to feel about my mother later."

Will squeezed his hand. He got up, pacing nervously across the room and back. "What if we had a distraction, then? Something to keep their eyes on Ramon or the goblin court?"

"Something magical?" Luc asked. "Would that be safe?"

"Maybe not." Will kept pacing. "What do the king and queen care about? What matters to them?"

"Marrying off their children," Luc said immediately. "But Felicity will claw out the eyes of anyone who tries to propose, and Ramon doesn't care for marriage. He thinks it tarnishes love. He suspects that any woman who wants him would only want the crown, not his affection."

Will paused. He seemed conflicted, his brows pinched, hands twitching as though he needed to twist or break something. "And if there *were* a woman who didn't want the crown?"

"You don't mean your sister?" Luc asked. "It's true that Ramon fancies her, but I don't believe it's love, and the king and queen wouldn't approve. They can't have magic in their family line. It would remind people of the god-kings."

"We could make it look like love," Will said, "only for a night. That's all Ella wants. She doesn't want to be queen, and Ramon doesn't want a social climber. We don't have to convince the king or queen that she's perfect. We just need to make her look so exceptional that everyone *thinks* the prince is in love. If I use magic to draw attention to her, the wizards might be too curious to wonder if someone's rummaging around in their rooms."

"That might suit Ramon as well," Luc said. "If they think he'll choose her, he could use her magical bloodline to delay a betrothal. But will that distract the guards?"

"It will if we turn it into a spectacle," Will said. "If you set Ramon up with the most unsuitable partners that first night, I can use my magic to make everyone look Ella's way. That can distract people enough for me to slip away. And if your family is already there... would there be someone who can get you home?"

"They'd be risking treason to do it," Luc said. He remembered Jade forsaking the crown on his behalf, calling him *mine, my son*. His memories of her were so dim, but she'd already loved him enough to turn her back on the throne. "My sister Jade. She might help. But Will, there's a chance we'll be on our own, and if the king knows you helped me, you won't be safe here."

Will went quiet. He checked the windowsill as though spies could crawl through the cracks in the wood, then closed the shutters. "I can get you through the thorns into the Brightwood," he said at last.

Luc wanted to ask Will if he would stay when it was over, but whatever lay between them was still too new. He couldn't ask Will to risk being labeled a traitor *and* leave his home behind. "Thank you."

"Don't thank me yet," Will said. He turned to face Luc. "Are you sure that you're all right with the goblin court being invited?"

"I don't know. No one may come at all." Luc sat down on the bed again. Will joined him, lacing their fingers together. It was such a small, intimate gesture that Luc had to stop to process it, his chest tight. "I think that my true feelings about it may be too deep to draw up right now. Westwood probably suppressed them when he replaced my heart."

"That fucking monster," Will said. "I believe you. The things he said in his notes about *me*... He only tried *spoiling* me because my magic worked better when I was happy. He used to give me something new from the capital every other week for a while. It's a good thing that I'm an obstinate brat by nature. He could never keep his cheerful facade around me."

"Does your magic work better for *you* when you're happy?" Luc asked.

"I don't know. I only just started using it," Will said. "The silencing spell worked too well, and I was... I mean, I was pretty... you could *say* I was happy."

"We can try again," Luc said. He kissed him softly, pleased to find Will leaning into his touch. "How about now? Happier yet?"

Will raised his brows. "So this is research, is it?"

"Sure," Luc said. He leaned closer, bracing his arms on either side of Will. "Research."

"My clothes are too wet for this," Will said. Luc kissed his neck, mimicking how Will had kissed *him* the last time. Will gasped, and when Luc scraped his skin with his sharp teeth, he shivered deliciously.

"Take them off, then," Luc said.

Will was close enough that Luc could hear his muttered, "*Entitled little princes.*"

"I'm hardly little," Luc said, drawing back as Will struggled to take off his tunic.

"I know," Will said, his voice muffled through the fabric. "I felt it."

"*Felt* it?" Luc helped Will shrug off his tunic. He had stays with a thin cotton shirt underneath, which must have been uncomfortable after his swim. He stripped them off with a sigh of relief.

"I'm amazed you can walk with that thing," Will said, and pointedly looked down to the bulge of Luc's cock through his clothes.

"I was talking about my *height,*" Luc cried.

Will lay back on the bed and rolled his eyes. "Tall men and their preoccupation with whether they can crack their skulls on door frames." He kicked off his boots, which were thankfully dry. He must have carried them in his bag while he crossed the river. "Take off my hose for me."

"You don't usually wear hose," Luc pointed out. He climbed over Will to start untying the belts holding his hose up, but Will pulled him down for a fierce kiss instead, biting his lower lip.

"I wore them especially for you," he said, "since you're always so formal about your clothes." He tweaked Luc's vest.

Luc untied Will's belt and rolled his hose down his legs. For a man who worked with his arms, he had surprisingly firm thighs. It must have come from all the walking people did in the country; it seemed as though he had to cross a dozen fields to get anywhere. He let Will's hose drop to the floor and gazed down at him, sprawled beneath Luc on the bed with a sly grin on his face.

"I wouldn't mind seeing *you*, either," he said.

Luc hesitated. He was used to people looking at him askance, wondering loudly if, like some of his kin, he had feathers hidden beneath his clothes. The royal family of the Brightwood had too much elf blood in their lineage to look too much like the goblins of Morvanish nightmares. Most goblin folk had a little elf in their ancestry, since elven commoners had fled to the Brightwood when Elfhame fell.

His family looked more human than most, but their goblin heritage came out in noticeable ways. Wren had been born with her back covered in pinfeathers like a baby bird. Jade had crystalline nails and scaled limbs that glittered like jewels. Alara used to have wings strong enough to lift her a foot or two off the ground, but they'd been amputated during the war, when she'd used them to shield herself from a volley of arrows.

Luc had scales like Jade, but instead of covering most of his body, they appeared in uneven patches. Most were centered on his lower back, shining a silvery-green in his mirror at the palace. He knew that Will had been to the Brightwood more than almost any other Morvanish human, but he still wasn't sure how he'd react.

"Is it your heart?" Will asked. "Has it been too long since the last time I called you through the spell?"

"It isn't that," Luc said. He took off his vest. Will sat up to kneel on the bed before him. He ran his hands through Luc's hair, teasing his fingers through the strands and scratching the back of Luc's head.

"One of my closest friends has the head of an owl," Will said.

"My sister had wings." Luc smiled when Will perked up, looking around at his shoulders. "I didn't inherit that trait."

"Oh. I suppose I would have noticed."

"Are you disappointed?" Luc stopped halfway through pulling off his undershirt. "You *want* me to have feathers? They aren't as soft as you think, you know."

"I'll believe it when I feel it," Will said. "So what is it? If it's your cock, I'm going to bite you. No one would be insecure about *that.*"

"It's perfectly normal," Luc said, hurriedly undoing his trousers to end Will's deluded fixation altogether. But Will had already seen the silvery scales on Luc's left arm, and he stopped Luc with a hand on his shoulder.

"Can I touch them?" he asked.

Luc could feel his face starting to grow warm. "If you'd like to."

Will trailed his fingers down the scales on Luc's skin and Luc shivered at the sensation. "I can feel the ridges. They're like snake scales."

"Or dragon," Luc said. "We like to be close to things that can fly."

"I don't blame you." Will seemed entranced, his voice soft. "I wonder if dragons ever looked like this. Like they were lined in liquid silver."

"You make them sound beautiful," Luc said.

Will's expression turned stern again. "I already said that you are. You don't think I'm a liar, do you?"

"No! No, I just... it's strange," Luc said weakly.

Will shrugged. "So am I, to *them*." He gestured toward the general direction of the palace. "I exist to spite them." He pulled Luc down to the bed and started undoing the points of Luc's hose. "You really haven't had a man's mouth on your cock before?"

"I hadn't been *kissed* before you," Luc said.

"Then you'll love this." Will shuffled back between Luc's legs, framed by his thighs. He pulled his hose off just enough to reveal Luc's cock. The hose would probably stretch horribly after this, but Luc couldn't bring himself to care.

Will lowered his head, and Luc dug his clawed nails into the bedsheets as he felt a tongue slide along the underside of his cock. Will wrapped his fingers around the base, just tight enough to make Luc's cock jump and his body thrum with a sudden, urgent need.

"Imagine how good it will feel when I ride you," Will said, and Luc's mind took that moment to shut the doors and shutter the windows, because Will took Luc's cock in his mouth and swallowed it down to the base.

"Fuck me," Luc whispered. He breathed shallowly as Will bobbed his head up again, his cheeks hollowing in a way that made his mouth tight, a slick, glorious pressure on his cock. Luc had to stop himself from bucking his hips, desperate for more, and Will put a hand on his thigh to steady him. Somehow, even with Will naked between his legs with his mouth on Luc's cock, he seemed utterly in control. Luc felt wild, unhinged, just a mess of breathlessness and heat, but Will was calm and steady, his gaze fixed on Luc. It was as though the more Luc lost control, the more Will gained it, which only made Luc more desperate with want.

Will's lips stretched over Luc's cock, his mouth stuffed so wide that Luc wondered if he could reach down and feel his cock distending Will's throat on the way down. Luc groaned, dropping his head on the bed.

"Gods," he said. "That was... I don't think I can conjure the words."

Will's breath came hot on his skin as Will drew back off Luc's cock. "Oh, it's adorable that you think it's over."

He enveloped Luc again, moving faster now, fingers slipping away to grip Luc's thigh as he went all the way down. Will's throat seized around him, but he didn't stop, and Luc felt it as Will removed his hand from Luc's thigh. He propped himself up on his elbows to find Will with his hand between his own thighs, his face flushed as he worked Luc's cock with a fierce determination that reminded Luc of all the times Will had called him forth out of the spell in his chest. If a man could break a spell simply by the enthusiasm with which he sucked a cock, Will would be the greatest curse-breaker in Morvane.

Will moaned around him, his thighs shifting together, and Luc couldn't hold himself back any longer. He barely had a moment to warn Will, his release crashing over him all at once. He cried out, coming down Will's throat, hips moving despite his best efforts.

Will tilted his head up, Luc's cock sliding over his lips as he pulled away. He met Luc's eyes as he swallowed his spend. Luc sat up to smooth down his unkempt hair for him.

"You are *magnificent*," Luc said.

Will caught Luc's hand and kissed it, not breaking his gaze. "My pleasure, I assure you."

"I want to do the same for you," Luc said, as Will lazily kissed his inner wrist. "I don't know exactly how humans are... are *built*, but we're roughly the same, aren't we?"

"My cock's a little smaller," Will said, "and I might have been enjoying myself already. I know I have a reputation as a selfish brat, but it's nice to take care of people."

"You don't seem selfish to me."

Will raised his brows. "And the part about me being a brat?"

"Certainly not selfish," Luc said, laughing as Will rolled his eyes.

"I was *going* to teach you how to pleasure me," Will said, reaching for his clothes, "but if you're going to be *insulting...*"

"There's the brat," Luc said, and rolled Will away from the edge of the bed, kissing him thoroughly. He was starting to figure out when Will was only pretending to be outraged. "Show me, Will. I want to return the favor."

"I suppose I don't have any *other* pressing things to do," Will said, "like stealing your heart back from the king."

"You'll do that anyway," Luc said, and the fond look Will gave him made warmth fill his false heart.

"That's right," Will said. He kissed Luc again, softer this time. "I suppose I can teach you, then. If you insist."

# Chapter Eight

Will could think of a hundred things he needed to do before the festival, but none of them seemed quite so important as sitting on the edge of the bed with Luc kneeling on the floor between his legs. The room was dark with the shutters closed, and with the magicked lock creating a protective bubble from the outside world, Will felt like he could take a minute to breathe.

"That's right," he said, as Luc, with the enthusiasm of someone who'd only just learned what his tongue could do, buried himself between Will's legs. Will could probably come just from the sight of Luc trying so earnestly to get him off, but he held himself on the edge, preferring to appreciate the low hum of pleasure spreading through his limbs.

Luc's grip on Will's thighs tightened, his claws scraping lightly over Will's skin. Will shivered, and Luc looked up with his mouth wet and his pupils blown wide with need.

"Did you... did you like that?" he asked, panting slightly.

"Try it again and see," Will said. Luc raised his hands higher, scratching down Will's side. Will moaned at the sensation. "Yes. Yes, I think I like that."

"It isn't painful?" Luc asked.

"Could be more." Luc dug his nails deeper into Will's skin, making pink lines along his stomach, and Will shuddered, thighs clenching around Luc's head. "Gods."

Will had knelt for enough men to find that he enjoyed the feeling of his throat constricting around someone's cock, the pain sending shivers of pleasure through his body as he made the man above him lose control. He just hadn't realized how deep his propensity for pain went. Will let out another shuddering gasp as Luc scratched his inner thighs. He ground into his mouth, shaking through his second wave of release that afternoon with the marks of Luc's claws on his body.

When he finally caught his breath, Luc was kissing the scratches on his thighs. He looked up, his eyes dark, hair a mess, silvery scales on his arms shimmering in the dim light.

He knew that Luc's guard was outside, listening to nothing but the sounds of voices in the dining area below. Beyond that was the palace, the king's wizards, and somewhere in the depths of it all, Luc's true heart. But Will couldn't help himself. He wanted to stay there, just him and Luc, secure in a small, protected room.

They sprawled on the bed together, lazy and languid, Will idly running his fingers through Luc's white hair.

"I made a needle come to life the other day," he said. Luc turned in his arms to face him properly, the bed sinking beneath them. "It isn't a heart, but it's something. I'll try to make the compass the next time I'm in the Brightwood. I just wish I had someone to explain why my magic only works half the time. Perhaps my father would have known."

Luc sat up. "What hasn't worked?"

"Lighting candles," Will said, frustration creeping into his voice as he rattled off the list. "Making bread rise. Oh, and I tried to make my clothes dry faster when I jumped in the river earlier, and you can see how *that* went."

Luc tapped his clawed nails on his knee, looking into the middle distance. "But you *did* open a lock, make a needle move, and you broke that sphere apart. Not to mention whatever you do when you call me through my false heart."

Will shrugged. "I suppose."

"My *brass* heart," Luc said. "Your theory about being connected to metal might be right."

Will felt oddly lightheaded. "But I can see through the thorns."

Except it was a miracle he could see at all, wasn't it? His glasses had been given to him by Westwood, but they'd been a new invention, the glass warped and thick. Will had discarded them for weeks after Westwood had died, but then he'd given up fumbling awkwardly through the house.

"You'd better work properly this time," he'd grumbled at them, blinking hard. "What's the point of you if you won't show me what's actually out there?"

He hadn't replaced his glasses in over a decade, but they still worked perfectly. Will picked them up from where they'd fallen on the pillow and rubbed the silver wire between his fingers. Then, feeling more than a little nervous, he worked the glass lenses free.

He put the frames back on. The world came into clear focus again, no longer a distant, murky haze a few paces away.

"I magicked the frames," he said softly. "Maybe my magic is why I'm so comfortable in a forge. It's been calling me all along."

Luc smiled and kissed him. "You, Will Fletcher, are the only wizard in Morvane who's worth knowing. I've half a mind to steal you away to the Brightwood when I go."

"Only half?"

They kissed lazily, tangling the sheets on the bed and almost tipping the journal onto the floor. When Will came up for air again, he was wrapped in Luc's arms, stroking the scales near his hipbones.

"What will you do with your magic after this?" Luc asked.

"I don't know. I had ideas of starting a smithy before. If I can stay hidden from the king's wizards, I might still do it. Wizards here are bound to the king. Even if there weren't the risk of someone finding out the name I used to go by, I wouldn't want to serve the man who hurt you."

Luc kissed Will's temple. "I thought I would always be Ramon's companion. I never considered anything else. I don't even know what I'd be in the Brightwood. But if you..." his voice faltered. "If you wanted something different, you could always join me."

"I like the Brightwood," Will said, "even if the goblins there keep expecting me to start frothing at the mouth and swinging axes around. I don't think I have the skill to start my own smithy yet. But if I could work with Olven and make chains that can't break, or hinges that don't rust..." He sighed. "That sounds rather silly and small, doesn't it?"

"Not really," Luc said. "I'd like to see it one day."

Will felt a small, fluttery hope building in his chest. If he *could* go into the Brightwood with Luc, and if the queen didn't try to take their heads off for breaking the peace, maybe he could build something there. Maybe they both could.

"I don't know if I'll still be a prince when this is over," Luc said, "but no matter where it leads us, I'd still like to be..." He paused, and Will saw something in his eyes that made his stomach swoop dangerously. "...your friend."

Will kissed him. "I think we're in this together," he said, "no matter what we are."

Luc cupped his head in one hand and kissed him back.

By the time they'd brought their clothes and hair to some semblance of order, Luc's guard was half asleep outside the door. He jumped when they stepped out, stifling a yawn.

"Your Highness," he said with a quick bow.

"Sorry to keep you, Alistair," Luc said. "We're both a little too passionate about philosophy, I'm afraid."

Will only just stopped himself from barking out a laugh.

He took a mail cart back to Westwood, hanging off the handrails at the back with a pair of teenagers. The city gave way to small villages huddled by the riverbank, crossing stone field markers and flocks of geese. Young shepherds splashed in the river while their dogs watched the birds, and in the distance, the tree line of the Brightwood rose like a heavy blanket draping the horizon.

Despite the looming festival, the heart hidden in the depths of the palace, and his mother waiting for him at home, Will was too distracted by the thought of running away into the Brightwood with Luc to care. It was a dangerous idea, and possibly a foolish one. It might not work at all. Nevertheless, he let himself dwell on fanciful thoughts of building a smithy with Luc standing at the entrance, his true heart beating in his chest. He was so caught up in daydreams that he nearly missed his chance to jump off the mail cart. He stepped down closer to the border of the Brightwood, where farms gave way to fields of wildflowers.

Something clicked nearby, and Will staggered to a halt. He looked down at his bag. A shiny black beetle crawled out of it, wings barely visible as it prepared to take off. Will grabbed it, tightening his grip as the creature buzzed frantically in an attempt to escape.

"What are you?" Will asked. "There have been too many of you around lately. Are you magical? A spy from the palace?"

The beetle clicked and buzzed angrily in his hands. He felt more than a little foolish, standing in an empty lane and yelling at a beetle, but he couldn't ignore the eerie way the creatures seemed to always be around when he was talking about Luc.

"If you're something magical, show me who sent you," Will ordered. He let go, and the beetle dropped to the ground, still buzzing.

Nothing happened. Will sighed, frustrated at himself for being so paranoid that the appearance of a few insects would rattle him, and started marching back to the house.

Then he heard it. Buzzing, soft at first but building to an incessant hum, rising all around him in the high grass. Beetles emerged from the fields, hundreds of them, all black and glossy, all nearly the size of his palm, converging where the first beetle fell.

Will drew back as the beetles rose in one horrible writhing mass, a misshapen lump heaving and twisting before him. It grew taller than Will, a swarm of insects in the loose shape of a person, humming and clicking. It turned its faceless head his way.

"Show..." He took a step back, his stomach lurching at the way the body swayed and shifted. "Show me to the people who sent you." If they'd been sent by the palace, then he would need to find Luc before the king and his wizards could lock him away, or worse, turn him into someone so pleasant and compliant that he'd never look at Will again.

The humming figure turned toward the trees and took off. It didn't run like a mortal, but broke apart into a cloud of beetles below the waist, the rest of its form expanding and shrinking like the beating of a heart. Will ran after it, kicking up soft earth as he cut through furrowed fields and over irrigation canals. The cloud of beetles flew before him, and the air filled with angry buzzing and clicking as Will flung himself forward.

It didn't take long to see where the beetles were going. They cut straight toward the Brightwood, undulating as Will struggled to keep up. He burst through the trees as the sun started sinking over the horizon. He was heading east of Olven's smithy, toward a part of the Brightwood he'd never been to before, where the little village faded into nothing but light-strewn trees and mossy creeks. Will stumbled over tree roots and scraped against branches as he ran, the light fading through the trees. He'd passed the border at last, but his lungs burned and his legs felt like they might give out beneath him as he ran.

If the beetles belonged to the goblin queen, that could be as bad as the king of Morvane knowing their plans. She'd given Luc to the humans in the first place, and there was no telling what else she'd sacrifice to keep the peace between their countries.

The beetles took Will to a small clearing, where the light in the trees nestled so high in the branches that Will felt like he was staggering into a starlit forest. The beetles dispersed, spreading into the trees and burrowing in the ground.

"Wait," Will panted. "Wait. I told you to... to show me where..."

Something whistled sharply past his ear. An arrow landed in the grass at his feet, and Will twisted around to find a dark figure in the branches of a tree behind him. They were small and vaguely lizardlike, with a long tail that wrapped around one leg as they drew another arrow back on a shortbow.

"On your knees, wizard." A woman's voice spoke behind him, warm and imperious. Will glimpsed other figures in the trees, some standing just behind them, others in the branches, all brandishing weapons. He fell to his knees, still breathing hard, and one of them ran over. She was about three feet tall, with fur down her arms and a ratlike tail whipping behind her. She held a knife out to Will as she approached, her eyes bright with fear. Someone behind him grabbed his arms, and terror surged through his weary limbs. He struggled out of his captor's grip and fell back as the goblins crept closer. He drew up his magic, eyeing the metal in their weapons.

"Remember the heat of the forge," he said. The knives and swords in their hands burned hot, and several goblins yelped and dropped them in the grass. Will got to his feet, narrowly dodging the ratlike goblin and stumbling over a small, moss-covered stone.

A clawed hand grabbed his left arm, lifting him up to his toes like a child dangling their least favorite doll. He looked up into the face of a tall goblin woman with white hair braided out of her face, her violet eyes gleaming with a cold fire. Her skin was almost entirely scaled, glittering like dark jewels in the light of the trees.

"Who are you?" Will asked. "Are you working for the queen? Why are you following me?"

The goblin woman dropped him, and the others swarmed Will, hands grasping and clawing, yanking his arms behind his back, wrapping his limbs with thick, heavy rope. Someone tied a cloth around his head in a makeshift gag, and Will glared up at the cold, commanding woman standing over him.

"Bring him to the safehouse," she said to the others. Will writhed as he was dragged to his feet, his legs too tightly bound to move more than a few mincing steps at a time. "I would like to speak with this wizard who tarries so long with my brother."

***

If Will weren't crammed into a decrepit cabin with a gaggle of roughly dressed goblins, he would assume he was being kidnapped by the queen.

Luc's sister bore herself with the confidence of someone used to command. She may have been dressed in worn leathers and dark linens, but it didn't matter when she wore them like a noble, striding to the head of her company with a quick, self-assured gait. She had Luc's eyes, but there was no warmth in them, and she stared down at Will with a stern, dispassionate gaze.

He was still gagged. The goblins had covered his eyes with a cloth through their journey, which he'd spent slung over a goblin's back like a sack of potatoes. The cabin they'd taken him to was falling apart, wind whistling through gaps in the wood and water pooling in murky puddles on the floor. Black beetles crawled up the walls, and one landed on Luc's sister's shoulder before flying off again.

Luc's sister propped her hands on her hips. "Do you know who I am, wizard? If you're half as clever as you should be, you suspect." Will rolled his eyes. It wasn't as though he could actually answer her, even if he did have his suspicions. "You may call me Jade of the Hanish Tree. You have asked my spies to bring you to me, yes? Well, here you are. So let's have a conversation."

A rational man would have pleaded for his life. Will's tongue, clearly devoid of any self-preservation, ran away before his brain could catch up. "You're the one who gagged me, smartass." Thankfully, it came out too muffled for most people to interpret.

"Untie him," Jade ordered. She kept her gaze fixed on Will. "If he tries to use magic, stick an arrow through his throat."

Will snorted derisively. Someone untied his bonds, and when his gag was whipped away, Will shakily got to his feet. It didn't help much. Jade was still taller than Luc, towering over Will even at his full height.

"You've been spying on us," Will said. "On whose behalf?"

Jade smiled. "Us? You're an us?" She walked around him, slowly, taking him in. "You, a human wizard, one of those who spat fire on our people on the battlefield?"

The other goblins in the cabin were still and quiet, watching him.

"I would hope it would be obvious to see," Will said, "that I was a *child* when the war ended."

"I don't concern myself with human aging," Jade said.

"The passage of time is pretty important," Will said, gesturing wildly with both hands, "since I wasn't old enough to actually read a clock when war wizards were setting things on fire!"

Jade drew back. "Do you *want* me to kill you?"

Will felt feverish and hot with terror, but it only pushed the blunt, spiteful core of him to the surface. "This is what happens when you shoot arrows at me!"

"And my brother is fond of you." It wasn't a question. It sounded more like dumbfounded resignation, which was somehow worse.

"He wouldn't be if I belonged to the king, would he?" Will asked. "And you did—and I only say this again because I don't think you understood me the first time—*shoot an arrow at me.*"

"It was a warning shot."

"Right, because *that's* how you calm down a wizard!" Will cried, throwing his hands up in a helpless gesture. "Shoot at him!"

"Princess," the ratlike goblin said hesitantly, "would you like me to *actually* shoot him this time?"

Will whipped around to face them. "No!"

Jade pinched the bridge of her nose. "Leave us."

"Princess, I'm not sure if that's wise," the goblin said.

"Now," Jade ordered.

The goblins under her command left the cabin, moving so silently that Will couldn't hear their footfalls on the creaky wooden floor. When the last of them were gone, Jade and Will faced each other in the middle of the gutted cabin.

"There," Jade said. "We're alone. No arrows."

"You're wearing a sword," Will pointed out, nodding to the sheathed weapon at her hip.

"And you can speak magic," Jade said. "We all need some protection." She drew the sword. The sharp edge gleamed in a shaft of moonlight shining through a hole in the roof. "It's a good blade, made by a commendable smith. Perhaps you know him."

Will examined the sword, his heartbeat hammering so hard, he could feel it in his throat. He caught the mark at the hilt, a symbol of a talon clutching a rose, and his outrage staggered to a halt to make way for utter confusion.

"That's Olven's work," he said. Olven *had* been working on a sword recently, but why would it be for Jade, who was clearly hiding out in the woods with a cloud of beetles?

There had been a beetle in Olven's kitchen, Will remembered. And Olven had tried to stop Will from talking about Luc at first. Had he known that they were being spied on, or had he been wary after making weapons for a princess with a tendency to fire warning shots?

"He's a good goblin," Jade said. "He likes you, and that is one of the few things that kept you alive after you barreled into my camp."

"Was he spying on me?" Will didn't think he could handle it if Olven were a spy. It would be too much of a betrayal.

"No," Jade said. "He just likes to talk."

Will sighed heavily. That, at least, was believable.

"Olven's opinion notwithstanding," Jade said, "you're still a human. And a wizard raised you."

"If you've been listening to us with your beetles, then you know that he didn't do anything close to raising me," Will said. "He used me, just like he used Luc. Like your queen used Luc."

Jade stilled, her gaze flicking up to Will's eyes. "Those are dangerous words to say to a princess."

"They're true, though," Will said.

Jade held his gaze for a long time, the air around them charged like the air in a heavy storm.

"They truly ripped out his heart, then," Jade said softly. She didn't look like the haughty queen she'd appeared to be a moment before, but Will couldn't quite place the change in her face. "To make him... agreeable."

"Yes."

"And you intend to set it right?" Jade seemed to be searching his face for the answer, her brows lowered in the same way Luc's did when he was worried. The comparison made Will chafe less at being dragged across the Brightwood, but not by much. "Why? For revenge against the people who hurt you?"

"Because he doesn't deserve this," Will said. He took a step forward. "You heard us talking, didn't you? You know I'm not lying."

"I know you didn't *seem* to be lying," Jade said. She sheathed her sword again. "Except when you spoke to that pretty sister of yours. Do you distrust her?"

"What? Wait, which sister?" Will remembered Ella holding the beetle in the study. "You mean Ella? When did I lie to her?"

"You lied about your stepfather," Jade said. Will bristled at that, uncomfortable with this stranger judging him for sparing his own sister. *Stepsister*, he thought quickly, but the impulse to make the distinction had faded of late. "Do you think she's loyal to the king? Would she betray you?"

"No. It's her father," Will said. "I don't have to justify that to you. She wouldn't betray us, because I'm not telling her what we're doing. The fewer people know, the better. And what about you? What are you doing with this information? Handing it over to the queen?"

"I am most certainly not in contact with my mother," Jade said. "I can't enter the Morvanish palace, and all my spies there have been repelled save one. But I can take my brother to safety, if you bring him to me."

"Come get him," Will said. Jade frowned slightly. "Come to the festival. If we escape, we'll need help. It's a half of a day's ride to the Brightwood from the capital, and the king has an army at his disposal. There's only so much my magic can do."

"The queen would not permit me to attend," Jade said. "Even if I tried to infiltrate this festival on my own, the woods at the border are impenetrable."

"Not to me," Will said. "He needs you. He's been alone there, leashed to them by his heart."

"I know." Jade's voice took on that low, dangerous timbre of displeasure. "I know far more than you, wizard."

"Do you?" Will asked. "Then help us. Help *him*. We'll need a distraction at the festival. We have an idea for one, but if *you* show up..." He looked around the ruined cabin. "I take it that you and your friends aren't on good terms with the queen."

"Her magistrates call us bandits," Jade said, "so no, we aren't on the best of terms with my mother."

"The arrival of a bandit queen should make everyone turn their heads," Will said. "Just think about it. And if you don't come to the festival, how do I call on you when I bring Luc through the border?"

"Stop tossing my spies out of your windows and I'll keep one nearby," Jade said. "And get that horrible little urchin to stop stepping on them."

She had to mean Louisa this time. "She's twenty-three, by the by," Will said.

"How?" Jade asked, her haughty demeanor collapsing entirely. Will almost laughed.

"That's what happens when you spoil someone," Will said. "But she's showing flashes of disenchantment lately. It's strange to talk about this with someone who's been spying on my family with beetles."

Jade shrugged. "I have magic of my own. It isn't like yours. It runs through nature—roots, insects, lichen, the things most people ignore. Of course I'd watch the family of the wizard who sliced open my brother's chest."

"A family that will be missing me soon," Will said.

Jade nodded. "I'll escort you to the border. I'd apologize for our rough handling, but I had to determine if you were using my brother for your own ends."

"And you're satisfied?"

"Satisfied enough," Jade said. "But if you get him killed," she leveled a cold, dark look into his eyes, "then there is nowhere in Morvane that will be safe from me. I hope you understand."

Will bowed low enough to be more mocking than polite. "The bandit queen has made her point."

"You'll be a bad influence on him," Jade muttered. She strode past Will, the commanding demeanor emerging once more. "Come. The border isn't far."

This time, Jade didn't bind Will as he walked through the forest beyond Olven's village. The goblins under Jade's command followed them as Will tried to keep up with Jade's brisk gait. The woods at the border seemed dim and lifeless without the thick undergrowth that threatened to trip Will at every turn.

Jade pulled Will aside when they reached the border. Her claws were sharper than Luc's, pricking his shoulder, and he thought dimly of Luc scratching his thighs only that afternoon.

"I'll keep my spies nearby," Jade said, "should you need to speak to me."

"Think about the festival," Will said.

Jade looked toward the woods. Will wondered what she saw there. Were the thorns unnaturally thick, or a forest of nettles that crawled up the trees and latched on to goblins passing through? He lifted his glasses and recoiled. The vines twisting around the trees were the size of his waist, with slender thorns that jutted out like the prickles of a hedgehog. He settled his glasses on his nose again, and the thorns disappeared.

"Deliver my brother to me, and I will keep him safe," Jade said. "It may not be my place to say it... but mind that lovely sister of yours, wizard. I should not know more of her life than you do."

"You didn't *have* to spy on us," Will said. He already felt guilty enough about letting Ella shoulder the burden of keeping the household running. He didn't need a goblin princess to drive that guilt home.

"She deserves to know about her father," Jade said. "No one wants to take comfort in the memory of a monster. She should have the freedom to make that choice herself."

"Now you *are* overstepping," Will said. His stomach twisted with the miserable truth of her words.

"Do as you wish." She nodded toward the trees in a clear dismissal.

Rather than argue with a woman who thought beetles could give her insight into his life, Will bowed again, turned on his heel, and stalked off into the quiet, starlit woods.

# Chapter Nine

Luc was being followed again.

This wasn't an uncommon occurrence in Morvane. As Ramon's companion, he was used to being tailed by guards. Alistair usually kept close, but he was hard to miss with his bright uniform and scarred face. The few courtiers who sought to gain favor with Ramon were also easy enough to spot.

Felicity was another matter entirely.

"It looks like that statue sprouted shoes," Alistair said one morning. They were winding down from a long bout with heavy training swords, leaning against a fountain in an unused courtyard. Alistair pointed, and Luc saw a figure scurry out from behind a large statue of a bird to duck under a bush.

"Felicity again," Luc said. He stood with a sigh.

Alistair crossed his feet at the ankles with the air of a man with nowhere to be. "I'll stay here, if you don't mind, Your Highness. *That* one spat at me like a cat the last time I got too close."

Luc shook his head and approached the bushes. He found Felicity crouching there, glaring up at him as though *he'd* been the one hiding behind statues all morning. She was dressed in the uniform of a wizard's page, with dark blue hose and a tunic with blue stripes on the chest, and her yellow hair curled around her ears.

"He told you, didn't he?" Felicity asked, jerking her head toward where Alistair lounged on the fountain.

"Maybe."

Felicity's scowl deepened. "Meddlesome little *spy.*" She got to her feet before Luc could chide her for it and grabbed his sleeve. "Follow me."

"People might wonder why the princess is ordering the king's ward around," Luc said, bemused, as Felicity dragged him toward an inner hallway.

"I don't see a princess," she whispered. She pulled Luc through the hall and into a small room. It looked like it used to be a storage room for old furniture, but it was heaped with piles of old, dusty gowns. Luc turned to examine them, running his hands over delicate lacework and embroidery.

"They're mine," Felicity said. "No one comes this way anymore, so I've started hiding them here." She kicked one of the lumps.

"Why?" Luc picked up one of the gowns. "They're finely made. Is something wrong with them?"

"If enough go missing, Mother will stop trying to shrink my waist and let me wear what I like," Felicity said. "Or what I *can* like." She sat on one of the piles, causing a diamond-studded bodice to go tumbling to the floor. "I've been watching you lately."

"I've noticed." Luc gingerly sat on one of the other piles.

"You don't always notice." Felicity grabbed a piece of a gown and started viciously ripping out beads, letting them clatter at her feet. "Not when you ran off with *him* to see that funny little wizard of yours."

It took Luc a moment to realize that *him* was Alistair. "You shouldn't have been following us, Felicity. It could be dangerous."

"For *Felicity,* perhaps. But I wasn't Felicity. I'm not. Not like this."

Luc watched the beads pile up on the floor. "Is there something else you'd like to be called?"

Felicity shrugged, still ripping out beads.

"You know," Luc said, feeling as though he were in a room with a high-strung panther, "my sister Wren—"

"Was born male," Felicity said, interrupting him. "I know. That guard of yours told me. And the king of Telmar's uncle was born female, but no one cares there either." Felicity scowled at the gown. "Lucky Wren. Lucky Telmar."

"Alistair told you about Wren?" Luc asked.

"He knows all about the goblin court," Felicity said. "And it doesn't matter what I like to be called."

"If you had a choice, though," Luc started to say. "What would you—"

"Kit," Felicity said immediately. "If I had a choice, I'd be Kit."

"And is that a man's name?"

That got him another sullen look. "Yes. Obviously."

Luc sat back, trying to readjust how he saw the young man before him. Kit held himself tightly, a thread pulled too taut. His movements were jerky, sharp, brimming with an energy he had to keep hidden, and his legs kept jiggling as though he couldn't bear sitting still. He was constantly running from his ladies-in-waiting, stealing correspondence, and hiding short-cropped hair behind long, thick veils; a man desperately trying to carve out a place to breathe in the shadows.

"It hurts to keep a piece of yourself hidden," Luc said at last.

"You'd know more than most," Kit said. He glanced at Luc's chest. "You've been different lately."

"Well," Luc said, still unsure how much he could tell Kit in confidence, "it's been a busy time, with the festival and all."

"I know when people are hiding things," Kit said, ripping at the beads again. "All I do is watch people. I have to know what's happening before anyone else does, so I can be ready. Lately, you've been acting like a dog who doesn't mind his leash. Before, you acted like a dog who didn't know the leash was there. It's a small difference, but you can see it if you know what to look for."

A ripple of fear ran through Luc. If Kit had noticed a change, then someone else would be bound to pick up on it. He needed to be careful before the festival.

"I won't tell anyone, if that's what you're worried about," Kit said. He ripped out another chunk of beading. "It's sick, what they do to you. And if Ramon suspects, then he doesn't care enough to find out. That'd mean losing a built-in brother."

"I didn't know that you felt that way," Luc said.

"It doesn't matter if I do." Kit finally looked up at him, his blue eyes shadowed in the dark storage room. "But you should leave, and soon. I don't know if that's what you're planning with that wizard, but it'll only get worse when Ramon figures out that he can control you."

"Ramon isn't that bad," Luc said, feeling an impulse to defend him in his absence. "A little flighty, perhaps."

"You say that because my father makes you," Kit said. "But he'll be a tyrant when he becomes king. I plan to be gone by then. You should, too."

Luc couldn't see Ramon becoming a tyrant, but he wondered how much of that came from the spell on his heart. Objectively, he knew that Ramon had a problem with his temper, but that he also felt a responsibility to prevent that temper from coming out. He remembered bouts of possessiveness and reckless behavior, but Ramon had grown up isolated, relying only on Luc for true companionship. He had many friends in the court, but they were all more acquaintances, too busy with their own lives to think about the pressure Ramon was facing.

"Where do you plan to go?" Luc asked. He didn't see the point in trying to convince Kit to stay. Regardless of what manner of king Ramon would make, Morvane was not kind to men like Kit.

"Telmar, probably," Kit said. "I'd go to the goblin court, but Alistair talks so much about how *good* and *perfect* they are and how all he wants is for Princess Jade to crush his head with her thighs while he whimpers and pisses himself."

Luc felt entirely lost. "Surely he doesn't say that." Alistair seemed to respect Luc's sisters, but that was the respect of a soldier acknowledging the strength of his enemy.

Kit snorted. "Not in so many words, but I got his meaning. I'd prefer to go to Telmar. The king has a man as his consort now, did you know that?"

"I might have heard a little about it," Luc said. "But why does Alistair know so much about the goblin court?"

"I suppose whatever you're doing with the wizard really *is* giving you your mind back," Kit said. "You're actually curious about things now."

"Kit," Luc said sternly, "we're talking about Alistair."

"Oh, just ask him yourself," Kit said, gesturing behind him. "He's been listening at the door for the past ten minutes."

Luc twisted around in time for the door to creak open. Alistair stepped in, his scar cutting deeper in the shadow of the room, mouth twisted in disapproval. When the door thudded shut, Luc felt dread drop like a stone in his stomach.

"That's enough, boy." Alistair's voice was a low rumble.

"Don't call me boy, old man," Kit said.

"Alistair?" Luc stood, stepping between Alistair and Kit.

Alistair turned to Luc, his grim expression fading. "Your Highness. I remain, as always, loyal to the royal family."

"Tell him which one," Kit said. He seemed less tense now, kicking his feet idly in the mess of beads on the floor. Alistair glanced at him, and Kit smiled back.

"The lad," Alistair said, still eyeing Kit warily, "is speaking of the orders I received from your sister, Jade."

"That's the one with skin that glimmers like jewels in a clear pool," Kit said. "And hair like starlight. And thighs like—"

"*Boy.*" Alistair's voice was practically a growl. He turned back to Luc. "I came here on your sister's behalf. During the war, the king of Telmar sent soldiers to the Brightwood to bolster their forces. I was only sixteen at the time, but I felt... strongly about Morvane."

"That's a diplomatic way to say that you hate us," Kit said.

Alistair dropped to a knee before Luc, holding his gaze. "I met your sisters there. When the war was done, Alara sent me to Jade. Alara couldn't defy the queen openly without losing her right to the crown, but Jade had already turned from her mother's side. She tasked me with watching you. Not protecting you," he added, with a grim twist of his mouth. "I couldn't protect you from the king's wizards. But I'm here for you, should you need me."

Luc stared down at his hands, unable to meet Alistair's eyes. Alistair had been a constant presence in Luc's life since he'd arrived. He'd taken over for Ramon's instructors training him in the sword. He'd whispered jokes and comments when Luc grew bored during royal engagements, and quietly eased the tension of Ramon's growing moodiness. One of the only truly good things about living in Morvane had come about because of his sisters.

Luc sucked in a sharp breath, trying to steady himself.

"Ah." Alistair pulled Luc into his arms. It was the first time he'd ever held Luc, but it felt familiar, like the warmth of a distant fire. "Your sisters haven't forgotten you, lad."

"Thank you," Luc said. "For being here. For doing this."

Alistair drew back. "I don't know the full details of what you and Will are planning, but if you need me, I will see you safely home."

Luc took a few seconds to control his breathing. "We're trying to find my heart while the guards are diverted at the festival. Will thinks he can replace it."

"I can look for it," Kit said.

"No, you fucking won't," Alistair growled.

Kit rolled his eyes. "Oh, so you treat Luc like a soap bubble, but I'm just a boy you can order around, is that it?"

"Yes," Alistair said, turning back to Luc. "Your Highness. While most of the palace guards will be posted around the festival grounds to protect the royal family, there's always one part of the palace that remains guarded."

"The stairs leading below, I assume?" Luc asked. Alistair nodded grimly. "So long as we can get inside, Will should have a spell to find my heart."

Alistair looked down. "If you signal me at the festival when you're ready, I'll do what I can. There are wards that prevent those who aren't born on Morvanish soil from crossing."

"Which means Will might have to go down alone," Luc said. He didn't like the thought of Will being stopped by whoever guarded his heart below. "What if he breaks the wards?"

"That'll probably signal every wizard in my father's employ," Kit said. "He'll *have* to go alone. Unless you want me to come with him, of course."

"No," Alistair snapped. "You hold a sword like a cudgel."

"You think that you know so much about me," Kit said hotly, "all because you caught me with a sword *one* time."

"One time was all I needed," Alistair said. "Stay out of it, boy. Tend to your own affairs."

"Maybe the man my father has been holding captive *is* my affair."

"I'll have to agree with Alistair," Luc said, and Kit sat back with an aggravated huff. "How are you two so familiar with each other?" Kit had made a few comments about Alistair now and then, but they'd barely said a word to one another in public.

"He caught me dressed as a page," Kit said, "and I caught *him* sending a message to your sister. I keep his secret and he keeps mine."

"What he means to say is that he tried blackmailing me," Alistair said in the driest tone yet. "Then he was insulted by my refusal to faint in shock at the thought of him being a man."

"You were so *boring* about it," Kit said. "I think the phrase you used when I told you was, *and?*"

"Telmar is too civilized to care what gender someone is."

"Well, good for Telmar."

Luc raised a hand to stop them. "Why didn't you tell me all of this?"

Kit and Alistair exchanged knowing looks. Alistair hesitated, scratching his beard, but Kit spoke up before he could answer. "You were tied pretty tight to that leash, Luc. What if you told someone?"

Luc wanted to say that he wouldn't have, but he wasn't so certain. Life before Will felt like a comfortable haze. Kit had been right about that; Luc hadn't even been curious, content to live at Ramon's whims without a second thought. There was no telling what he would have done if he'd known one of Ramon's guards was a spy, even one as familiar as Alistair.

"We'll need to be more careful from now on," Alistair said, with a grim look at Kit. "No reckless behavior. When the time comes, signal me and I'll see you safely out of Morvane."

"Why do I feel like the *no reckless behavior* part was for me?" Kit asked.

"Because you're the one who keeps poking into corners you'd be better off avoiding," Alistair said.

"I'll need to see Will soon," Luc said, before Kit and Alistair could start bickering again.

"That's easy enough," Kit said. "Father plans on taking Ramon to a hunt in a few days. He probably wants to appease Ramon before he stabs him for dragging him to party-planning meetings. They'll go right by Westwood."

"How do you know that?" Alistair asked. "*I* haven't been informed."

Kit looked smug. "I stole a letter to Lord Maven off Father's desk."

Alistair groaned.

"Kit," Luc said, "that's dangerous."

"No," Kit said with mock horror. "Is it? You're welcome, by the by. I'll insist on coming, faint at the thought of seeing Ramon try to skewer a fox, and insist on you taking me somewhere to calm down. Somewhere like the Westwood estate, which is full of noblewomen who might attend to my delicate nerves." He scoffed loudly.

"Women aren't generally delicate, as a rule," Luc said. "My sisters never fainted at the thought of skewering anything."

"Yes, but Father doesn't need to know that." Kit picked at his nails. "Since I'm clearly not allowed to do anything interesting, I might as well try something to help."

"That's kind of you," Luc said.

"Ugh." Kit curled his lip. "I'm not *kind.* I'm just sensible. Tell him, old man."

"You're the least sensible man I know," Alistair said.

"If you truly want to show your gratitude, Luc, all you need to do is keep quiet about me," Kit said. "You can tell your wizard if you must, but only because he's probably leaving Morvane with you."

Luc wanted to say that he wasn't sure of that, but Kit seemed lost in thought, his blue eyes narrowed. "All right."

"Good. The fewer people who know what I'm up to, the better."

"And what *are* you up to?" Alistair asked.

"Nothing." Kit shoved the remains of the beaded gown to the floor. "I'm going to be a good little princess and marry some hideous old councilor, and I have no plans to circumvent that whatsoever."

Alistair pinched the bridge of his nose. "I can only look after one prince at a time."

"Yes, you *are* rather limited in that regard," Kit said. "Don't worry. I'm used to going it alone."

Luc didn't like the sound of that. It was clear that he knew next to nothing about the true Kit. The sarcastic, sharp-tongued man lounging on a heap of expensive gowns was a far cry from the princess he thought he'd known. "If you do need an escape, find me at the ball. I can bring you into the Brightwood."

"That's thoughtful of you, but unnecessary." Kit got to his feet. "The thing about having a terrible reputation is that I'm practically invisible to the right people. *You* are as visible as they come." He strolled to the door. "I'll leave first. I know you can't bear to keep away from me, old man, but don't follow me this time."

Alistair let out a heavy sigh as the door closed behind Kit. "If he does get to Telmar, the king will personally send someone to lock me away for letting that menace loose."

Luc smiled. "I just wish I'd become better acquainted with him first."

Alistair shook his head with a dark look. "You'll find other companions in the Brightwood, Your Highness. Leave that one to his machinations. We'll have more than enough on our hands dealing with yours."

***

Flowers rustled in a breeze from Westwood as Will, having spent the past three days making useless lumps of scrap in Olven's forge, collapsed in the garden with a bucket of water.

"I can't figure this out, Olven."

He'd barely made it back to the Westwood estate before he'd turned around, books in hand, and crossed the border to Olven's forge again. He'd been determined to meet Luc not only with news of his sister, but with real, tangible magic that could find his heart *and* replace it. Instead, he'd agonized over his father's limited notes, wasted half the space in Olven's forge, and hadn't even bothered to go back to Westwood the night before.

Luc was depending on him. A terrifying woman living in the woods was depending on him. If he didn't manage this, there was no telling when he could slip past the king's wizards again. Every time an attempted spell went wrong, Will felt the walls closing in around him, choking off his air.

"It's like when I taught you how to make a fork for the first time," Olven said, standing over Will with his talons hooked in his apron belt. "You'd think the world was ending over a couple of tines."

"I was a child then," Will said. He dumped most of the bucket over his head. He felt like a piece of metal left too long in the fire, misshapen with the heat. "I should be able to make a compass that doesn't fall to pieces."

"No, a watchmaker should," Olven said. "You're trying to learn another trade with a blacksmith's tools."

Will barely registered his words, too caught up in the anxiety building in his chest. "That's only the start. Next there's making something that can fix a man's heart in place when half of his organs and bones are missing."

"Fix a man's what, now?" Olven asked.

"And then something to make Ella look magically interesting enough for most of the wizards in Morvane to watch her. And I haven't even told him about his *sister*!"

"I believe I may be a few leagues behind you," Olven said. He sat down in front of Will. "I know that your... friend in the palace is in trouble. What's this about a heart and a sister?"

"Several sisters," Will said. "But I don't have time to explain. The festival's almost here."

"Which is important because...?"

Will sighed. "I suppose I should start by saying that I know you made a sword for Jade."

Olven glanced toward the empty street. "And we will continue this inside," he said briskly. "Up, up, my boy. Indoors."

It took over an hour before Olven was satisfied with Will's explanation. They had to eat dinner first, and Olven kept making Will backtrack to explain little details before he could get to the point. He spent a good deal of time going over how Will had been using magic.

When Will was finally done, Olven skimmed through Will's father's notes, eyes narrowed.

"I think I see the problem," he said. "You aren't your father."

Will bristled, his shoulders hunching defensively. "I know that. He didn't exactly get to raise me."

"No, it's not that." Olven tapped the journal. "This is useful, and perhaps you may use it in the future, but it isn't how you do magic. Your father's notes involve pouring magic into the metal while it's in the fire. *You* put your magic into metal after it's been worked."

Will took off his glasses and stared down at them. The frame had been the first item he'd enchanted, and it had been made by some jeweler hundreds of leagues away. Every spell he'd successfully cast had only worked on something that had already been shaped to a purpose.

"It feels like I'm cheating, somehow," Will said. "I should make it myself."

"You didn't make your clothes, but you still wear them," Olven said. "So you need a compass, eh? Something to point you in the right direction?" He got up from his chair and rummaged through one of his drawers. "Ah. I thought it'd be here." He came back cradling something in his talons. He set it carefully down on the table, and Will leaned forward to examine a small, simple compass.

"It belonged to..." Olven paused and smoothed his ruffled feathers. "My husband."

Will looked up from the compass. "You never mentioned being married."

Will had thought he knew practically everything about Olven after years of listening to him amiably chatter away while they worked in the forge. He knew Olven's favorite tea, the feud he had with the florist in the capital, even that he liked to go two towns over just to see a very specific cobbler for his boots.

The house itself had no portraits. His clients never mentioned it, even the relentless gossips who shared scandals while Olven puffed up his feathers in excitement. There'd never been any sign that Olven had been anything but a resolute bachelor.

"We were young," Olven said. He stared down at the compass. "Bernard was a soldier. War came easily to him. A quiet life on the border of the human realm did not. When the queen sent her army through the gates the last time, Bernard left with her. I gave him this as a little joke, yes? To help him find his way back to me." He looked away, his feathers flat on his neck. "It was returned with the rest of his things after the war."

"Then I can't use this," Will insisted. He didn't know what to do about the quiet, haunted old goblin sitting at the table. He was so used to Olven being a steadying presence that he felt lost and young, a child thrust into a world they couldn't fully understand.

"You must know, my boy," Olven said, "I've never been alone here. Not once in my life. But grief is always lonely. You can surround yourself with people and remain trapped in the dark of one person's absence. It has been good to have you. You were so *angry* when you came to me—young and hurt and afraid, full of grief you shouldn't have felt yet. A human boy shaped like the men who killed Bernard, but not wicked, not hateful. Just lonely." He pushed the compass into Will's hands.

"Thank you," Will said. It seemed too weak and thin for what Olven had just offered him. "I... I was. I didn't realize how much, before. And I don't know if I'll be able to keep coming here when this is over. I might have to hide for a while. I might not see you at all."

"You're thinking too far ahead again," Olven said. "Focus on what you already have. That compass was meant to bring the man I loved back to me. Perhaps it will finally do the job for you."

"I never said I loved him," Will said, panic rising hot in his face and chest.

Olven clicked his beak in a laugh. "You didn't have to."

Will slept in Olven's little kitchen that night, wrapped up in knitted blankets on a cot by the stove. He examined the walls, laden with paintings, masks, and knickknacks from dozens of goblins throughout the Brightwood. He had knitted cozies for his mugs and kettles, a closet full of scarves and jackets that threatened to spill out like a woolen rockslide, and a piano in the corner of the drawing room that Will had never seen him play. He even had solstice gifts from Will on the wall shelves, displayed like small treasures alongside magical charms and antiques.

Will held the compass and thought of Olven waiting in that small kitchen, young and frightened, uncertain if Bernard would ever return. Will knew that Olven had other lovers. He'd engaged in dalliances with half of the artisans in the Brightwood by now. But they'd never lived with him. Bernard must have been singular, or the weight of his loss too great for Olven to bring in another. For all Will knew, *he* was the only one who'd slept in Olven's house in years.

"Maybe you don't find what's missing," he told the compass softly. His magic brought a slight warmth to his fingers, faint as the dying fire in the stove. "Olven knew where his husband had gone. He wasn't lost."

In the quiet dark of Olven's cottage, Will could say the words that had lingered beneath every attempt to call Luc forth from the spell on his chest, every failed magical working, and the terror of failing to save him. "Maybe you're meant to bring us to what we love," he said.

The needle wobbled, jostled by his hands, and went still. Then, slowly, it shifted. Will sat up, dislodging several blankets, and raised the compass to the dim light. It pointed south, toward the border of the Brightwood and to the capital beyond.

Toward Luc.

# Chapter Ten

Kit stayed true to his word. In less than three days, Ramon came swanning up to Luc with the news that they were going on a hunt in one of the overgrown forests near the Westwood estate.

"I feel like we haven't seen hide nor hair of one another in centuries," Ramon said, wrapping an arm around Luc. "And dull little Felicity's coming, so Father will be too distracted worrying about her to pay attention to the hunt. We can actually breathe for once."

Luc tried to smile. Traditional hunts were banned in the Brightwood. They were too reminiscent of the hunts the elves used to hold across the countryside, chasing down some poor goblin child with their hunting foxes and their uncanny weapons. The Morvanish royal family seemed to enjoy imitating them, making a spectacle out of slaughter.

Luc hadn't minded before, but now, he could feel an echo of discontent. The thought of having smiled and trotted along after the king and Ramon for so many years made his skin crawl. His family would have been mortified if they'd seen him.

"You know," Ramon said, "you usually would have asked me how I'm feeling by now."

Luc met Ramon's eyes. There was something strange there, a hunger that flickered like a dull fire. "I don't need to," he said quickly. "You're seconds from hiding in the summer palace with your great-uncle and letting the festival go on without you."

The odd light in Ramon's eyes faded. He sighed and jostled Luc's shoulders. "That's true enough. You might know me too well."

Luc's misgivings about the hunt only grew as they set out. They even rode in a loose formation like the elves had, with the king and Ramon at the front, Luc a few paces back with the king's courtiers, and guards fanning out behind them. Kit and a few of his ladies-in-waiting hovered at the rear, riding awkwardly in their gowns. Kit's gown was a pale blue with truly hideous flounces, and his hair was covered by a jeweled cap and a sheer blue veil. He caught Luc's eye and urged his horse forward, shoving through the astonished courtiers to reach Luc's side.

"I've never been on a hunt before," he said. He widened his big blue eyes. "Is it *dreadfully* violent?"

"Yes," Ramon said, twisting around in his saddle with every sign of annoyance. "So you should stay back with your ladies."

"That she's out at all is a miracle," the king said. "Embrace this rarity as it comes."

Kit smiled a little too brightly at Ramon and kept pace with Luc as they rode through the woods. Ramon failed to hide his irritation, imposing himself between them so that Kit had to ride closer to the guards.

"Try to enjoy yourself," Luc said. "At least we aren't trapped inside."

Ramon sighed heavily. "And how often will we be able to do this when I'm married?"

"As often as I do," the king said, "which is already more than necessary. A less compassionate father would have married you off to a cheerless shrew for your insolence. Count yourself lucky, boy."

"Lucky," Ramon muttered. "Right."

It didn't take long for them to spot a stag loping through the woods. A commoner would have simply shot an arrow through the creature's throat and been done with it, but the royal family of Morvane needed a challenge. The dogs started baying, startling the poor thing into a run, and the riders cheerfully gave chase. Luc hung back, letting Ramon take the lead, and Alistair slowed his horse to keep Luc in his sight.

"Disgusting, isn't it?" Kit asked. They were solidly in the middle of the party, with the ladies whispering to each other in the back while Ramon and King Tomas tried to race each other in the far distance. Kit scratched his head under his cap. "All this for a stag we *might* eat at the festival to show what good hunter boys they are." He adjusted his veil. "I believe I might have my hysterics a little early."

Before Luc could ask what he meant, Kit urged his horse forward. He caught up with his father far too easily, making Luc wonder if he'd been hiding riding skills as well as his true identity. He'd always come across as a deplorable horse rider, but he nevertheless managed to keep time with the others in that horrible blue gown.

The king slowed in alarm when he saw Kit, and the entire hunting party had to stagger to a halt. Ramon was red-faced in fury, but Kit seemed to enjoy putting on an act, trembling and sobbing over the *poor innocent creature.*

"We should have never let her come!" Ramon cried, turning on his father. "This is what happens when we bring women into our affairs!"

"You can stay back with your ladies," the king started to say, ignoring Ramon entirely.

"I'd feel much better in a *civilized* sitting room," Kit said, glancing at his brother with exaggerated fearfulness. "The Westwood house is nearby, and they have a young lady my age. If I could have a guard come with me, I can call on them."

"You aren't taking our guards because you're too weak to handle a little blood," Ramon said.

"Then I'll take Luc," Kit said. "He can protect me just as well, and he's like a brother to me. One who doesn't yell," he added, with another trembling look at Ramon.

"You can't take him." Ramon looked apoplectic with rage. His horse shifted uneasily beneath him, sensing his mood.

"Perhaps it would be best to separate you," King Tomas said, "so that you can better appreciate what you have. Luc, you and three guards will accompany Felicity and her ladies to—"

"No!" The words burst out of Ramon in a roar. Several courtiers gave him embarrassed, sidelong looks, trained not to object to a royal's moods. "He's *mine*. You gave him to *me!*"

Luc's blood ran cold. Ramon had always been possessive, but there was a dangerous edge to his voice, and his words rang through Luc's mind. Ramon knew. The king had given Luc to Ramon, and while Ramon might not know the extent of it, he knew enough.

"And I told you before that I can take him away," the king said. "Felicity could always use a guard when she marries."

"You wouldn't dare!" Ramon was screaming like a child, eyes squinted, fists clenched, his horse threatening to buck him in fear. "He doesn't *belong* to her!"

"Ramon," Luc said, his chest aching with something that felt too close to betrayal. "You know he wouldn't do that."

"Lucan," the king said, "escort Felicity to the Westwood estate. Do not speak to Ramon until I tell you. This is an order from your king."

Luc blinked heavily. He could feel the magic coiling in his chest, wrapping around his limbs, forcing him to obey. The king hadn't given him a direct order in so long that he'd forgotten how it felt. He bowed. "Your Majesty."

"Don't listen to him," Ramon begged. "Damn you, Luc, *damn* you, don't *listen* to him!"

Luc met Ramon's gaze, but he didn't speak. He turned away, gesturing for Kit to follow. Kit had gone pale, his mouth pinched as though he were biting the inside of his cheek. He followed Luc quietly, head bowed.

Three guards and two of Kit's ladies came with them, anxiously quiet as they left the hunting party. Alistair was one of the guards, and he rode next to Luc, his expression carefully blank. One of Kit's ladies approached him, but Kit shook his head, and she went back to the other young woman to whisper urgently.

"Are you well, Your Highness?" Alistair asked.

"Quite," Kit said. Alistair had been addressing Luc, but Kit straightened his posture, drawing the attention of the other guards. "Thank you, Alistair."

Alistair inclined his head, still searching Luc's face, and withdrew.

"I'll need someone to ride ahead to inform Lady Westwood and her daughter," Kit said, regarding his ladies. "You two, go with them," he pointed to the other two guards, "so the Westwoods aren't surprised by our appearance."

"But my lady," one of the women said, "we can't leave you alone with two men."

"My guard and the man who might as well be my brother?" Kit asked, voice going cold. "The man who is loyal to my family alone?"

His lady blanched and shook her head. "I apologize, my lady. We'll go on ahead."

Kit slid down from the saddle as soon as they'd rounded the bend in the road, and Luc dropped down to join him.

"That was expertly done," Luc said.

"They're terrified of me." Kit's voice was still cold and hard, his hand curled tight around his horse's lead reins. "They have to be. It's the only way they'll leave me alone." He took a few slow steps, his gown sweeping up dust from the path, before he turned on Luc. "I'm sorry about Ramon."

"It's..." Luc wanted to say that it was fine. Part of him insisted on it, already bending before he was asked to bow. "I wanted to think that he didn't know."

"He loves having a pet friend," Kit said. "Someone who can't deny him."

Luc struggled with that knowledge. "But he still cares for me. He's just... he's..." He couldn't say it. He could barely think it. Every time he tried to remember Ramon's red face, the snarl in his voice, or even the words he'd spoken, his mind slid over the memory like glass. "I can't say."

"They must've really hammered that part in deep," Kit said. A beetle landed on his horse's saddle, and he stopped to shoo it away. It buzzed around them, trying vainly to find a place to land before flying to Alistair. He made no move to brush it off. "I didn't think asking for you to come with me would make Ramon erupt like that. When you get your heart back... it's all right if you hate him. If you want to hurt him."

"Kit," Luc admonished, "that's too far."

"I know why you're saying that," Kit said.

Luc tried to find a place for the anger he knew he should feel. It couldn't be toward Ramon. He'd been shaped by the king's wizards to be his friend, his life twisted inexorably around Ramon's. He *could* hate the wizards. Berenger and Aengus, with their dark blue robes and their condescending looks, holding his heart in their bare hands as they gave him orders. Murtagh Westwood, using the old elves' tactics to drain Will's magic. They were tools of the king, but willing ones, with every chance to refuse their orders. He could hate them with impunity.

The Westwood home was in its usual state of disarray when they arrived. Alistair clapped Luc once on the shoulder before he joined the other guards, enlisting them in stabling the horses. Ella was nowhere to be seen, but Luc could have sworn that he'd spotted a flash of yellow hair in the kitchen window.

Kit looked gleeful to find that there was no proper tea waiting for him, and despite Lady Westwood's fawning apologies, he swept into the house with the dirt of the road on his clothes and riding boots.

"Your Highness!" Will's youngest sister trembled as she curtsied. "You honor us."

"No, I don't," Kit said. "You're Lucy, right?"

"Louisa, Your Highness."

"Right." Kit hooked his arm around hers. "I suppose we're friends today. Unlucky you, I'm sure."

Will came thumping down the stairs behind Louisa, his hair slightly messy and his jacket hanging off his shoulders. He met Luc's eyes, and suddenly, the tension of the day came crashing over Luc like a rockfall. He didn't want to think about Ramon, the king, or his wizards. He felt drawn to Will like an instinctive pull, flowers turning to the sun.

Kit glanced at Will, then raised his brows at Luc. "Can my brother annoy yours for a while? I'm that tired of men today, aren't you?"

"I have that book of philosophy upstairs," Will said tightly.

"Yes," Luc said. His throat felt compressed, his pulse roaring in his ears. "Philosophy."

"But Will doesn't like philosophy," Louisa said loudly. "He's always reading those horrible little novels."

"Oh, yes, I do *hate* reading," Kit said, towing Louisa away. "Why should ink on a page try to tell *me* how to feel?"

Luc tried not to race up the stairs after Will. He felt jittery, the king's voice echoing in his ears. *I can take him away.* He needed the touch of someone who wanted him without possessing him, someone who cared if his soul was in one piece.

Will locked the door to his bedroom and whispered his silencing spell when Luc entered. "Luc. I need to tell you—"

"Don't," Luc said. He grabbed Will hungrily, pushing him against the wall. "Don't tell me anything."

"But your..."

"No." Luc kissed him hard before Will could continue. He tugged at Will's jacket, letting it fall at their feet.

"You're shaking," Will said. His brow was furrowed, but he kissed Luc back all the same. He gasped into Luc's mouth when Luc rucked up his tunic. "What happened to you? Do you need..." He gasped again as Luc pressed their mouths together. "Did they... your heart..."

"Go ahead," Luc said. He grabbed Will's hand and pressed it to his chest. "Make me feel something."

"Lucan," Will said. Luc felt another rush of nervous terror, but desperate need filled his veins. "Come to me, Lucan."

"Yes, I'm here," Luc said, and bit Will's neck. Will let out a sharp, shivery moan at that, and he fumbled with Luc's tunic, his palm sliding over Luc's cock. "Gods, I need you. I need to feel this. I'm so tired, Will. I'm so *sick* of it."

He bit Will again, higher on his neck this time, and Will cried out. The sound went right to his cock, heat building below the fear and nerves and tension, threatening to consume him.

"We can always set the palace on fire behind us when we go," Will said. Luc laughed, but it came out harsh and ragged. Will hooked one leg around Luc's thigh, pressing Luc's cock against him as they moved together. "Do you want me to? I'll do it for you. I'll throw those wizards inside first."

"We'll start with Murtagh's study," Luc said. Will slipped a hand between them, his fingers parting the folds between his thighs.

"Do you want to take me?" Will asked. "It feels like you do."

"Keep talking about destroying wizards and I will," Luc said.

"I can do that." Will kissed him, still moving his fingers in tight circles, his knuckles grazing Luc's cock. "Whatever you need."

"What I need is you," Luc said.

"Yes," Will said, and tipped his head back against the wall. He raised his free hand to his neck, fingers sliding over the marks Luc's teeth had made on his skin. "Yes, I think I can give you that easily enough."

***

Will could feel Luc's restless energy like the warmth of magic under his skin. Something had obviously happened to him, but with Luc holding Will up against the wall, it was hard to press the issue. Will kissed him as he worked himself open, already slick and hot between his thighs. He hadn't taken more than his own fingers before, and Luc's cock was long enough to be mildly alarming, but Will was nothing if not a stubborn bastard.

"You know," Will said, breathing hard as Luc ground against him, kissing every part of him he could reach, "this might be easier on the bed."

"I don't want easy," Luc said. He dug his clawed nails into Will's thighs, pricks of pain that sent a thrill rippling up Will's spine. "I want you, however I can have you." He hitched Will up by the hips, holding him there by the weight of his body alone as he freed his cock.

"Fuck," Will whispered. He tensed as he came on his fingers, the hot core of him pulsing, hips trying to jerk against Luc. Luc tilted his head slightly, bemused.

"Did you come just by seeing my cock?" he asked.

"Don't get too full of yourself," Will said, "just fuck me."

Luc flashed his sharp teeth in a smile. "Are you certain? You aren't exactly..." He trailed a claw along Will's skin. "Big," he said at last, with a teasing glint in his eyes.

"I nearly came when you bit me earlier," Will admitted. "A little pain won't stop me."

Luc held Will by the hips, grinding his hard cock against the heat of him. Will's toes barely touched the floor, so he gave up trying to stand altogether and wrapped his legs around Luc's. Luc's cock nearly slipped inside, and Will made a truly desperate sound, digging his nails into Luc's shoulders.

"Are you all right?" Luc asked.

"Just impatient," Will said. He wriggled, trying to slip down onto Luc's cock, but Luc held him fast. "You *said* you wanted to take me."

Luc leaned in to kiss him, and Will moaned as he felt the head of Luc's cock stretch him wide. The pain was fainter than Will expected, not at all the sharp jolt some of the ladies in town had described, just a low ache of discomfort as his body opened up around Luc's cock. Luc closed his eyes and pressed his head to Will's shoulder. His teeth grazed Will's skin, and when Will shivered in response, he tightened around Luc.

"Gods," Luc said, like a prayer. He pushed deeper still, making Will shudder and tighten his legs around him. "Gods, I want to... I want..."

"Do it," Will said.

Luc thrust into him, not even sheathed all the way but filling him so thoroughly that Will thought he might be irrevocably changed to fit on his cock, molded to the shape of him. Will tried to move against him, and Luc drew back to thrust into him again, deliberately careful but deep, pushing a low cry from Will's throat.

Will could hear Luc's cock sliding into him as he moved, claws digging into Will in an effort to keep him still. The stone wall brushed against Will's shoulders, pulling up his tunic and exposing his stomach as he heaved for breath. Luc held him up with one arm, muscles bunching in his shoulders. His claws scraped hot lines over Will's neck as he tilted Will's head to the side.

When he bit down, Luc's teeth broke the skin. Will tried to speak, to tell him to go harder, deeper, but all that came from his tongue was a low, broken cry as he came on Luc's cock. Luc jerked his hips, groaning into Will's neck.

"I can't," he said. "I'm going to come. Will, I—"

"Do it," Will said, too lost in pleasure to care. "Do it, Luc, *Luc.*"

Luc ground his hips against Will as he came with a shaky inhalation, blood welling where his claws pricked Will's body. He panted over Will, face flushed a darker green, eyes bright, white hair falling over his face in messy strands. Will kissed him through it, savoring the way Luc went breathless with desire.

Luc drew out of him slowly, and Will finally dropped to his feet. His thighs were slick, his legs shaky, and his hose was a wrinkled, shredded ruin, tangled up in his jacket on the floor.

"You'll owe me a new tunic at this rate," he said.

"I'm not done yet," Luc said, and dropped to his knees.

"Oh." Will felt a little wild, gripping Luc's silken hair as Luc pressed his mouth to his thigh. "Oh, you're not done. I see."

"Still haven't had you yet." Luc's voice trembled against Will's skin. "Not fully."

Will laughed, but it turned into a whine as Luc sucked on the sensitive nub of Will's cock.

He barely managed another word. Luc worked him through release after release, relentless and desperate beyond hunger. By the third, Will could hardly stand, held upright by Luc's hands on his hips. On the fourth, he slid to the floor, legs shaking through the quakes of another heaving wave of bright, overwhelming pleasure. He lay there, insensible and weightless, staring up at the ceiling as Luc draped over him, resting his chin on Will's belly.

"You do know that I had something to tell you," Will whispered.

"I'm certain that you did." Luc sounded far too smug, but Will supposed he could be allowed, this once. He moved over Will, looking down at him on the old, warped boards of his bedroom floor. "Come with me to the Brightwood. Stay with me."

"You're just saying that because you spent the last hour making me come," Will said, stroking Luc's hair.

"But will you?" Luc asked.

Will didn't have to think about it. When there was Murtagh Westwood's house on one side of the woods and Luc on the other, he didn't have much of a choice. "Yes. Of course."

"Good." Luc rolled to his back. "Because I'll need to do that again. Preferably for the rest of our lives."

Will glanced at him. That came very close to a declaration, which they'd both been dancing around for some time. He thought of the compass in his bedside drawers, pointing inexorably toward Luc.

Still, he understood Luc's meaning. They'd always been tied together, forced into it by Murtagh Westwood and the king, but this was something they could choose.

"Ramon knows that I'm being magically controlled," Luc said, and Will sat up. Luc was staring up at the ceiling, his hands clasped over his chest. "I can't feel anything about it, even now. I need you to feel it for me."

Will lay a hand on Luc's shoulder. Anger was always close at hand in his own life. It had only been since Luc's arrival that he'd managed to build a place for something more. The anger returned to him now, mingled with the unspoken bond he felt for Luc, the word for it as yet unspoken.

"I'm sorry," he said. "And if he's been using you... if he's been influencing what the wizards tell you to feel..."

"Don't finish that," Luc said, finally meeting his gaze. "Not until I have my heart back."

"I have to tell you something else." Will kept his hand on Luc, trying to steady him. "Your sister found me. Jade. She's been watching you. Or watching me, I suppose."

Luc's eyes widened. "I was about to tell *you* that. Alistair—you remember Alistair? The guard who's always with me? He's been sending her messages. He says he's sworn to me." His expression darkened. "He also says that there are wards that can prevent any non-Morvanish visitors from reaching the lower levels of the palace."

"So I'll have to find your heart on my own," Will said.

Luc sat up, gripping Will's arm. "You can't. We'll have to find a way around it."

"There isn't time, Luc." Will held his gaze. "I'm already sneaking over to Olven's every chance I get to figure out the illusion for Ella. Not to mention replacing your heart when we find it. That's why I haven't seen you these past few days. If I can get down there, then I can find it. I'll be fine alone." He swallowed, trying to force a confidence in his voice that he didn't feel. "I'm a wizard, after all."

"You're *my* wizard," Luc said. He recoiled suddenly, as though something in those words had hurt him. "I don't mean to say that I own you. I mean you're... you're more important than..."

"I'm not more important than your heart," Will said. "Or your freedom. I know that you're used to people forcing you to show your fealty, but when you have the freedom to make your own choices, you can still do terrifying things for people. Because they mean something to you. You called me kind before. I'm not."

Will refused to look away, keeping Luc in his gaze. "I've been selfish and withdrawn. I'm more likely to snap at someone than speak kindly. I almost lost my chance at becoming close to Ella, and I know I'm still not doing enough. But I don't have to be kind to do the right thing, Luc. I just have to want it. I have to want it enough to be a stubborn ass about it. So that's what I'm doing. I'm being a stubborn ass again, and I'm going to go down into that palace on my own and get your heart back. And I can do that now."

Will rose to fish the compass out of his drawer. He held it out to Luc, watching the needle wobble from Luc to a spot just past his shoulder. "It's pointing to your heart, Luc."

"It's also pointing to me," Luc said, gazing down at the compass. Will felt heat rise to his face.

"Well. Yes. It's supposed to lead you to what you... care for," Will finished weakly, unable to say it aloud.

Luc took the compass out of Will's hands, and Will watched the needle swing firmly in his direction.

"I see," Luc said. He leaned in to kiss Will tenderly. "I love you."

Will felt more lightheaded than when Luc had him pressed to the wall. "So do I."

"I had a feeling," Luc said, and kissed him again. "We should clean up before Kit scares off your sister."

Will hesitated, momentarily lost. "Who's Kit?"

Luc grinned. "It seems that I have more to tell you than I thought. Let's find some clean hose, and I'll explain."

# Chapter Eleven

Kit held his composure until precisely five seconds after his ladies-in-waiting had walked out down the path out of the Westwood estate.

"I'm going to scream," he said, covering his face with both hands.

"Ah," Alistair said in a low voice, "the famous Morvanish self-restraint."

"Shut up," Kit said, laughing through his hands. "Oh, Luc. You and that wizard practically raced upstairs, were silent as death for *hours*, and came back with your hair undone and his hose a different color. Gods, I *adore* you. You're so indiscreet."

"He had a tear in his hose," Luc said, trying to regain a semblance of dignity in front of a man who was openly chortling at him. "I helped him find something else to wear."

"Like what, your fingers?" Kit asked.

"That isn't appropriate behavior toward a prince," Alistair said softly.

Kit sneered at him. "And I'm not one?"

Alistair shrugged. "His line extends to the rebellion. *Your* family only took control three centuries ago."

"And who were your people back then?" Kit asked. "Professional nuisances?"

"Try not to antagonize him, Kit," Luc said. He wondered how old the royal family in Telmar was to make Alistair so pretentious about noble bloodlines. He hadn't paid much attention in the lessons he'd shared with Ramon, since Ramon had always needed someone to watch him before he started fussing at his tutors. Telmar had come up once or twice, but even the tutors hadn't seemed that interested in a country whose people enjoyed romping around in elven ruins.

He couldn't help feeling lighter as he walked back with Kit and Alistair. Kit's ladies inevitably tried to edge closer to their charge, but Kit kept scaring them off again, prompting Alistair to sigh and mutter. That would start Kit up again, and Luc found himself trying not to laugh as he watched his even-tempered guard lose his composure in the face of one twenty-year-old prince.

Luc had always assumed that he'd been content with Ramon, but there was a comfort in Kit and Alistair's company that felt *safe.* They were all a part of the conspiracy, such as it was, and with Will behind him and the festival quickly approaching, even the threat of the king and Ramon's discontent couldn't dampen his mood.

Ramon certainly tried. As soon as they returned to the tents in the field where the hunting party had retired, Ramon came storming over. He glared briefly at Kit, then turned to Luc.

"You could have at least *tried* to deny him," he said. Luc opened his mouth to respond, but he felt as though a fist had closed around his throat.

"He can't," Kit said. "Don't blame Luc for what Father did to him."

"Luc?" Ramon tried to grab Luc's shoulder, but Kit shoved between them, and Ramon gripped Kit's arm instead. "He's *Luc* now? Don't presume to know him simply because Father let you borrow him for a day."

His fingers had to have been digging painfully into Kit's flesh, but Kit didn't look away. Luc placed a hand on Ramon's shoulder, and Ramon twitched back as though it burned.

"Your Highness," Luc said to Kit. Ramon must have realized that Luc was trying to speak to him around the magical compulsion, because he clasped Luc's hand so hard that his bones ached.

"I'll fix this," Ramon said, and let go. He strode off toward his tent, leaving Luc and Kit with Kit's anxious ladies-in-waiting.

"Well," Kit said brusquely, "*that* was mortifying."

The king didn't permit Luc to speak to Ramon for the rest of the hunt. He waited until they were at the palace to rescind the order, and Luc spent most of the journey trying to swallow a knot of outrage in his throat. Without Will to draw him further out of the spell, Luc's fury was contained, unable to be directed at the man who'd given the order. He tried to hold on to it, but it faded as he crossed the entrance to the palace, simmering beneath the familiar fog.

Kit pulled Luc aside before he ascended the stairs to his and Ramon's rooms.

"This has been enlightening," Kit whispered, "but I'm leaving before the horde descends."

"What horde?" Luc asked.

"Your Highness!" The rest of Kit's ladies appeared at the end of the hall, dressed in similar shades of blue and gray. At their head was a young woman that Luc was fairly sure had tried to court Ramon once, the daughter of a lord near the coast. She came running over, keeping her knees together in an attempt to look dignified, but it made her look more like a hobbled marionette. "We heard that you had a swoon at the hunt. Oh, was it terrible? Are you well? This is precisely why I keep *insisting* that we go to my aunt's by the sea."

"Shit," Kit whispered, and darted off down a servant's stairwell. His head lady-in-waiting stopped next to Luc, balling her fists at her sides.

"You slippery little *eel,*" she hissed, and clattered off down the steps after Kit. "Why do you keep *doing* this?"

"At least we can say we've lived in the palace," another lady said, holding her skirts above her ankles as she descended the stairs.

"Yes, but at what cost?"

Luc shook his head, smiling, and went upstairs.

Ramon was already in his rooms by the time Luc arrived, but he didn't answer when Luc knocked on the door. He didn't wait for Luc before dinner, either, and he remained oddly reticent throughout, keeping his gaze focused on his plate and avoiding Luc as they left the dining hall.

"Ramon," Luc said, trying to catch him at the door. "Ramon, honestly. I wasn't *trying* to ignore you."

Ramon kept walking, his back straight, hand clenching too tight on the banister.

Luc spent the next two days alone. He trained with Alistair and watched for Kit, who had gone back to slinking around in the shadows. Flower garlands rose around the festival square near the palace. Wizards showed their prowess at night, crafting elaborate designs out of fire that had once been used to decimate battlefields. Luc watched them twist ropes of fire and wondered what Alara had seen when she'd gone to battle. Had the fire seemed beautiful then, if only for a moment? Would she ever separate the fire of the human mages from the fire that made roses and braided ladders in the night sky?

He would see her soon enough. Perhaps he could ask her one day, if she ever forgave him for upending the fragile peace between the Brightwood and Morvane.

Ramon finally broke the silence three days before the festival.

He knocked at Luc's door in the night, startling him out of a restless sleep. The knock was an old code, three short taps and two long ones, meant to distinguish Ramon and Luc from meddlesome parents and tutors. Luc flung the sheets from his bed and threw on a pair of loose trousers as the knocking became more insistent.

"I'm not about to open the door nude, Ramon," he said. He heard an answering chuckle in the hall.

"Don't be such a girl about it and quit dithering," Ramon said. Luc grimaced in disapproval and opened the door to find Ramon fully dressed, grinning like a cat in a cheesemonger's shop. "Good. Come with me. I want to show you something."

"This couldn't wait?" Luc asked, following Ramon out of his room. Ramon rolled his eyes. "I'm glad you finally decided to stop giving me the cold shoulder, but you could have let me sleep."

"You always wake up early," Ramon said. "And I'm sorry for being such a brat, but I couldn't let Father suspect."

"Suspect what?"

Ramon smiled. "You'll see."

"I can't help you flee Morvane," Luc said as Ramon led him to Ramon's chambers. "So if you've tied your bedsheets together and thrown them out the window, I'm afraid you're out of luck."

"Oh, my plans are much better than that," Ramon said. He opened the door and ushered Luc inside. "Just sit down and I'll explain everything."

"We can't exile all the eligible women from Morvane, either," Luc joked. Then he turned to see the man sitting in a chair next to Ramon's bed.

Aengus, the lead apprentice to the king's wizard, sat in a shaft of moonlight, holding Luc's heart in both hands.

"Ramon." Luc reached behind him for the door. The heart pulsed softly, and Luc's head throbbed in time with it. Terror rose like bile in his throat, and when Aengus flexed his fingers around Luc's heart, Luc lunged for him, desperate to keep it from bursting.

"Sit," Aengus ordered. Luc collapsed on the rug, breathing hard.

Ramon knelt at his side. "No," he said, gently brushing Luc's cheeks with both hands. Luc only realized that he was crying when Ramon's hands came away wet. "No, no, no, Luc, it isn't like that. It isn't like that at all."

"Are you..." Luc could barely get the words out. "Are you returning it to me?"

Ramon looked pained. "One day," he said, and Luc felt a cold wave rush through him. "One day, if you're good. Which you are.

You're always good, Luc, you've always been so good to me. I just need to make sure you're safe, don't you see?"

"I'm not safe without it," Luc whispered. He could feel the weight of the betrayal, but the love he had for Ramon clouded it, and his stomach rolled with conflicting emotion.

"But you do have it. You have it with me," Ramon said. "So long as my father has your reins, you're his to lead about. But we can fix that now, Luc. We can fix all of it."

"You don't have to convince him, Your Highness," Aengus said. Luc shot him a hard glare. He couldn't hate Ramon, but he *could* hate Aengus, holding his heart so casually, his fingers slick with a thin sheen of blood.

"I'll *kill* you," Luc said. Aengus had told him to sit, but he hadn't told him to sit still. Luc pushed past Ramon, crawling across the floor. His claws dug into the rug, pulling up silken threads. "I'll rip your heart from your chest myself."

"Stay," Aengus ordered. He looked at Ramon from over Luc's shoulder. "Your Highness, he can be volatile in the presence of his heart. This is not the man you know."

"Of course he is," Ramon said. He hurried over to Luc. "Of course you are. You're still Luc. You still love me."

"And if you love me, you'll give it back," Luc said. "You won't use it against me. Ramon. I've never done anything to hurt you. Never."

"Not unless my father ordered you to," Ramon said. "That's all I'm doing. I'm making sure that he can't use you against me again."

"And *him?*" Luc spat the word, glaring at Aengus.

"I could use a loyal head wizard when I'm king," Ramon said. "Don't worry about Aengus, Luc. This is about us." He held out a hand to Aengus. "Give it to me."

"Your Highness," Aengus said, as Luc's world shrank to Ramon's outstretched hand, "remember what I told you."

"Do you want to take Berenger's position or don't you?" Ramon snapped.

"Faramond," Luc begged. "Please don't do this."

Aengus gingerly handed Ramon the heart. It was so small in Ramon's hand, glistening with the magic that kept it beating.

"Lucan," Ramon said, turning to him. "Answer me truthfully. Do you care for me?"

"Yes," Luc said, unable to stop himself. "I have to."

A crease formed in Ramon's brow. "But you'd love me if my father and his wizards hadn't ordered you to. You'd love me on your own if you could."

"Your Highness, that isn't how he functions," Aengus said.

"Be silent." Ramon turned back to Luc. "Would you love me, Luc? Even if you weren't told to?"

Luc stared up at him, and for the first time, with Ramon's orders forcing him to speak the truth, he saw Ramon as he was. Ramon had always been the child screaming in red-faced fury every time a tutor told him no, a small-minded bully with the reach of a crown. Luc had been his minder, anticipating his moods, easing the way before Ramon could howl and thrash uselessly in a humiliating tantrum.

"No," Luc said. "I would not."

Ramon breathed in sharply through his nose. "Did my father tell you to say that?"

"No," Luc said. "Perhaps if you'd been allowed to mature, you would be someone worth loving."

Ramon looked for a second as though he were about to dash Luc's heart on the ground and shriek on the rug like a child. He gathered himself with visible effort before he spoke again. "But William. You love him."

"Yes," Luc said softly.

"*Him.*" Ramon's voice dripped with scorn. "He isn't even a man, did you know that? All it took was a little digging to find that out, thanks to Aengus here."

Fear lanced through Luc's chest, and the heart on Ramon's hand started beating faster. "No, he's a man."

"She's a woman," Ramon said. "A daughter of a smith pretending to have a man's magic. I could have her killed for that, even if she did save your life when you fell off your horse."

"Him," Luc said. "*He's* a wizard, and a damn sight better than the one you have leashed like a dog."

Ramon was breathing faster, his neck and cheeks a splotchy red. "I told you to tell me the truth."

"I did," Luc said. "It isn't my fault that Morvane is a degenerate cesspit of pseudo-elven prejudices."

"Enough." Ramon held the heart out as though he wanted to crush it in his fist. "You are *mine,* Lucan. You belong to *me.* You love *me.* You can have your William, or whatever you call that thing of yours in the country, but in the end, your loyalty belongs to me. You don't take orders from my father, my mother, and certainly not from my conniving little sister, but from me."

Luc could already feel himself slipping away. The terror was still there, winding about him like a constricting snake, but the part of him that was Lucan was drifting beneath it all. The last true thought of his own was small and seemingly useless. *But Ramon doesn't have a sister.*

Then even the terror was gone, and the goblin known as Luc knelt beneath the man he loved, watching him lift his beating heart aloft.

"You'll do anything for me," Ramon said.

"Yes," said the creature that has once been Lucan.

"You'll follow me." Ramon's eyes gleamed in the moonlight. What lay there wasn't nobility or even fury, but the cold, unfeeling selfishness of a petty tyrant. If Luc were there, he would have felt disgust, perhaps fear. The mind moving his body now only watched in reverence. "You'll kill for me, if I ask you to."

"Yes."

"Even your mother. Even *my* mother." Ramon glanced at Aengus, who sat quietly with his hands folded in his lap. "If I tell you to, you'll kill my father for me."

Luc's voice was a whisper. "Yes."

"Good. Good. Then I'm done." Ramon handed the heart back to Aengus. "Put that back where it belongs."

"Of course, Your Highness," Aengus said. Magic glimmered in his hands, and the heart vanished.

"It'll be *your majesty* soon," Ramon said. "Remember that. You." He snapped his fingers at Luc. "Fetch me something to wash my hands. That was disgusting."

Luc silently rose to his feet.

Aengus had left by the time Luc found something suitable for Ramon. Luc watched numbly as Ramon cleaned blood off his fingers, trying to understand what was happening beneath the fog in his mind. It was as though someone were screaming far below, a tinny whine that Luc couldn't quite make out.

"What are you doing staring at me like that?" Ramon asked. "Gods. I assume you want me to give clemency to that wizard of yours."

Luc blinked heavily. The wizard. Yes. William. The whine rose in pitch, thin but insistent, tickling his mind.

"Not to worry, old friend," Ramon said, throwing his cloth on the floor and clapping Luc on the shoulder. "I have that well in hand already. I always look after you, don't I?"

Luc gazed at him. He wasn't certain what Ramon wanted. He wasn't certain what *he* wanted. All he could think about was the whine in his ear, and the thick, full feeling of nothingness rapidly consuming his heart.

Ramon grabbed a fistful of Luc's hair and yanked, forcing him to nod his head. "There you go," he said. "I may have been too rough this time, but we'll work on it, you and I. Because I do love you, Luc. You know that, don't you? I love you more than life itself." He made Luc nod his head again. "That's right. Now, why don't you go back to bed, and *I'll* take care of everything you need."

***

"You're being ridiculous, Will."

"No, I'm not." Will stood behind Ella in the study of the Westwood house, pinning a thin band of silver over her hair. It had come from a tiara that Halpernia had gutted for its diamonds, and it looked cheap and pitiful in the dim evening light. "Trust my process."

"I don't know why you're so invested in my going to the festival," Ella said, twisting to try and get a glimpse of the band in the mirror.

"Well, excuse me for wanting to give you something nice," Will muttered. Ella sighed and smacked him on the arm. "Hey. No hitting me. Hit the silver. Two taps and it should do *something.*" He hoped it would, in any case. He'd been so preoccupied with the question of how to get Luc's heart back into his chest that he had thrown together the spell on Ella's band at the last minute.

"That's promising," Ella said, and tapped the hair band twice.

The study immediately disappeared in a blast of white light. Ella shrieked and covered her eyes. Will stumbled into her, unable to see past the spots in his vision, and Ella accidentally dragged him down. The hair band went clattering over the floor, sliding under Will's old bed. With the frame blocking some of the light, the bed was haloed as though it were burning with a white flame.

"What on earth was *that* supposed to be?" Ella cried.

"It was supposed to make you look wreathed in fucking starlight," Will said. "Like a delicate fucking princess or something. *Fuck*, my *eyes.*"

"You should have said metaphorical starlight, not an inferno from an actual star." Ella crawled toward the bed, tears in her eyes. "How do I stop it?"

"Tap it again! Two times!"

Ella grunted as she fumbled for the band. Finally, the light pooling under the bed faded, and Ella collapsed against the bed frame.

"Starlight," she said, and burst out laughing.

"I wanted you to make an impression," Will said. He flopped down next to her.

"Yes, let's blind the prince." Ella wiped her eyes, still laughing. "I'm sure he'll love that!"

"Oh, he's just a pretty little brat, regardless," Will said. "But maybe you'll find someone else who would like to know where his wife is at all times. He'll just have to follow the trail of screaming people covering their eyes."

"Perfect," Ella said. "I will commission you for hair jewelry for every festival from now on."

They sat there for a few minutes, the spots gradually fading as Will adjusted to the dark.

"You've been gone quite a bit lately," Ella said. "I can't say I miss being blasted with magic, but I do miss *you.*"

Will chose his words carefully. "I might be gone longer."

"I suspected that you might." Ella propped her arms over her knees, not at all the proper young woman she always tried to be. "You like it over there, with the goblins. You're always happier when you've been to the Brightwood."

"I could make a life there if I wanted one," Will said. "But I don't want you to stay here when I go, Ella. These people don't deserve you."

Ella bumped Will's shoulder with hers. "So that's why you're trying to help me make an impression."

*I'm also using you,* Will thought, guilt tugging at his gut. "Well, maybe someone will see you at the festival and want to hire you as a seamstress, or some rich old man will want to give you his inheritance before he dies."

"And now I'm less charmed," Ella said, and laughed again. "Thank you, Will. I'll find my way, somehow."

"I'll work on that hair band in the meantime," Will said.

Ella raised both hands in mock horror. "Please, no more!"

"William?" Will groaned as he heard his mother's footsteps on the stairs. "William, what was that? We could see the light coming through the floorboards! And when we have important guests!"

"Why would we have important guests after sundown?" Ella whispered.

"It's probably the mayor's wife again," Will whispered back. He got shakily to his feet. "Sorry, Mother!"

"What... why are you..." Halpernia opened the door to the study, her face pale. "What are you doing in here?"

"Talking," Will said. Ella hurriedly stood, head bowed. "I got carried away with a little experiment."

"You shouldn't be experimenting at all," Halpernia said. Her voice was a strained hiss. "You know what the king's wizards will do if they know you're—if you're not practicing *men's* magic."

"How kind of you to care," Will said. "But they won't."

"Not if you're careful," Halpernia said. She grabbed Will's arm. "And you must be very careful now, do you understand?"

Will frowned at Ella, confused. Halpernia had largely left him to his own devices, for the most part. She certainly hadn't tried to be an actual mother, not behind some halfhearted apologies and fussing over his health. Ella looked as bewildered as Will felt, following them out of the study and down the narrow stairs.

"What's happened?" Will asked. His mother was practically dragging him, her arm hooked tight around his. "You're acting strange."

"It's a good thing, darling," Halpernia said. "*Very* good. You just have to trust me. I've been speaking to a friend from the capital, you see. He came by after the princess visited, while you were—away."

Will must have been with Olven in the Brightwood then. He'd been slipping away practically every day after Luc's last visit, returning to the Westwood estate to sleep and work on Ella's entrance to the festival. He didn't know what *friend* Halpernia could be talking about, though. All her friends in the capital were connected to his great-aunt, too busy caring for their own descendants to concern themselves with hers.

She ushered Will toward the dimly lit drawing room before whipping around to glare at Ella.

"I'd better not catch you eavesdropping, girl," she said.

"Her name's Ella," Will said. "Not *girl.* Not *you.* Use her name, Halpernia."

Halpernia looked as though she would rather eat nails. She stared at Ella for a long breath, then turned toward the drawing room without a word.

Will shrugged at Ella. "I tried," he mouthed silently. Ella waved a hand dismissively.

Halpernia closed the door to the drawing room the moment he entered. A young man in blue wizard's robes sat in the least decrepit chair they owned, looking entirely uncomfortable amid the fading wallpaper and drooping furniture. He couldn't have been older than Louisa, with a mop of curly red hair and the skinny frame of someone who had grown like a weed as a boy and had yet to catch up. He adjusted his robes, smiling a little too brightly.

"You must be William Westwood," he said. Halpernia sat next to him, her smile nervous and strained.

"William Fletcher." Will didn't move to sit. There were only a few reasons why a wizard would call on him, and none of them were good. He tried to suppress the nagging fear that he and Luc had been found out. If that were true, the king wouldn't have sent just one wizard, and he wouldn't be inviting Will to talk like a stately old grandmama hosting tea.

"Will Fletcher," the wizard said. "That was your father's name. Robert, I believe? He was a gifted smith, they say. Quite gifted."

Will didn't answer. Halpernia shifted in her seat, simpering at the world at large, her eyes wide and pleading.

"My name is Aengus," the wizard said. "I work at the palace, under the king's head wizard. Your mother says that you may have a touch of magic. Was that your working that we saw earlier?"

"No," Will said shortly. "Freak accident. Someone dropped a candle."

Aengus' smile remained fixed in place. "There's no need to obfuscate matters, William. My mentor worked under Murtagh Westwood. He spoke at length about Murtagh's... curious style of magic, and the boy living with him who called himself William. Or I *suppose* we could call him a boy. He had a different name, once, but perhaps I heard incorrectly."

Will looked at Halpernia. A momentary glimmer of guilt crossed her face. "How much did you tell him?"

"I'm only saying," Aengus said, interrupting as Halpernia opened her mouth to speak, "that there's no reason to keep secrets here. I'm a wizard, William. I know magic well enough to recognize that it doesn't matter what sex the caster is."

"How progressive of you," Will said. He clasped his hands behind his back to keep them from shaking. Aengus hadn't mentioned Luc yet. So long as he only knew of Murtagh Westwood and Will's old name, Will could handle him.

"However," Aengus said, looking down to pluck invisible lint off his immaculate robes, "there's the matter of your education."

"Yeah, I missed that while Murtagh had me hooked up to his machines," Will said. "Your mentor told you about that, I assume."

Halpernia flinched, but Aengus didn't even blink. "I've seen the mechanism in his old study, yes."

"The one in the palace," Will said. "The one made by the elves. The one he *modified* for a *child*. That mechanism."

"We all do what we must to maintain the peace of the realm," Aengus said. Will clenched his fists tight. "The prince has informed me that you would be better suited studying with the other apprentices in the palace."

"It's a great honor," Halpernia said, clasping her own hands in her lap. "Will, they'll give you a wizard's salary, perhaps even lodging of your own in the capital. We could afford a dowry for Louisa."

"So you're selling me again," Will said. The old, familiar outrage rose like a forge fire in his veins. "And there's no telling if *this* one won't hook me up to the same machines Murtagh did, to drain my magic for his own purpose."

"I didn't sell you, William," Halpernia said.

"You did." Will's voice rose, echoing off the sad, decaying walls. "You sold me to Murtagh, and now you're trying to sell me to his successor."

"No one is selling you," Aengus said, "and I'm certainly not about to use Murtagh's methods. We're just ensuring that you have a proper education. Besides, the prince said this would keep you close to our friend Lucan."

Will's reply died on his tongue. His mouth went dry, a cold rush of fear threatening to dampen his rage. "Our friend."

"Yes." Aengus gestured for Will to sit. He didn't move. "The prince knows that you're close. As a wizard, I can train you *personally*, and you would live in the palace with me and my mentor. You could see him as often as you like. And of course, there's the matter of his heart."

Will searched the room. There were butter knives on a discarded tea tray. The tray itself was tin polished to look like silver. There were nails in the couch and chairs, hinges on the doors, rings on Halpernia's fingers. Nothing he could use as a weapon.

"His heart," Will repeated.

"Yes, it's quite sad. He might not have told you." Aengus smiled pityingly at Halpernia like an aunt soothing a mother with a temperamental child. "His heart is volatile. Most goblins' are, you know. Their feral nature can't help but come out in moments of stress. But a few select wizards, ones with talent like you and I... we can help him regulate those emotions. The prince suggested bringing you on as an apprentice, and I agree with his reasoning. Who better to tend to his heart than a friend?"

"And if I refuse?" Will asked.

"That would be unfortunate," Aengus said, "but I'm sure alternate arrangements can be made. Murtagh's notes were *very* thorough, and the king would be displeased to know that a female has been practicing unlawful magic around his ward. We'd have to find another way to ensure that your talents don't go to waste."

Will looked to his mother. She sat quietly, her gaze fixed straight ahead, refusing to look at him.

"So that's it," he said. They clearly didn't know about his plans with Luc, but if Will went with Aengus under the guise of apprenticeship, there was no telling what Aengus would do. He could simply trap Will in the box again, and Luc would be stuck in the palace, never knowing why Will had disappeared. "I go with you, or you force me to go. And Mother gets her pension either way, I suppose."

"You can't punish me for the rest of my life, William," Halpernia cried. "Murtagh never intended to hurt you. He only needed a little magic, just a touch, but you were so stubborn. You kept refusing him, *just* like your father, denying him to the last when you could have spared yourself so much pain by simply being good and obedient."

"I refused him like my father?" Will asked. Halpernia flinched back when he turned on her, hands raised to her mouth. "How did my father refuse him?"

"Perhaps this would be better explained on the way to the palace," Aengus said delicately.

"How did my father refuse him?" Will asked. His voice was so cold that he almost didn't recognize it.

"He only wanted to borrow you," Halpernia said, "like an apprentice. He offered us enough for Robert to close that horrible smithy for good, but Robert insisted on denying him."

"Murtagh tried to buy me when my father was still alive," Will said. "When? How soon before he died?" He approached his mother, fury crystallizing in his heart like a cold spike of ice. "What did you and Murtagh do after my father refused to sell me?"

Halpernia was shaking. "You don't understand, William. He wasn't trying to *hurt* you."

"I see that you don't have the temperament for wizardry," Aengus said, rising from his seat. "The female humors conflict too strongly with the power necessary for spellcraft."

"A tidy excuse," Will said. "You were always going to use me like him. Like *her.*" He took a step closer to his trembling mother. "Did you kill my father? You and Murtagh? It's much easier to sell your child to a monster when he's living in your house, isn't it?"

"That's enough," Aengus said, and moved his hand in a slow circle. Magic shone around his fingers, a pale orange like the flicker of a candle flame.

Will's magic surged to his skin like fire consuming tinder. "No." His magic burst free of him, raw power with no intent, reacting to the urgent need to stop Aengus' spell.

Halpernia screamed as fabric tore around her, cloth and padding shredding to pieces as nails ripped out of the couches, chairs, and walls. They slammed into Aengus' hands with the force of a blacksmith's hammer, and he cried out in wordless pain as he was flung into the wall behind him. Nails sprouted from his hands like weeds jutting from the ground, blood oozing over his skin.

"Go on," Will said, as Aengus heaved for breath, eyes wide with pain. "Cast your spell, wizard. Leash me. *Use* me. Do it."

Aengus tried to pull his hands from the wall and whined, deep in his throat. Halpernia fell to the floor, hands over her face, as Will approached him.

"Do it," Will said.

Aengus mouthed something, lips moving through the tremors rippling over his body, and Will felt bars of magic forming around him like a steel trap closing shut. He shuddered with the weight of what he'd have to do. He couldn't let Aengus go back to the palace. He had too much power over Luc. He couldn't be trusted not to punish him in Will's stead.

He looked at the nails in Aengus's hands. "Stop him."

Aengus screamed and thrashed, legs kicking uselessly as the nails burrowed like grubs into his arms. They squirmed through his flesh, digging toward his heart, and Halpernia screamed shrilly behind him. He dimly heard a door slam open, and slim hands grabbed his shoulders.

"Will. Will, you have to stop."

"He can't hurt Luc again," Will said. He was breathing hard, his gaze unfocused despite his magicked glasses, Aengus' face too close to make out. "He can't tell them what happened here."

"He won't." That was Ella's voice. Ella shouldn't have been there. She wasn't supposed to know. Will let her draw him away from the body nailed to the wall. "Will, he's dead."

Someone was sobbing behind him. Will turned to see his mother weeping on the floor at his feet. Louisa was shaking in the hallway, staring wide-eyed through the door. Ella looked pale, but she kept her hands on Will's shoulders, guiding him away from the body. Blood pooled under Will's shoes, spreading over the worn wooden floor.

"That's what will happen to you if you tell anyone what he came here for," Will told Halpernia. He could feel the bile threatening to rise in his stomach, but he forced it down. "If you breathe a word to anyone, if you *touch* Ella, if you say one word against her—"

"Will, don't." Ella tried to pull Will away. He wrenched out of her grip, stopping before Halpernia.

"Did you kill my father?" he asked. Halpernia only let out a wrenching sob. Will raised his voice. "Did you kill him so you could sell me properly?"

"Please," Ella begged.

Will turned away from the woman sobbing on the drawing room floor and rushed past Louisa, who cringed against the wall. He pounded up the stairs and flung open his bedroom door.

He'd ruined everything. Word would get back to Luc eventually. With any luck, he'd only be deemed a witch, a fraud, casting magic in disguise and killing the wizard sent to bring him to justice. But he still needed to find Luc at the festival. He'd have to hide at Olven's, find a disguise, and slip into the festival that way. He couldn't rely on Ella as a distraction anymore. He needed to rethink it all. He needed

Olven's forge, his quiet kitchen, and a silence that wasn't filled with the soft, organic sound of nails digging into flesh.

He stopped halfway through throwing things into his bag to heave for breath, hand pressed to the wall for balance. Nothing came up, but he could taste the bile in the back of his throat. He shoved his father's journals into his bag and put the compass in his pocket.

When he stepped outside the Westwood house, Ella was waiting for him.

"You can't come with me, Ella," Will said. He couldn't look at her. She was a pale ghost in the dark, with her yellow hair and white gown blowing in the wind.

"I'm not leaving you," she said. She followed him, striding through the grass. "Will, you killed that man."

"I know." The words came out breathy and too high.

"You said that Halpernia sold you to my father," Ella said.

"I can't talk about that." Will tried to walk faster, but Ella kept up with him, the wind tossing her gown about her knees.

"Yes, you can." She raised her voice over the wind. "You said that he used you. How did he use you, Will? What did he do that you're so damned scared to tell me?"

Will turned to her. "He put me in a box," he said, "and he used *my* magic to rip out Luc's heart. And now Luc's forced to be friendly and nice and *loyal* to the people who gave Murtagh his orders, and if I don't do something about it, he'll be stuck like that for the rest of his life!"

Tears glistened in Ella's eyes. "Why didn't you tell me?"

"Westwood was your father!" Will shouted.

"I should know if I'm loving someone who's hurting you," Ella shouted back. "All those years you were in pain, and you never gave me the choice to be on your side!"

"I didn't want to hurt you!" Will turned back toward the Brightwood. "And now I've killed someone. So you should go home."

"Home with the woman who sold you to my father?" Ella cried. "Home to the girl who treats me like her servant? To the place where my *father* used my brother's magic to take out some poor boy's heart?"

"He did that in the palace," Will muttered.

"I didn't hear you, and it doesn't matter," Ella shouted. The wind kept tossing her hair in her face, and she pushed it aside with a frustrated groan. "I'm furious with you! I'm terrified! I just saw you nail a man to the wall! And I'm coming with you, Will Fletcher, because you're my *fucking* brother!"

"That's the second time you've cursed at me," Will said.

"That's because you're a terrible influence!" Ella shouted, and stormed off toward the Brightwood.

Will raced to keep up with her. "You didn't pack any clothes!"

"I'll manage!"

"You can't even get through the thorns," Will cried, grabbing her hand. That was a mistake, because she held on tight, squeezing his fingers together.

"You can."

The one good thing about Ella stubbornly wrenching him forward by the hand was that it distracted Will from thinking about the dead man in the Westwood drawing room. His real problem was marching ahead of him in a white nightgown and house shoes, not bleeding out over the floor while his mother and younger sister wept in terror.

Ella only hesitated when they reached the edge of the Brightwood. She stopped a few paces ahead of the trees, frowning into the dark, quiet shadows of the beech forest. The wind that swept over the fields of Westwood was muted there, gently rocking the canopy and tickling the grass.

"All right," she said. "How do we get through this?"

Will supposed he should have already made another pair of glasses for Luc, but he hadn't reached that part yet. "I don't know. I wasn't planning to lead anyone through here until the night of the festival."

"Another thing you need to explain," Ella said tightly. "But not right now."

Will sighed. "Do you have any metal on you? Iron, silver, brass? Tin?"

Ella gestured widely to her nightgown and soft slippers.

"Right," Will said. He opened his bag. The only metal he could find were silver buttons on a fine jacket he'd received from Olven as a solstice gift. He peered at them, trying to figure out what good they'd do against a forest of illusory thorns.

His father had written that silver was best for protection. Will didn't have much choice, so he shook the jacket out in front of him. "Anyone who wears this can pass through the thorns unharmed," he said, trying not to sound like he disbelieved himself.

"Oh, come now," Ella said.

"Do you have any better ideas?" Will asked. "Look. Buttons keep things closed, don't they? That's a form of protection. Silver is apparently good for protection, so silver buttons are what you're getting, Ella."

Ella silently put on the jacket. She eyed the forest warily. "The thorns are still there."

"They only look like it to you," Will said. "On a bright day, I can see clear through the trees."

Ella shuddered and reached for his hand again. "Don't let go."

Will squeezed her hand and stepped forward. Ella took a long, shivery breath, then stepped into the soft grass under the beech trees. "Oh gods, it's like I'm inside them."

"But they aren't hurting you?" Will asked.

"No..." Ella drew out the word, examining her arms and legs. "I don't think so."

"Then let's keep moving," Will said. "We have a long way yet to go."

He led Ella slowly into the dark woods at the edge of the goblin court. Above them, the boughs of the beech trees tossed in the wind rising from Morvane, rustling like a chorus of voices whispering in shock at their arrival. Then they passed the reach of even the wind. The forest was still, the silence broken only by the sound of Will's footsteps and Ella's soft, hitching breaths as she finally began to cry.

# Chapter Twelve

It was nearly midnight by the time they made it to Olven's cottage. Ella had to move slowly, unnerved by passing through the thorns, and Will kept thinking back to the man nailed to the wall of the drawing room. Aengus had been a horrible, small-minded ass, but Will couldn't help feeling worse. There had to have been a thousand other ways to keep Aengus from returning to the capital. He simply couldn't think of them with Ella clinging to his hand.

He nearly collapsed when he saw the light shining through Olven's cottage window. "It'll be all right," he said. "Olven's fantastic, you'll see. He'll probably love you. He'll make you drink gallons of tea and give him all the gossip in Westwood."

Ella didn't answer. She looked thin and spent, her mouth pressed tight together. He squeezed her hand, and she squeezed back, faintly.

"It'll be all right," Will said again.

He knocked lightly on the cottage door, eyeing the other small houses lining the street. Olven's was one of the only ones with candlelight still streaming through the windows, but a lack of light never stopped people from watching their neighbors.

Olven opened the door. He was dressed in one of his thick wool robes and his enormous rainbow scarf, and Will felt Ella's fingers tense as he turned to look at her.

"Will," Olven said. "You've brought a young lady."

"My sister," Will said. "Ella."

"How do you do," Ella whispered, with the smallest bob of a curtsy.

"Oh, much better with guests," Olven said. "My Will told me so much about you. Come in, my dear, I have tea already prepared and scones in the oven. I do hope you like scones. I have strawberries and honey if you like them sweet."

"Oh," Ella said, already being whisked away from Will by Olven's feathery embrace. "That would be very nice."

"There's a guest in the drawing room," Olven said to Will over his shoulder as he steered Ella like a dumbfounded puppet. "You look like you've had a horrible shock, my love. I hope you like crocheted robes, because I have one just your size. Don't mind the woman on my couch."

The woman on Olven's couch looked up from a full mug of tea, her white hair braided loosely over one shoulder, scaled skin glimmering.

Jade nodded to Will. "I see you made it through the thorns."

"You were watching us," William said. His chest clenched uncomfortably. He'd wanted to tell Olven the truth in his own time. Now, he glanced nervously at Olven, searching for any sign of disapproval or disgust.

"I told you that I'd keep spies near you," Jade said. She stood, setting down her mug. "You must be the lovely Ella Westwood," she said, bowing to Ella.

Ella shrank back against Olven, her face going a curious red. "Pleased to make—how do you do your acquaintance," she said, stumbling over her words.

"You don't have to worry," Will said. Ella must have been terrified. "Jade's a princess. Luc's sister. She's too proper to go around shooting people with warning arrows."

"Former princess," Jade said, ignoring Will. She held out her palm, and Ella put a trembling hand into it. Jade raised Ella's knuckles to her lips. "I've been keeping an eye on your brother. You may have seen my servants in your garden. You sang a little song to one of them, once."

Ella flushed red to her ears. "The beetles? Oh, that was just... it was something to pass the time."

"You also sang to the cat," Jade said. Her sharp teeth flashed in a smile.

Ella was still holding Jade's hand. "The beetles were yours? Like the one that flew at Louisa when she called me..."

"Called you what?" Will asked, but Ella and Jade seemed to be in a glass bubble, gazes fixed on each other.

"She deserved worse," Jade said. "I'm sorry for encroaching on your privacy, but as you can see," she gestured vaguely in Will's direction, "the men in our lives do need looking after."

"Yes," Ella said, in a dazed voice.

"Will," Olven said, as Jade led Ella to the couch. Olven was already bearing an enormous heap of knitted blankets, scarves, and robes. "Give these to your sister and help me with the scones."

Ella seemed surprised to find Will there at all when he dumped the mountain of wool in her arms, and Will left her sinking on the couch under the weight of it. Olven ushered him into the kitchen and stopped him near the stove, eyes bright with concern.

"The princess told me that one of the king's wizards came for you," Olven said. "Did he hurt you? Are you well?"

"I killed him," Will said. "He would have reported to the prince. I couldn't let him—if he brought me to the capital... I'm so sorry, Olven."

Olven pulled Will into a feathery embrace. Will felt suddenly young again, a scrawny, unkempt teenager hovering at the entrance to Olven's forge. Olven didn't mind if he let out a ragged sob into his impossibly large scarf, or held on a moment too long. He just stood there, holding him, his feathers obscuring Will's vision.

"Perhaps I'm a selfish old goblin," Olven said, "but I prefer you coming home at that wizard's expense than not coming home at all."

Will thought of the compass in his pocket, and this cluttered cottage haunted by the absence of a goblin he'd never known. "I think I might be in over my head, Olven."

"I suspected," Olven said. He waited for Will to step back and smoothed down his feathers. "Let's see about those scones."

Olven insisted on whipping cream to go with the strawberries, and brought the whole mess of them into the drawing room on several mismatched plates. It felt strange to wrap himself up in a knitted robe with Ella, a disgraced goblin princess, and Olven over scones only hours after making nails burrow into a man's flesh. He stared at the sliced strawberry sliding down a mountain of cream and tried not to think about the blood staining his shoes.

"So you're trying to steal Luc's heart," Ella said. She was practically drowning in Olven's thickest robe, which was dyed the colors of a sunset. Her hands kept disappearing in the sleeves, and her hair was a rat's nest after being tossed in the wind. "The heart that my father took from him. And you need to go to the festival for that?"

"We need a distraction," Will said, staring down at his plate. "To keep the wizards and guards busy."

Ella's voice went cold. "Ah. You just wanted me to make a good impression, then?"

"I'm sorry," Will said. "You seemed to like the prince, and I didn't want to drag you into trouble."

"Consider me dragged," Ella said. "What will you do without a proper distraction now?"

"I can find a way to sneak in," Will said. "Maybe in disguise."

"You'll go back." Ella was glaring holes into Will, her brows lowered. "Even though you're probably wanted for murder. Even knowing what they'll do when they find you. What that *man* wanted to do to you." She finally looked away, her jaw clenched. "What my father did to you."

"I have to go," Will said. "They have Luc's heart."

"You really do love him," Ella said.

"And you can't go alone." Jade spoke around a mouthful of scone and strawberries. "You clearly can't be trusted when you're backed into a corner. My people and I will go with you. I *am* a member of the royal family," she added, when Olven and Will looked at her in surprise. "And my people will be enough of a distraction, I think."

"Maybe not enough," Ella said. "You still need to distract the prince. I know he seems to favor me." She met Will's gaze again. "If you can get me there, I'll keep him occupied."

"Ella," Will said. He couldn't imagine how it must have felt to learn tonight that her own father had used Will like wood in an oven for half of his life.

"I'm still angry with you," Ella said. "And I'm sorry, and I'm confused, and I don't know what to think. But I love you, gods help me."

"You're the best sister a man could have," Will said, and he knew as he said it that it was true. Ella was often frustrating and sanctimonious, but despite everything, he was glad she was there.

"Oh, I know," Ella said darkly, and took a dainty bite of her scone.

"I'll find you a dress," Jade said. "Something in silver, perhaps, to match those pretty eyes."

Ella blushed. "They're hardly as nice as yours."

It finally struck Will what was happening. "Hold on," he said to Jade. "That's my sister."

"Yes, you've made that clear," Jade said.

"My *sister,*" Will repeated.

"We can accommodate you before the festival, if you like," Jade said to Ella, once again pointedly ignoring him. "Our lives may be a little rough and tumble at the moment, but we'll always welcome a young lady with promise."

"Or you can stay here," Olven said.

"That might put you at risk." Jade laid her hand on Ella's arm, and Ella seemed uninclined to shake it off. "We'll need to consult with them as the festival approaches."

"And *I'll* need to consult with Olven," Will said, "since I still have to make something to return Luc's heart to him safely."

Jade sighed. "I suppose there's no helping it. I'll send for you once we've gathered our resources for the festival." She got to her feet. "If your actions tonight hurt Luc, we'll have words. My spies say that he's been acting strangely lately. The wizards might have strengthened the spell on his heart again."

"I can fix that," Will said. He could only hope that Luc was safe. He couldn't risk going back to Morvane until the festival, now. "I promise."

"See to it that you do," Jade said. She nodded goodbye to Ella and swept out of the drawing room, her steel-toed boots thumping on the floor.

"So that's what a goblin princess is like," Ella whispered.

"She did shoot at me once," Will said. "And she was dangerously forward just now."

"Was she?" Ella smiled softly and touched her messy hair. "I had no notion."

"That might be enough speculation for the night," Olven said. He started gathering the plates. "I'll make up beds for you here, and I will draw a hot bath for you in the morning."

"Thank you," Ella said. She looked like she wanted to get up to help clean, but Olven waved her back to the couch.

"No need to thank me, my dear. Any family of Will's is family of mine."

Ella hovered as Olven brought even more quilts, knitted blankets, and pillows, easing almost guiltily into her makeshift nest on the couch. When Olven and Will had set up his cot and Olven had retreated to his bedroom, Ella slipped back out from under the blankets.

"Help me," she said, and started dragging Will's cot over to the couch. She pressed it up against the cushions and climbed back into bed. "I don't think I can be alone right now."

"I know what you mean," Will said, getting under his own pile of quilts. Ella rolled so she was facing him and reached for his hand, lacing their fingers together.

"I think I might be a horrible person," she whispered.

"You're the nicest person on earth, Ella," Will said. "It's highly aggravating at times, I assure you."

For once, Ella didn't rise to his teasing. "No, I'm not," she said. "I thought that man was going to take you away tonight. Even when he was bleeding from his hands, with those things moving around inside of him, I was relieved. I'm glad that he's dead," she added, and Will realized that she wasn't talking about Aengus now.

He clasped her hand in both of his. "Your father still loved you."

"Not enough to excuse what he did to you," Ella said, "or to Luc. If I had to choose, I'd choose you, Will."

Will felt a knot growing in his throat. He'd grown used to being a sacrifice. His mother's sacrifice for a title, Murtagh's sacrifice for power, a means to an end. It only struck him now how many people had deliberately chosen *him*, not what he could give them. Olven. Luc. And now Ella.

"I'd choose you too," Will said. "Thank you for coming with me."

Ella laughed softly and released his hands to tousle his hair. "Oh, Will. As though I could ever leave you on your own."

***

A vase older than the Morvanish royal family shattered against the wall of Ramon's bedroom, breaking into a dozen pieces. Luc stared at it dispassionately, wondering what he was supposed to feel. No one had told him yet, so he waited, trying to ignore the strange disquiet in the back of his mind.

"That *wizard* of yours must have done something to Aengus." Ramon paced the room, raking his fingers through his hair. "He was found dead in a field in Westwood. Father is sending people to investigate. Even that blasted toady of his, Berenger, has been asking me questions. Do you hear me, Luc? Berenger is sending people there. Wizards who can track the scent of a body, with spells to divine a man's last moments. If he said something to implicate me before he died, I'll be ruined."

Luc nodded. "Yes. The king would be concerned to find a wizard dead so close to the Brightwood."

"I *know* that." Ramon kicked a chair and cursed softly. "I wasn't trying to make you repeat everything I say. We need to *fix* this."

Luc picked up one of the shards. It was a fine vase, sturdily made, but the broken edge was rough and pebbled. Luc scraped it experimentally against one of his claws. It made a satisfying sound, reminding him of his boyhood, when he'd watch Alara file her claws to sharp points. He scraped his claw again.

"I'll need to find another wizard," Ramon said. "I thought keeping yours close at hand would help. We could use a strong base. But if he turned on us... Perhaps *Aengus* turned on me. He was a sly, power-grubbing little commoner, after all. Would your Will betray us?"

Luc's claw was nearly sharp enough to cut the skin now. He kept going. "He wouldn't betray me."

"Then Aengus must have double-crossed us," Ramon said, "and your wizard wouldn't go along with him. That has to be it. Yes. Aengus was the wrong choice. I need to find another, and soon. Not Berenger. He's too loyal to my father. Your Will must have gone into hiding, if he's clever. Perhaps his sister knows where he is."

Luc watched Ramon pace the room like a trapped wolf. If he didn't love Ramon dearly, Luc might feel no small amount of pleasure in the exhaustion in Ramon's eyes and his nervous habit of picking his nails raw. If he hated Ramon—if he despised him for holding his heart in his hands and shaping his mind to suit his needs, Luc might stop him by the window. He might back him against the glass, gently, gently, and dig his sharpest claw into the fragile skin of Ramon's throat until his heart pumped a torrent of blood out of the gash he made there.

Yes. If he hated Ramon, it would be so very easy.

"I'm going to petition Father to keep you armed," Ramon said. "I need protection. Someone I can trust. Someone who won't turn on me."

It wouldn't take much pressure. Just a push, and Luc could open Ramon's throat for him. He wondered what it would sound like.

"If you're just going to sit there, you might as well leave," Ramon said. "*Gods*, you're so *dull* these days. The moment I have a wizard I can trust, I'm making you interesting again."

Luc scraped the shard against his claw. Not sharp enough yet, no. Not yet.

He dutifully left Ramon to his pacing. Alistair tried to speak to him, but Luc didn't know how he was meant to feel about Alistair now. Alistair was a spy, which could put him at odds with Ramon. If Luc never spoke to him, then he wouldn't have to report him to Ramon one day. It would be bad, he thought, to report Alistair. He simply couldn't remember why.

He kept idly scraping his claws into sharp points until he heard voices down the hall. Alistair was whispering to someone in an alcove, his face half hidden in shadow. After a minute of furious whispering and gesturing, Kit marched out of the alcove, dressed as a page with his arms swinging. He grabbed Luc without preamble, yanking him away from the wall.

"Come with me," he hissed.

Ramon had ordered Luc not to listen to his family, but Luc found himself following Kit regardless. After a minute or two of struggling to work through the fog in his mind, he realized that it was because Ramon had ordered him not to listen to his sister. Kit wasn't Ramon's sister. Something stirred in Luc's mind, trying to force itself through the haze.

Kit practically shoved Luc into the storage closet.

"What the *fuck* did my father do to you?" he asked.

Luc searched for the shard he'd been using on his claws. He picked it up from where it had rolled under a violet gown and got back to work. "It wasn't your father."

"Was it Ramon?" Kit braced his hands on Luc's shoulders. He nodded slowly. "Shit. Does he know about you and Will?"

"He knows that I love him."

"Oh, love." Kit didn't sound particularly interested in love. "Does he know what you're planning?"

"No," Luc said. "He never asked."

"And you won't tell him." Kit shook him slightly, and Luc stared up at him. "You won't tell him, because if you do, Will is going to *die.*"

Something unpleasant threatened to rise in Luc's chest. "I don't think I would like that. Would I?"

"No," Kit said. "No, you won't." He let go of Luc. "And since you don't seem like you can do much of anything on your own, you can't stop me from helping you."

Luc shrugged, scraping his claws against the shard. They were nearly all wickedly sharp, too short for most goblins, but with an edge that could tear open a man's belly.

"Right," Kit said. "If Alistair asks, you don't know where I've gone."

"No," Luc said softly. "I don't."

Kit sighed heavily. His eyes were wet, but Luc couldn't imagine why. "I was just starting to like you," he said.

"I like you very much, Kit," Luc said.

Kit wiped his eyes with the back of his hand. "Of course. Of course you do."

Kit took Luc to Alistair in the training grounds. He was already having a hard time remembering what Kit had said. So much was harder, lately. Every time he thought of Ramon, the world seemed to tilt beneath his feet, and the indescribable mass beneath the fog boiled dangerously. Whatever was left of Luc could only focus on propelling his body forward.

Kit paused in front of Luc for a minute, jaw working as though he wanted to speak. Then he turned on his heel, disappearing into the belly of the palace.

He did not return.

# Chapter Thirteen

Will woke up on Olven's couch with daylight streaming through the narrow windows. Voices rose from the kitchen, and it took Will longer than he'd care to admit to recognize that they belonged to Ella and Olven. They were singing one of the little working songs Olven liked to hum at the forge, something about wheels of cheese and unreliable sailors. It was hard to imagine how anyone could sing when everything had gone so wrong the night before.

Will sat up slowly, swinging his legs off the couch. Someone must have moved him off the cot while he slept, because the cot was leaning flat against the far wall with a pile of blankets neatly folded nearby. He groaned as he stood, his legs one massive ache, and the singing in the kitchen stumbled to a halt.

"Will?" Ella appeared at the door. She was wearing one of Olven's tunics, which was big enough to be a gown. She'd cinched it with a belt, but it still swallowed her. "I was so worried. You slept most of the day."

"What?" Will turned to the window. The sun was already creeping below the trees. "The festival is *tomorrow.* Why didn't you wake me?"

"You can't help anyone when you're exhausted," Olven said, "let alone hungry. Come in, dinner's almost ready."

"But the festival," Will protested weakly.

"Eat," Olven ordered. Will entered the kitchen, where one of Olven's seed loaves was resting on the table. Robert Fletcher's journals were open next to it, along with a few scraps of paper and a bottle of ink.

Ella pulled Will into a seat. "I went through them while you were resting. I hope you don't mind. But Olven told me a little of what you're trying to do, and I thought it might be nice to have some notes."

"Of course you'd organize everything," Will said, but there wasn't any heat to his words.

He pulled out the first paper. Will had a habit of skipping over important thoughts on the way to a solution, but Ella had a clear, concise way of attacking a problem. There were lists. There were little boxes to go with the lists. There were additional boxes to support the first round of little boxes. It was so neat and tidy that Will felt like a grubby imposter who'd stumbled across the paper by mistake.

"I thought that it might be important to list what metals had certain magical properties," Ella said, pointing to one of the lists. "Silver for protection. Iron for matters of the body. Steel for cleansing. Brass for magic."

"What about gold?" Will asked.

"According to your father, gold is rubbish at holding magic." Ella pulled up a seat next to Will. "Though his handwriting was a little difficult to read. Does this help at all?"

"I think so," Will said. He stared at her careful lists. The panel in Luc's chest was big enough for his hands to slip through with a bit of twisting. He could wear studded gloves, perhaps, or...

"Rings," he said. "I can use rings. One on every finger."

Ella grabbed another paper and uncapped the ink bottle. "Silver to protect his heart, right?"

A seed of excitement started to grow in Will's chest, pushing through the fear and misery of the night before. "And iron to make sure his organs knit together again."

"Brass for the magic that keeps everything else working," Ella said, scribbling furiously. "Unless you can heal the other pieces of him that are missing?"

"I don't think I can," Will said. "Write down steel for cleansing, too."

"Right. Though I've never seen a brass ring before," Ella said.

"It can corrode," Will said, "but that's fine. Olven, do you have any rings I can borrow?"

"Dozens," Olven said, pulling a truly enormous meat pie out of the oven. "We'll need to resize them, but that should be easy enough. But put that away for now and eat something. When was the last time you had a proper meal?"

Will hesitated, trying to sift through the chaos of the past few days. "I had a scone?"

Ella and Olven both groaned. Olven plopped the pie on the table, making it rattle slightly.

"Food first," he said sternly, "then conspiracies."

Will didn't realize how ravenous he was until he started eating. It didn't settle his concern for Luc, but it made him feel less like a jittery collection of nerves. Olven insisted on Will taking a bath afterward, and when Will left to pump water for the tub outside, he spotted Olven and Ella talking quietly like old friends. A small knot of tension unwound as he watched Ella smile at something Olven said. He hadn't known how she would react to suddenly finding herself in the Brightwood, but Olven was charming enough to win anyone over.

He hurriedly washed and changed into some of the spare clothes he'd kept in Olven's house. The sun had already set by the time he was done, but Will finally felt awake, his mind reeling with possibilities. He and Olven gathered as many rings as they could find, and Will laid them out on the table, splitting them up by type of metal. They'd have to make the brass rings, but while Olven and Will weren't jewelers, they could probably manage with the tools they used for chains. No one said that the rings had to *look* nice. They just had to function.

He worked into the night, shaping and refitting rings, until he had a motley collection piled up on a tray before him.

He lifted two silver rings into the air. He felt the magic in his chest, the river that had flowed so painfully out of him and into Murtagh long ago. Once, it had been used to hurt Luc. He hadn't seen Luc then, trapped in the elven wizard's box, but they'd been entwined then, their lives inexorably bound together. Now, twenty years later, he would use his magic to heal.

"You deserve to be protected," he said, thinking of Luc alone in the palace, living above the dark, horrible room where his heart had been ripped out of his chest. Magic trickled out of him, filling the rings, making the silver warm to the touch. "That's what I'm going to do, Luc. Not just because I love you. You'd deserve it even if we'd never met. You deserve to feel, to be fucked up or kind or unpleasant, because everyone deserves that. You should know what it's like to be who you are without someone forcing your loyalty. You should be loyal to *yourself* first."

The rings grew so hot that they nearly burned his fingers, but Will refused to let go until he knew that the magic held. When he finally set them down, his fingertips were marked with two half circles.

He shook his hands out and picked up the steel rings. "Now you," he said, bracing himself for the warmth of his magic. "It's time to listen to me."

Olven found him a few hours later, rousing him from an uneasy sleep. Will's hands were marked with faint burns, interwoven rings crossing over each other as he'd tried to find a less painful way to hold them. Olven clucked over his hands and fetched a burn balm, but Will barely felt it. Will had stuffed the rings with so much of his power that he felt lightheaded and dizzy, drifting back to sleep before he could understand what Olven was saying.

When he woke the next morning, he found that Olven had carefully put the rings in a pouch by his cot. Will tied the pouch to his belt for safekeeping and staggered into the kitchen, praying that Ella hadn't let him sleep through the day a second time.

Jade nodded from the doorway, arms crossed over her chest. Her sword hung loosely at her side in a plain leather scabbard, and jewels glittered in her braid. Ella stood nervously near Olven, fussing with her oversized tunic.

"Hello, wizard," Jade said. She flashed her sharp teeth in a mirthless smile. "The festival is tonight. It's time that we borrowed you. By your leave, Olven," she added.

"Just return him to me safely," Olven said, laying a talon on Will's shoulder. Will didn't bother arguing that he was no one's to borrow or give away. Olven had earned the right to be a little protective.

"We could also use your help, if you don't mind," Jade told Ella, with much more care than she reserved for Will.

"Of course," Ella said. She looked down at her tunic. "But I don't know how much help I can be."

"Not to worry," Jade said, taking Ella's hand with a slight bow. "I'm sure you'll prove to be an asset."

Olven pulled Will aside as Jade led Ella out through the door to the garden. His dark eyes were troubled, his feathers ruffling with unease.

"Promise me that you'll take care of yourself," he said. His voice was low and soft, and Will could feel the fear building in the air around him, tangible as the prickle of energy before a heavy storm. "Don't do anything too rash."

"Olven, all of this is rash." Will touched his shoulder. Olven was as tightly wound as a sprung wire. "But I'll be careful."

"Those people will not hesitate to kill you," Olven said. "Remember that."

Will thought of Olven's Bernard lying in some field beyond the border, and pulled Olven into a tight embrace. "I'll come back, Olven. And I'll introduce you to Luc. I think you'll like him."

"I'll like anyone you love," Olven said. He sighed, his feathers brushing Will's cheek as he breathed in. "Just stay out of reach of their swords."

"You'll see me again soon," Will said, drawing back. "I swear."

***

Jade's bandits were far more welcoming in the daylight.

They met Will and Ella near the abandoned cabin, their swords and bows sheathed. Ella seemed reticent at first, sticking close to Will as Jade stepped away to speak to one of her subordinates. Then a goblin with moth wings and pale fur along her arms and leg came flying over the grass. She was about two feet tall, stocky, and bristling with daggers.

"I'm Fern," she said. "You must be the woman who sings to Lady Jade's beetles."

Ella blushed. "Oh, not *regularly.* Fern's a lovely name."

"Isn't it?" Fern said, preening.

"And I'm Giselle," the ratlike goblin said, pushing Fern out of the way. "That's practically the same as Ella, you know."

"It is," Ella said, "I suppose."

"Don't crowd her," another goblin said. She was nearly eight feet tall, broad as a tree trunk, and covered in lichen. She bowed and extended a furred hand to Ella. "M'name's Daisy. I used to be the princess' seamstress."

Ella took Daisy's hand and curtseyed. Daisy stared at her for a few seconds and tried to curtsy back. "I quite like sewing, myself," Ella said. "I used to want to be a seamstress, but... oh! Oh, have you met my brother?"

The goblins looked in Will's direction.

"He's fine," Daisy said. She gestured toward the cabin. "I've been making a gown for you, miss, but it might need alterations. If you'd step inside?"

"I thought I was escorting her," Fern mumbled as Ella was ushered away.

"Why is *she* the guest of honor while I get shot at?" Will asked.

Jade glanced his way and grinned. "She isn't wielding magic that has been known to kill our kind," she said. "Besides, everyone favors a girl in a pretty dress."

"You seem to be favoring her more than most," Will said, unsure how worried he should be about Ella blushing over a bandit queen.

"Perhaps," Jade said. She towered over him, her hand resting casually on her sword hilt. "I hope you aren't one of those *Morvanish* types who keeps women locked away until they're married off."

"What? No!"

Jade's smile was too vulpine for comfort. "Good. Come with me."

Will followed her through the woods. The goblins in her company huddled in small groups, some whispering, some gesturing widely, others stretching and testing the weight of their swords. Jade led Will to a quiet part of the forest and drew him in close.

"I need to know that you have a plan to return my brother's heart," she said. The veneer of a confident, unshakable leader had faded again, revealing a goblin in desperate need of comfort. It reminded Will of Olven, and it struck him how agonizing it must have been for Jade to rely only on her spies for word of the brother who'd been taken from her.

"I do," Will said. He jingled the bag of rings, and Jade looked at them sharply. "I can do this. I'll bring him home."

Jade closed her eyes. Will could see her try to regain her composure, unable to show weakness for more than a moment. "Good. Good."

"I don't know if I can get all of your goblins out of the Brightwood, though."

"I've made arrangements," Jade said. "We'll leave through the main gate of the Brightwood, with the queen's party."

"She allowed you to go?" Will asked.

Jade didn't answer his question. "My concern lies in what happens when we return. Most of my people will go through the gate as a distraction. That will give me, Luc, you, and your sister the chance to sneak safely past the thorns, where others won't follow. But I need you for that."

"Do you have glasses?" Will asked. He lifted his empty frames. "So long as the frames are metal, I can enchant them."

"Can you enchant masks?" Jade asked. "I'm fairly sure I can get my claws on a few of those."

"I think so," Will said. "It's the same principle, I suppose. But aren't most masks made of cloth?"

"Ours have metal frames." Jade paused as though choosing her words delicately. "They might be a little alarming to someone with a sensitive disposition."

"Ella thinks praying mantises are cute," Will said, guessing where Jade's reticence was coming from. "Not much scares her."

"I knew she was a reasonable woman," Jade said. She clapped her hands together and straightened her shoulders. "Right. Follow me, then. We don't have long before my mother's carriage arrives at the gate to the Brightwood. *That's* where we'll find your masks. And a suitable disguise, I suppose, since you might be a wanted man."

"Your mother is helping us?" Will asked, flabbergasted.

Jade laughed brightly, drawing the attention of several of her people. "Absolutely not," she said.

"But... but how?" Will asked.

Jade's smile broadened, her eyes glimmering. "If she calls me a bandit, then I might as well act like one. Come along, wizard. We're going to steal the queen's carriage."

***

Luc examined himself in the mirror.

The queen had given him a new suit for the festival. It was mostly in the Morvanish style, laced up the front with a dark sash over one shoulder to signify him as a member of the royal family. A sword hung from his hip, the result of a furious argument between Ramon and his father. His tunic was cut at an odd angle, however. It draped downward from his left thigh, and when Luc leaned down to touch it, his sharp claws sliced easily through the fabric.

The queen clasped her hands tightly together. "It's what the goblin noblemen were wearing when the treaty was signed," she said. Luc turned around, brows furrowed. She rocked forward on one foot, then back. "I thought it might be fitting."

"The king wouldn't approve," Luc said. The king wouldn't approve of many things in Luc's life. In his head. In the invisible weight on his claws, an itch he couldn't satisfy, the unspoken, primal urge to tear and gouge.

"He won't notice," the queen said. She stepped closer, brushing Luc's hair out of his eyes. Her voice dropped to a whisper. "He doesn't notice many things. Like the page who looks like my daughter running through the palace. You haven't seen them, have you?"

Luc met the queen's gaze. No one had seen Kit in days. Even Alistair, who could find Kit in a hedge maze with his eyes closed, hadn't seen hide nor hair of him. That should bother Luc. But it was another dangerous feeling, one that threatened to tip everything out of balance if he gave any thought to it.

"I'm sorry," he said, because that's what Luc would say if he were truly there. "I haven't."

The queen patted Luc's shoulders with shaking hands. "If you need to leave the festival at any time, I'll allow it. I know that Ramon wanted your family to come, but it must feel..." Her voice was so soft that Luc had to strain to hear. "Humiliating. Being paraded in front of everyone like a horse, day after day. No end to it."

Ramon had ordered Luc not to obey his mother or father. Accepting a gift wasn't an order, but the queen permitting him to leave the festival felt like one.

Luc's voice emerged dully through the fog, like a marionette trying to form words in a wooden throat. "I'm quite happy as I am."

"Of course you are," the queen said softly, gaze lowered.

Someone knocked on the door, and the queen pulled away.

"Time to find my wife, I suppose," Ramon called, swinging the door open. He strode into the room in a white suit with a dark blue sash, his golden hair combed and shining. He stopped when he saw Luc. "Don't you look tidy. What did you do with your claws?"

"Sharpened them," Luc said.

Ramon shuddered dramatically. "It must be a competitive thing with your more feral relatives," he said. "Some things can't be helped."

"Ramon," the queen said. "I'd best not catch you speaking that way to a visiting monarch."

"And what will you do if I did, Mother?" Ramon drawled. "Cluck at me?" He grabbed Luc's arm. "Come, Luc. I need you to weed out the thoroughly unbearable ladies before my father takes a shine to one of them."

He drew Luc away from the queen and into the hall. Luc looked back over his shoulder at her as they left. She was standing in his room with her hands held loosely before her, and in that one, brief instant before the door closed, her face was twisted in helpless fury.

# Chapter Fourteen

The gates of the Brightwood used to be a terrible omen.

In Morvane, people still held their breath when they crossed the worn, beaten road leading out of the gates. It was bad luck to hold a wedding in sight of them, and people built their houses facing away from them, even if that meant having to walk around the house just to get to the door.

In the Brightwood, the gates just looked like a tunnel through the trees.

"They say the trees used to reach out and grab people during the war," Ella whispered.

She huddled next to Will in the shadows of the ordinary, thorn-free forest that spread out around the road like the wings of a bird, cutting off the village beyond. Jade had insisted on Will and Ella staying behind while her people got into position, which meant they were hunched next to the enormous, good-natured Daisy.

Daisy looked up when Ella spoke, her long brown fur hiding her face. "They did," she said. She kept her voice soft. "The Brightwood has its defenses."

Ella blanched, smoothing her hands nervously over her dress. Daisy must have worked magic of her own when she tailored it, because Will hadn't seen anything quite like it before. It was enormous, blooming out from Ella's waist in light blue petals resembling a moth's wings. The sleeves were equally voluminous, and Daisy had cunningly cut a bit of lace to go over her hair like a veil. Crystals glimmered on her bodice and under the sheer petals of the gown, but her shoes were still the old, worn house shoes she'd brought from Westwood. So long as she kept her feet hidden, Will was pretty sure she didn't need any magic to draw the eye of every bachelor in Morvane.

Not, however, that she seemed to care for any of them. Will hadn't caught her looking away from Jade since they'd crept into their hiding place, and if she kept worrying at her gown, it would be hopelessly wrinkled by the time they reached the capital.

"Jade will be fine," Will whispered, "if that's what you're worried about."

"I'm not worried," Ella whispered back. She watched Jade walk along the side of the road, the only member of her company that would be visible to an approaching carriage. She cut a fine figure there, upright with her sword in one hand, her sharp claws bared on the other.

"I'm worried," Daisy said. "She's reckless where her brother is concerned. But I suppose that can't be helped. She practically raised him, poor dear."

"Were you around when Luc was a boy?" Will asked. "What was he like?"

Daisy tilted her head. "Oh, he was a cute little thing, always following his sisters. He wanted to be a soldier like Alara, but when she lost her wings, well... Jade wouldn't have it. It was bad enough to have Alara and Wren fighting, especially after Alara sent Wren home for the shakes."

"The shakes?" Will asked. A shadow appeared on the road, imperceptible through the trees, and Jade stopped pacing.

"Many soldiers have them," Daisy said. "Some have it worse than others. It comes from getting too close to magefire. Wren has tremors, or she did the last I saw her. She couldn't even walk in a straight line for a while. Alara's shakes are all in her head. It changes you, you know. Leaving home, killing people."

Will thought of Aengus bleeding out in the drawing room and looked down. Ella grabbed his hand in silent understanding.

"Here it comes," Daisy said. "Stay quiet now."

Will had no idea how Daisy could see at all through her curtain of fur, but she must have had keen eyesight, because Will didn't see it until it was nearly upon them. The queen's carriage was shaped like a sphere, broad and white with delicate, almost lacelike designs on the outside. It was larger than Will had expected, with space for soldiers to cling to the back, and it was open enough that Will could see at least seven people inside.

Jade stepped into the middle of the path. The horses drawing the carriage slowed and tossed their heads in alarm, and an older woman with long, curling ram horns appeared at the window.

"Hello, Mother." Jade's voice carried over the sound of shuffling horse hooves and the creak of carriage wheels. "If you'd be so kind as to step outside, we can do this with as much dignity as possible."

"Jade." The queen opened the door to the carriage and stepped out. She looked remarkably like Luc, with gray-green skin and white hair, but the horns and the absence of claws marked the difference. Will gently pulled Ella a little further into the shadows as Jade's company appeared in the trees and along the path. "I should have known that you would try something like this."

Jade hefted her sword in one hand. "Yes, you should have. Now, Mother, just sit down and we'll be having that carriage. If you don't mind, Alara."

Alara stepped out of the carriage. She held no sword, but her claws were nearly four inches long and terribly sharp, and she walked toward Jade with an air of purpose that made Will's breath catch.

"Not to worry, Mother," she said. "We'll be on the road soon enough."

With that, she threw herself at her sister with a snarl. Ella covered her mouth with a muffled scream, and Daisy wrapped a large arm around her shoulders as Jade and Alara went tumbling into the dirt.

Goblin warfare was clearly nothing like the exhibitions the palace threw every now and then in Morvane. Instead of slow, heavy swings and careful footwork, Jade and Alara fought like cats, growling and snapping, kicking dust in each other's eyes. Jade slammed Alara into the ground with a shoulder, only to be thrown backward. She and Alara went skidding not ten paces from where Will, Ella, and Daisy were hiding, and Ella pressed her hands harder over her mouth as Alara pinned Jade beneath her elbow.

"You're taking him to my villa when this is done?" she asked. She'd spoken softly, but Will was close enough to hear, and he glanced at Ella in confusion.

"Not if you keep insisting," Jade said. "How's Wren?"

"At home, probably chewing her claws off. She misses you."

"Tell her I'll get her a souvenir from Morvane," Jade said. "And let me *beat* you. That last hit hurt."

"Well, excuse me for trying to make it look convincing," Alara said. She went limp, letting Jade get up and wrench her arms behind her back.

Will suppressed a smile. He wondered if Luc knew that Jade wasn't the only sister in the conspiracy. Perhaps even some of the guards were on their side, because as soon as the crown princess surrendered, Jade's people easily took the rest of the carriage.

"Don't worry, Mother," Jade called as she marched Alara back toward the group of outraged goblin nobility. "We'll keep Alara safe with us so you don't try anything unpleasant on our way home."

"You're jeopardizing our peace," the queen said, wrenching against her bonds. "All for one petty, inconsequential resentment."

"I wouldn't call Luc's heart being ripped out of his chest by a human wizard inconsequential," Jade said. The queen went still. "Or did the Morvanish king not tell you that in his letters?"

"That's an outlandish lie," the queen snapped.

"Yes, believe a Morvanish human over your own daughter," Jade said. She stopped before a young goblin woman sitting glumly next to the queen. "Chrys, let me see your shoes. Yes, they look about the right size."

She bent down and pulled a pair of glittering shoes from Chrys' feet. Chrys spat at her, but Jade didn't flinch.

"You've doomed yourself with this," Alara said.

"Oh, I know," Jade said, shoving Alara into the carriage. She turned to give her mother a simpering smile. "I'll return your daughter in one piece. Though you didn't offer the same courtesy to my boy, so who's to say?"

"There's bad blood there," Ella whispered.

"And there isn't with *my* mother?" Will whispered back. "Imagine the two of them together."

Ella shuddered. "I'd rather not, thank you."

Jade hopped onto the bench at the front of the carriage and urged the horses forward. The carriage moved slowly toward them, and a handful of goblins jumped aboard from their hiding places in the trees. Another group led the queen's company into the forest, leaving no sign that the carriage had been waylaid. When the carriage creaked to a stop near Will, Ella, and Daisy, the road leading to the gates was clear.

"Your carriage awaits, my lady," Jade said, and lifted a pair of shoes in one hand. They shone like glass, mirroring the tiny crystals in Ella's gown.

Ella mumbled her thanks and took the shoes. They fit her perfectly, and she nervously handed her old shoes to Will before climbing into the carriage.

"You too, wizard," Jade said, jerking her head, "and be polite. There's a crown princess in there."

"Take care of your sister," Daisy said, waving an enormous hand. Will waved back sheepishly and stepped into the carriage.

For a carriage that already seemed too big to be possible, the inside was surprisingly roomy. Several of Jade's company were inside, dividing up cloaks, masks, and gloves that they'd stolen from the royal entourage. Alara sat among them all, legs crossed, her shoulders not quite touching the back of the seat. Will wondered if the stumps of her wings hurt if she leaned back too far.

Alara caught his gaze and raised an eyebrow. "You must be the wizard who's charmed my brother."

Will tried to bow, but it was hard to do when Ella's dress kept spilling over his side of the bench. "I'm trying to *remove* a charm, actually."

"He means to say that he's honored to make your acquaintance," Ella said. "As am I."

Alara leaned forward to take Ella's hand. "A pleasure."

"Will your sister be upset by my wearing her shoes, though?" Ella whispered.

Alara grinned. "Only a little. She knows what we're doing here. She's simply a better actress than I am."

"Speaking of," Jade called through the window, "I'll need the resident wizard to start enchanting those masks."

Giselle scurried over with a bundle of masks in her arms, dropping them at Will's feet. She also handed him a hooded crimson cloak. It was embroidered with golden feathers and held with a jeweled clasp.

"For a disguise," she said, "if you can manage it."

Will draped the cloak over his lap before picking up one of the masks. It was shaped like an owl head, with a thin metal webbing stretched over the frame like cloth. Will had never seen the like before, and he examined it carefully, wondering if he could recreate it at Olven's forge. It looked like the work of a jeweler, not a smith, but he could probably figure it out.

Seven metal masks lay on the carriage floor, jostled slightly by the bump of the wheels.

"I think I can work with this," he said, and called the magic to his hands, feeling it sink comfortably into the mask on his lap. The rings on his fingers gleamed in the light flickering through the window, and Will thought of Luc in the royal palace, waiting for him to arrive.

"We're coming, Luc," he whispered, and got to work.

***

Night fell over Morvane. Wizards at the main square cast pale illusions of flowers opening over the darkened sky, stars rising from their petals. The royal family of Morvane stood on a dais overlooking the plaza, with Luc a step behind. Only he could see the tension in the way they held themselves.

Kit still hadn't appeared. The person who'd killed Aengus had not been found. An uneasy air had settled over the family, despite all attempts to look calm and collected. The king kept close to Queen Imogen, and Ramon kept clenching and unclenching his hands.

Luc kept his gaze on the road stretching toward the Brightwood, uncertain why he couldn't tear himself away. Every time he thought of his mother attending the festival, his mind went oddly blank. It was as though the fog had to fill every piece of his body to keep the chaos beneath from spilling over. He checked his claws. They shone in the light of the wizards' illusions, sharp and cold as steel.

A horn blew over the gathered revelers, and Luc's head snapped up instinctively. A round carriage raced through the city streets, accompanied by the faint howling, hooting, and cheering of goblins clinging to every handle and bench. The carriage bristled with them, goblins in fine cloaks and outlandish masks, a severe-looking woman at their head with dark skin that gleamed like it was inlaid with jewels.

*Jade.* He wasn't sure where the word came from. It simply came to him, hard and swift as a blow to the stomach. Jade called the horses to a halt, veering the carriage dangerously at the edge of the plaza. She stood on the bench, cupping her clawed hands around her mouth, and the fog threatened to fill Luc again as her voice carried over the hushed crowd.

"Introducing Crown Princess Alara of the Brightwood, General of the Unbowed Legion, Victor of the Battle of Halted Ridge!"

The king shifted uncomfortably, likely displeased to hear of his own failures on the battlefield. The carriage opened to reveal a slim, tall figure all in black. Luc hadn't seen her in so long that it was hard to tell how much she had aged, but she stood ramrod straight, and only a slight bump to her jacket hinted at the stumps of her wings. She wore a mask shaped like a ram's head with horns like the ones Luc remembered growing from his mother's pale hair.

"And Jade," Jade shouted, "guardian of Prince Luc, son of the Brightwood!"

Ramon glanced at Luc, but Luc could barely think through the fog. It was getting hard to breathe. He laid a hand on his chest, trying to force his lungs to work, and his fingers shook with a faint tremor.

"And finally," Jade called, jumping down from the bench, "Lady Ella Westwood, daughter of wizards and friend of the goblin court."

"*Westwood?*" Ramon asked. He reached for Luc, pulling him closer. "That Ella? The pretty little nothing from the country?"

Luc shrugged. Ramon kept his grip tight on Luc's arm as a young woman stepped down from the carriage. Her gown was full and pale blue, feathered like a moth's wings. Her shoes sparkled as she moved, and she wore a birdlike mask over her face. She lifted it, revealing Will's stepsister, smiling anxiously in the wake of a chorus of shocked whispers.

"Why is she a *goblin* friend?" Ramon whispered.

"I don't know," Luc said. Something struggled to work its way out of the fog, and he added, "but that would make her thoroughly unsuitable, don't you think?"

"Yes," Ramon said, staring at her with a fierce, bright light in his eyes. "Yes, it would."

Other goblins poured out of the carriage, bearing themselves with none of the elegance of Ella or Luc's sisters. One of them, a goblin in an owl mask with feathers poking through his crimson robe, touched Ella's mask and leaned in to whisper in her ear. The mask shone with a faint light, a gentle radiance that cast a glow over Ella's skin and dress.

Ramon released Luc. "We should greet them, Father."

"The queen should have come with them," the king said. He turned to Luc. "Would this be an insult in goblin culture?"

"I can't say," Luc said, trying to think clearly. "The crown princess often does the work of a queen."

"I'd hardly call it work," the king said. "It's unnatural, having so many children without a king. Do they even have the same father?"

"It isn't our place to speak on it," the queen said shortly.

The king sighed. "Very well." He gestured for Ramon and Queen Imogen to follow him off the dais. Luc stayed a few steps behind, examining the people who had come with the goblin court. Will was nowhere to be found. Still, Ella being there had to be a sign. Perhaps he was somewhere in the crowd, watching.

Alara didn't bow to the king or queen, and she approached the queen first, holding her arms out for an embrace. The queen looked shocked and held her back, looking at her husband for help.

"I wanted to properly meet the woman who helped raise my brother," Alara said. "I'm sure that you safeguarded his heart as closely as we would."

The queen went pink. King Tomas stepped forward, and Alara nodded to him. "King Tomas."

"General," King Tomas said.

"Which one of you is Jade again?" Ramon asked. He leapt forward, taking Jade's hand. "Luc seems to hold you in high regard. I feel like I know you already. Luc, come over here and greet your sisters."

The tension between Alara and King Tomas remained thick as smoke, but Luc staggered forward, drawn by the compulsion on his heart.

"Jade." His voice came out cracked, too young. His brass heart hammered in his chest.

Jade closed the distance between them. She pulled him into her arms, a clawed hand around the back of his head. The fog shifted. Luc pressed his cheek to hers, unable to speak.

"I'm sorry that it took so long," she whispered. She drew back, but she held Luc's arm a moment longer before letting go.

"Perhaps I could offer you a dance," Alara said to Ramon. Her eyes were carefully blank, her smile too polite.

Ramon looked toward Ella, standing in the back of the goblin entourage with a glow like starlight over her lovely dress. "I thought... perhaps..."

"Ella," Jade said, gesturing toward her, "have you been introduced to his highness, Prince Faramond?"

Ella approached with a faint blush over her cheeks. "A pleasure, Your Highness."

"The pleasure is mine," Ramon said, taking Ella's hand. In the corner of his eye, Luc caught the king making a sharp gesture, and several of his wizards left their posts to drift toward them.

"Then I must take your hand, Your Highness," Alara said to the king, he politely pulled her onto the dance floor, leaving Luc with Jade and the queen.

"Allow me to escort you to the dais," Jade said, taking the queen's hand with a warm smile. Luc moved as though to follow, but someone grabbed him by the wrist, holding him there.

"Luc." The owlish goblin stood there, his mask glittering in the magelight. He had tawny feathers under his robes, but his talons felt like a human hand, and Luc could just see the glimmer of human eyes behind the mask. His voice lowered, and Luc felt something tug at the fog in his chest. "Lucan."

Magic filled him, familiar as the warmth of his bed after a long day of riding. "Will," Luc breathed, and gasped as Will swept him into the throng of dancers.

The world spun, becoming a mass of color and expensive cloth, masks and illusions, boots and jeweled slippers. Will didn't seem to know the steps to the dance, but he whirled Luc away from the royal family, deeper into the riot of music and dancers.

Will pressed his hand to Luc's chest and spoke his name with a yearning that pulled Luc out of the fog for one bright, terrible second. Then he fell back in again, but shallower this time, not quite drowning.

"Lucan," Will said again.

"Will." Luc tried to push Will's mask up to kiss him, but Will gently brushed his hand away.

"Not yet. When you're whole again. You'll break the illusion if you remove the mask."

Luc gripped Will, drawn through the crowd of dancers toward the edge of the square. "Will. Ramon had my heart. He forced me to... I have to be loyal to him alone. He sent a wizard after you."

"The wizard isn't a problem," Will said tightly. "Can you get away?"

"Ramon didn't order me to stay." Luc felt wetness on his cheeks and tried to push the tears back. "I still can't think properly. Not fully. It's as though I'm gasping for air. I'll sink under again, and I won't... you might..."

"I have you," Will said. "I promise."

The music swelled in another reel. The king returned to the dais, speaking with Jade and the queen, but Ramon was still with Ella, her glowing mask shining brighter than the illusory flowers over the square. "Your sister—"

"She knows," Will said softly. "She'll keep him busy. Where's your guard?"

Luc hadn't even thought of Alistair. He searched for him, trying to resist the urge to sink deeper into the fog. He finally spotted Alistair behind the dais, his gaze flicking from Jade to Luc. When he caught Luc watching, Alistair straightened. Luc nodded carefully, and Alistair took a measured step back to speak to one of the other guards.

"Are you ready?" Luc whispered. "I don't know how much help I can be."

"Don't worry. We'll handle it." Will pulled Luc deeper into the crowd at the edge of the square. Luc could still see Ella and Ramon dancing, Ella's gown swirling like a cloud as they moved. Ramon's face turned their way, but with the goblins leaping and crowing in the crowd of scandalized humans, surely he couldn't have seen him.

"I'm not disobeying him," Luc said to himself. "He didn't *tell* me not to take my heart back."

"That's right," Will said. "Keep repeating that, Luc."

He took Luc's hand and drew him out of the throng. He took off his mask as soon as they crossed the edge of the square, and the feathery illusion over his hands and chest faded. Rings glinted on every finger, and his eyes were shadowed with lack of sleep, but the sight of Will's face made Luc's chest ache despite the fog that threatened to engulf him.

Ella's arrival with the goblin court had done what no amount of magic could accomplish. Every wizard in the king's employ had their eyes on her, and even some of the guards followed her path, ignoring Luc and Will as they passed by. A shadow flickered along the route to the palace, and Alistair appeared from behind a barrel of flowers.

"Luc?" he whispered.

"I'm here," Luc whispered back. "As much as I can be."

Alistair nodded. "There are still guards at the palace entrance," he said. He put a hand on his sword. "Can the princess provide a way out?"

"We're to meet her at the carriage at midnight," Will said.

"That's plenty of time for something to go wrong." Alistair walked ahead of them, his movements sure, fingers wrapping around his sword hilt. "I can lead the guards away from the palace doors."

"Alistair." Luc swallowed a heavy knot of dread in his throat. "You're coming with us when this is over, aren't you?" Alistair didn't answer. "Aren't you?"

"I knew the risks when I came here, Your Highness," Alistair said. Luc lurched forward to stop him, but Will shook his head.

"You have to let us help you," Will said.

"Stay close." Alistair's voice went curt with fear. "There should be more guards here. At least five were stationed by the doors, but all I see is..." He slowed to a halt, his hand slipping off his sword hilt. "No."

Luc squinted in the darkness. A shape moved slowly before the doors to the palace, bent at an awkward angle. He wore a dress with a skirt tied to the waist and sensible workman's trousers underneath, and he was trying to move an unconscious guard down the steps.

Kit turned to look at them, his sweaty hair hanging in his eyes.

"Oh, thank the gods," he said. "I thought I'd have to move them all myself."

"Kit?" Luc asked, as Alistair said, "move *who?*"

"The guards, obviously." Kit wiped his forehead with his arm. "It turns out that my father's guards are *very* trusting of strange people walking around with bottles of wine. Even when that wine has enough Night Thistle to take down a bear."

"You did *not* just poison all the palace guards," Alistair said, striding forward.

"No, I poisoned half of them." Kit grunted as he tried to haul the guard further away from the door. "I couldn't get to everyone. Are you going to help me or not?"

Alistair pulled Kit out of the way so he could grab the fallen guard. "Where are you putting them?"

"In the moat. It's *dry,*" he said, when Will made a sound of dismay. "Gods. I'm not a monster."

Luc glanced over the edge of the moat surrounding the outer keep and spotted several guards groaning softly and rolling ineffectively in the dirt. "How did you manage that?"

"Rolled them, mostly," Kit said. "You don't have long before replacements arrive, and I don't think they'll want a drink once they see my..." He gestured vaguely toward the moat. "...guard collection."

"I'll lead them away," Alistair said. He pointed to Kit. "*You* need to make yourself scarce."

"You're welcome," Kit said. He made no effort to move. "You two should go."

"Come with us," Luc said. He reached for Kit's hand, but Kit pulled away.

"I told you before, I have a plan." He shoved his skirts over his trousers and swished them dramatically. "If anyone gives us trouble, I'll just scream. There's nothing like a shrieking princess to draw someone's attention."

"If I don't see you again—" Luc started to say, but Kit shook his head.

"Don't start. I can't stand sentimental goodbyes." He sat on the edge of the drawbridge instead, dangling his feet over the edge. Luc turned to Alistair, who stepped forward and clasped his arm.

"Return with us," Luc said. "If you can."

Alistair just squeezed his arm once and turned away, facing the dark path to the palace doors.

Luc and Will left Kit and Alistair on the bridge, an odd pair silhouetted against the light streaming from the palace. Luc watched them until they'd disappeared into the shadows, unable to shake the feeling that this was the last time he'd see either of them again.

The palace entrance was strangely quiet. The servants must have been watching the festival from the upper floors, but without the guards at the doors, the front hall felt small and drab. He was suddenly aware of the dust clinging to the rafters and the smudged windows, the glass warped and discolored. Will took out the compass, which reflected off the polished rings on his left hand.

"Do you know the way down?" he whispered.

"Yes, but I can't follow." Luc pulled Will toward the lower stairs, which were tucked away behind a small dais. The last time he'd been there, he and Ramon had been turned aside by a guard before they reached the wards. Now, there was no guard to sternly usher them back, but Luc still felt reticent, descending the steps with care. Will held no such reverence, idly tapping the stone wall with every step.

He stopped at the first landing, arm outstretched to halt Luc's progress. His hood was still covering his face, but Luc could see the tension in his hands as they flexed against the wall.

"The ward is in the stone," Will said, staring up at a rune etched on the wall next to the stairs leading down. "I can't remove it." He turned to Luc. "Do you have somewhere to hide?"

"I'll be safe," Luc said, thinking of Kit and Alistair at the entrance. "Go."

Will hesitated, then snatched up Luc's hand and kissed it. "If you hear someone, run. I'll find you."

"I love you," Luc said.

"Tell me again when you have your heart," Will said, and broke free, racing down the winding stairs. His cloak swirled behind him like a bird's wing, then was gone, leaving Luc facing the dark, yawning stair alone.

# Chapter Fifteen

Will thumped down the stairs, holding the compass before him like a lantern in the dark. Runes flickered on the walls as he passed, gleaming with power. This was the heart of Morvane's greatest strength—wizards trained in war magic, learning spellcraft that could blanket a battlefield in fire. If even one wizard had been left behind, there was no telling what could happen. They might not be as slow to act as Aengus had been.

The compass shifted slightly, and Will stopped at a lower landing, gazing through a stone archway. A narrow hall lay beyond, unadorned with the tapestries and wall hangings Will had seen on the way down. He tried to remember if Murtagh had led him there as a boy, but his memory of the night Luc had lost his heart was disjointed at best. There were no sudden jolts of familiarity, nothing but a low, creeping dread as Will passed the empty hall.

The air was colder there, dampness clinging to the stone. The compass pointed Will past a closed door and toward another open arch. The stair behind it smelled stale and wet, and Will's shoes slid on the stone steps going down. He grabbed the walls for balance and stumbled to the next landing, where the stair opened up to a small, cramped stone room.

Will sucked in a sharp breath. He knew this room. The door was gone, and there were no lights to illuminate the crowded shelves or the heavy brass box, but he knew they were there. He could sense them, aware of their presence like a small animal scenting an owl on the wind.

He took a step forward. Light shone under his boots, and before Will could react, tendrils of stone snaked out of the walls and wrapped around his arms like thick vines. He struggled against them, but they held fast, pinning him in place.

"That's far enough, I would think." A figure appeared in the dark room beyond, a formless shadow stirring the cold air. Will heard the sound of paper tearing, and a pale light shone around the hands of a man in dark blue robes. He seemed to be in his fifties, with white in his beard and laugh lines at his eyes, but his expression was as hard as steel.

Will could taste the coppery tang of fear on his tongue, but he didn't cower or tremble. He resorted to the same response that he'd honed through years of spitting insults in Murtagh Westwood's face.

"Who the fuck are you supposed to be?" he asked.

"Oh, that's refreshingly familiar." The man made a gesture in the air, and Will's throat locked up as though someone were squeezing the base of his neck. "You'd think you'd recognize me. I'm the man you came here to kill."

Will tried to say, "what?" but the pressure on his throat strengthened, cutting off his air. When it finally released him enough to breathe, the man was facing him, brows raised curiously.

"My name is Berenger Devorath," he said. "I was your stepfather's assistant, once upon a time."

Will wanted to say that he didn't recognize *or* remember Berenger, but he didn't want the spell to start strangling him. Murtagh had spoken of an assistant once or twice, but Will hadn't cared enough to ask for his name.

"I knew you would come here," Berenger said. "When I investigated Aengus' body, I saw his last moments in a rune circle, fragmented as they were. You've changed some, but your mother was agreeable enough when I pressed her. She said that you've always been angry. Resentful. Jealous of Murtagh's power, perhaps, or the skill he used to siphon *yours*. But you have none of that skill."

He tipped Will's chin up with a finger, examining him. Will searched him for traces of metal as Berenger's pale gaze swept over him, but Berenger wasn't even wearing a brooch to hold his robes together.

"I don't blame you," Berenger said. "Murtagh should have been a weak man, insignificant and powerless. But he knew how to use the resources given to him, and I must respect him for that. I can't have you killing my wizards, though. If you were trained in runic magic, perhaps there would be some use for a man like you."

Will would have laughed if he could. Berenger had seen the last moments of Aengus' life and had come to a woefully wrong conclusion. Still, it didn't matter if Berenger was misinformed or if he knew why Will was truly there. The result was the same, Will trapped in stone vines while Berenger talked him to death.

Will shifted in his bonds. The stone wasn't thick, even if it wrapped snugly around his arms. He flexed, muscles swelling, and the stone groaned faintly.

"It's a pity," Berenger said. "You'd think that the son of a wizard would be less of a bloody-minded *goblin.*"

Will wrenched forward. Muscles that he'd honed in Olven's forge pressed against the stone vines and broke through, shattering them to pieces that rained over his legs and feet. Berenger opened his mouth in dumbfounded shock, and Will swung his fist with all the strength of a hammer blow. Bone cracked under his knuckles, and Berenger collapsed in a limp heap of skinny limbs and heavy blue robes. The pressure on Will's throat fell away, and Will kicked a lump of stone aside.

"I'm not the son of a wizard," he said. "I'm the son of a smith."

He stopped to tie Berenger's hands with strips of his own robes, to prevent him from sketching any runes while Will's back was turned. He probably should have killed him, but that was the sort of thing Berenger and his wizards would do, and one dead man was enough for Will. He gagged Berenger for good measure and left him drooling in pain on the cold stone floor.

Will stepped over Berenger's body and into the dark room beyond the hall, his breathing loud in the sudden silence. The light of Berenger's spell had faded when he fell, plunging the room into darkness.

The only light came from thin runes glowing faintly on the lid of a small jar at the far end of the room. Will could just see a swirling liquid moving slowly behind the glass, thick and viscous. He moved toward it, keeping low. The compass pointed directly at the jar, wobbling only slightly as Will stepped forward. He nearly bumped into something at knee height, and his stomach rolled as he looked down at the dim outline of a coffin-shaped brass box.

The box was so *small.* He knew that he'd been only a child when Murtagh had trapped him there, but the enormity of it only struck him now that he was older, practically towering over it. He couldn't imagine placing a child inside that box, let alone using them to maim another young boy on the king's orders. Perhaps some small part of him had wondered if Murtagh had ever regretted it, but that question died in that room as Will stared at the tiny box on the floor.

Aengus had threatened to trap Will inside it again. It wasn't even protected. If someone else wanted to trap some helpless commoner inside, a woman with illegal magic, a *child,* there would be no one to stop them.

Will glanced at the jar, then down at the box. Luc would forgive him.

Will placed both hands on the box. "Hey." His voice was low and rough, hoarse as though he'd just spent hours screaming in the dark box, fingers clawing uselessly at the sides. "Remember me? You took my magic once. Maybe that connects us. Maybe it's like a memory. So I want you to remember this." He felt the magic filling his skin, growing hot on the brass box. "I don't care if the old god-kings made you. I don't care how powerful you are. I was the last person you used, and I'll be the last person you ever use. You're done. You're just metal now."

The box trembled under his hands, fighting his magic. He could feel the ball beneath the lid like a chain dragging him closer, but he kept his feet planted, fingers curling around the lid.

"You're just metal," he repeated. "You're just a box. No magic will work on you again."

The air around Will grew warm. Steam rose from the stone at his feet, and the box rattled violently as though something were trying to escape through the brass itself. Will held it down, arms straining.

"You're *nothing*," he snarled.

The box went still. Will straightened, and when he let go of the lid, a shadow of his hands stayed on the brass like a brand. The box lay cold and dead on the stone, no longer a tool of the old god-kings and metal mages, but a lump of metal in the shape of a coffin.

He spat on the box and turned away.

The jar on the far shelf gleamed softly, as though it had been waiting for him. Will summoned his magic easily, warming the rings on his fingers.

"Open," he said.

The lid of the jar unscrewed itself and went clattering onto the shelf. Will lifted the jar, surprised to find it cool to the touch, and dipped his hand inside.

He touched something fleshy and soft. It pulsed against his fingers, and when he pulled it out, a heart thumped steadily in his palm.

Luc's heart.

"It's all right," he said. "I have you."

He left the jar where it was. Holding Luc's bare heart in his hand felt unnatural, but he didn't trust anything in that miserable cell, and he'd already lost enough time dealing with the box. He walked briskly past the cramped, cold hallway where Berenger was bound and ascended the stairs, checking the compass on the way up. The needle still wobbled between the heart and where Luc probably was upstairs, but it didn't seem like Luc had moved far. Will pocketed the compass. Blood oozed over the hand holding the heart, dripping over his clothes and spotting the stone stairs.

He was nearly up the lowest flight when he heard someone screaming his name.

It wasn't Luc. He'd heard this voice for most of his life, calling him from across the Westwood estate and over empty fields. It was Ella's voice, high and frightened, but Ella wasn't supposed to be in the palace at all. She was supposed to be with Prince Ramon, keeping him and the wizards distracted. Something must have gone terribly wrong for her to have fled the festival.

"Ella!" Will scrambled up the stairs, desperately holding the heart close to his own chest. He was practically flying, his cloak whipping behind him, fingers slick with blood.

"Will," Ella shouted, as Will rounded the final bend. "Will, don't!"

Will didn't have time to understand Ella's last, agonized plea. He barreled up the landing where he'd left Luc, gasping for breath, his mask hanging off his neck and tangling with his hood, to find Ella standing at the top of the stairs with Ramon's fist in her hair and his sword pressed to her throat. Luc stood before them, hands upraised, but Ramon's face was twisted in unthinking fury.

"I'm sorry," Ella said. "Will, I'm sorry."

"So glad you could join us," Ramon said, his voice cracking dangerously. He yanked Ella's hair, making her wince. "This *bitch* tried to stop me when I saw you and Luc leaving the festival, and I thought, how strange! How strange! But they said it when they introduced her, didn't they? Those creatures that call themselves royalty. She's a *goblin friend.* Both of you traitors, working with the Brightwood, trying to steal *my* Luc away from me."

Will tried to keep the hand holding Luc's heart under the folds of his cloak. "Your Highness, you misunderstand us."

"They aren't betraying you," Luc said.

"They're betraying my father and his treaty, which is close enough." Ramon's eyes were wild with a bright, terrible fire. "It's all right, Luc. I know you couldn't help it. They manipulated you. *You* wouldn't betray me. You love me."

"Let the girl go, Ramon." Luc took a step forward, but Ramon pressed the sword closer to Ella's neck.

"The girl. It's always girls. *Women,*" Ramon spat, "with their softness and their trickery, clawing away at you, trying to take pieces of you, making you *weak.*" He dragged Ella closer to Luc. "That's what they've done to you. My sister, my mother, this *thing.* That abomination behind you. They've weakened you."

"Will isn't," Ella started to say, and grimaced as Ramon pulled her hair again. Will examined the sword. He had to be careful, now that he was holding Luc's heart. The way Luc had described it, just touching it had been enough to twist his mind.

"The sword doesn't want to hurt her," Will whispered under his breath. "It's too dull to pierce the skin."

Ella's pained expression shifted, and she raised a hand to her neck curiously.

"Ramon, if you gave me a moment to explain," Luc begged.

"Stop treating me like a child!" Ramon practically shrieked the words. "You're mine! Father gave you to *me!* They have no right to take you! No right!"

Ella took a deep breath, leaning closer to Ramon as though to ease the pain in her scalp.

"I've had enough," Ramon said. "Luc. You swore you would protect me, so do it! *Will* is trying to steal what's mine. Kill him."

Luc moaned softly, turned on his heel, and drew his sword.

It would have been better if Ramon had forced Luc to want it. If he'd made Luc hate Will, it wouldn't hurt so much to see Luc's sword arcing swiftly toward him. But Ramon had given Luc no such orders. The grief and betrayal was stark in Luc's face, an agony that mirrored Will's, and Will stumbled back to avoid Luc's blow.

Behind Luc, Ella lifted her slippered foot and slammed the heel down on Ramon's boot. The glass pierced soft leather, and Ramon dropped the sword with a howl. Ella threw herself at him, grabbing fistfuls of his hair and dragging her nails down his beautiful face. She wrenched off her other heel and swung her arm back.

"Tell him to stop," she cried, as Will narrowly avoided a thrust from Luc's sword, "or the next one goes in your eye!"

"Will, please," Luc said. He moved slowly, deliberately, as though he were trying with every ounce of strength in his body to resist.

Will knew what he was pleading for. Will had Luc's heart. He could easily force him to stop with a word, but he couldn't speak. He felt frozen, his tongue leaden and slow. Stopping Luc with his heart would make him just another wizard giving him orders, a betrayal too deep to heal. There was only one way Will could get close enough to Luc to fix this.

Luc thrust the weapon toward Will's chest, a straight, clean stroke, and Will raised his arm. A line of pain slid across his forearm as he diverted the sword, and he let out a horrible gasp of air as the blade slid smoothly into his side. Luc's eyes widened in horror, but Will just grabbed the sword with his free hand, pulling Luc closer.

"It's okay," he said. Luc was leaning over him, tears in his lovely violet eyes, long hair falling over his face. "It's going to be okay."

Will ripped the laces of Luc's tunic down with one hand.

"What is he doing?" Ramon cried. "Get *off* me, you *viper!*"

"I love you," Will said. He took Luc's heart in both hands, calling on the magic in his rings, and watched as his fingers sank into the glass over Luc's chest.

Luc stiffened, his gaze going vague. The sword in Will's side was throbbing, but he shoved the pain to the back of his mind as he felt for Luc's brass heart.

"Come to me," he told it. "Come on."

The heart thumped into his right hand, and Will quickly pulled it out, letting it clatter at his feet. Before he could question whether the enchantment on the rings would work, Will gently placed Luc's true heart where the brass one had been.

"Stay there," Will said. He couldn't doubt himself now. He'd come too far. He'd survived Murtagh. He'd enchanted masks and rings and spectacles. He'd broken a piece of machinery from the time of the god-kings. It had all brought him here, holding Luc's heart tenderly in his hands.

The heart pulsed. It knitted itself into Luc's chest, no longer relying on Will to keep it in place, unable to be controlled by wizards or princes.

"There," Will said, drawing his blood-slick hands from Luc's chest. "You belong to Luc now. You're home."

***

*You're home.*

For the first time in twenty years, Prince Lucan of the Brightwood could feel his true heart beating.

His body was on fire. Decades of living in the fog that had consumed his life were stripped away in an instant, laying bare the long years of isolation, picking up after Ramon's tantrums, quiet obedience and forced smiles. He felt as though he'd spent his life underground, and found himself now standing under the beech trees of the Brightwood with a cool wind shaking the high boughs. He was a part of it now; the wind, the trees, the delicate structure of growth and decay.

Will's fingers left streaks of blood on Luc's chest as he collapsed, Luc's sword impaled through his side.

Luc felt everything stronger now. He knew, as he knelt before Will with his heart thumping frantically in his chest, that he loved Will truly, far beyond the thin artifice that had kept him loyal to Ramon. It was a cruel trick that he'd been forced to betray him.

"Will," he said, holding Will up by the shoulders. "I'm so sorry."

"For gods' sake!" Ramon's voice was a strangled shout. "Finish it and get this woman off me!"

Luc turned. Ramon was struggling ineffectively under Ella's onslaught, holding his arms over his face in a weak defense. Ella froze in the midst of reaching for Ramon's eyes, her gaze falling on Luc's chest. She grabbed Ramon's hair with both hands and yanked his head back, holding him still on the steps. With his face no longer hidden by his arms, Ramon finally saw the tatters of Luc's tunic. A pallor fell over his face, terror chasing out his impotent rage.

"Luc," he said, trying to wriggle out of Ella's grip. "Luc, we're brothers. We're *brothers*."

Luc didn't speak. Ramon didn't deserve an explanation. Luc crouched over him, claws extended, watching Ramon's throat work desperately, his mouth open in a broken plea.

"You *loved* me," Ramon whined.

Luc brought his claws down.

He didn't wait for Ramon to die. He left him convulsing on the steps, turning back to Will, who was leaning against the wall. He reached for the brass heart at his feet. He touched it with his fingertips, his face ashen, blood pouring from the blade in his side.

"You can't hurt him anymore," he told the brass heart, as Luc caught him in his arms. "You're nothing. Just metal."

Even in pain, even with his lover's sword impaling his body, Will was keeping Luc safe. Luc steadied him, laying a hand on his sword hilt.

"Will. I'm taking the sword out now," he said slowly.

"Wait!" Ella stepped over Ramon's twitching, gasping body, ripping long swathes of her beautiful gown in both hands. "He'll bleed out if you do that. Let me get behind him and I can staunch the wound."

"Since when..." Will groaned faintly as Ella brushed against him. "Since when do you know about that?"

"I bound a wounded rabbit once," Ella said. "It's probably the same principle."

"Great," Will whispered. He touched the sword, leaving bloody finger marks on the steel. "Steel is for cleansing. For... healing. Fuck. Maybe it'll work. Pull it out slowly."

Luc drew out the sword as gently as possible. Will bit the side of his hand as it pulled free, and Ella hurriedly started wrapping scraps of her dress around his waist. They ran out alarmingly fast, and Ella wasted no time ripping her gown to pieces. It was in shreds by the time they were done, tatters falling about her bare feet.

"Can you stand?" she asked Will.

"Might have to," Will said. He reached for Luc, staggered, and fell against the wall. "Just a moment."

"We don't have one," Ella said. "It's almost midnight, and when Ramon dragged me here, I heard fighting by the gates."

"That must have been Alistair and Kit," Luc said. "Someone saw the guards."

"They were bound to," Will said, trying to stand upright again. Luc gathered him in his arms instead. "I can walk, Luc."

"Walk later," Luc said. He carried Will past Ramon, refusing to look down at the bloody mess he'd once considered his only friend. Ella followed, holding her shredded gown well above her ankles.

There was no sign of Alistair or Kit when they reached the drawbridge. The body of a guard lay a few paces away, already dead, blood staining the earth beneath his tunic.

"Alistair!" The dark swallowed Luc's voice, making it thin and weak. "Kit!"

"We have to go," Ella said. She tugged at Luc's sleeve.

"But they're still out there," Luc said. He looked down at Will. He was still dangerously pale, his breathing shallow. Luc couldn't risk a fight with the guards with Will in this state.

"I'm sorry," Ella said, as though she could sense Luc's thoughts. "Jade's waiting for us."

Luc stared into the darkness, trying to summon Alistair and Kit with his thoughts alone. Above the royal plaza, brilliant illusions of fire bloomed in the night sky.

"Midnight," Will said. The light of the magefire reflected in his eyes. "Time to go."

Luc turned from the palace entrance with a grimace. Ella led them out, her bare feet thumping on the cobbles, her dress floating about her like wisps of cloud in a high wind. Will breathed shallowly in Luc's arms, his gaze fixed on the lights in the sky.

Luc struggled to rein in his emotions as they ran through the dark streets leading from the palace. Grief warred with the heady thrill of freedom. Fury choked him. Dread weighed his limbs like liquid lead. Fear was a copper taste in his mouth, like the blood that had sprayed over his chest when he'd ripped his claws through Ramon's throat.

"Thank the gods," Ella whispered. The goblin carriage waited at the end of the street, horses alert and jittery, figures hanging off the sides and draped over the bench. One jumped down, and Luc was consumed by a sudden rush of relief and aching loss.

"Jade," he said. She turned to look at him, her brows raised. "I can't find Alistair, and Will... Will's hurt." He felt like a child again, running to Jade every time he stumbled or lost something, seeking out the gentle, reliable oldest sister who always knew what to do.

"Just a scratch," Will said. Alara leapt down from the bench, landing as lightly as she would have with her wings to keep her aloft.

"Bring him into the carriage," Jade said. "I'll have my spies look for Alistair." Her gaze flicked down to Luc's chest, her eyes bright. "It's good to have you back."

Luc couldn't find the words to reply, but Jade didn't seem to need them. She kissed Luc's cheek, smiling fondly down at him. Alara helped Will into the carriage, laying him out on one of the benches, while Jade lifted Ella inside. Jade remained outside of the carriage with the others while Alara knelt by Will. The carriage jolted to life, wheels clacking over the cobbles as Alara checked Will's bandages.

"This was well done for an amateur," she said. She looked at Ella. "Was this your work? Watch me while I show you how to do it properly. Ideally, we'd have something to cleanse the wound, but we'll have to make use of what we have."

"Glad I could be a lesson," Will said.

"Don't spend all your energy on being smart," Ella said, but a slight tremor in her voice gave away her concern.

"Can't help it," Will said with a shaky smile. "It comes naturally."

Ella rolled her eyes.

Luc sat with Will, letting him rest his head on his lap and trying not to look at the blood soaking through the scraps of Ella's dress. Will breathed softly, staring up at him.

"How does it feel?" he whispered.

"It's impossible to describe," Luc whispered back. "Why didn't you order me to stop? You had my heart in your hand. You could have done it."

"What do you think I am?" Will asked derisively. "A *wizard?*"

Luc stroked Will's hair.

Something slammed into the side of the carriage, and an arrowhead bursting through the wood. Jade twisted round to shout from the window.

"Looks like someone caught on!" she shouted. "Alara, I need you!"

"One moment!" Alara called. She finished wrapping Will's wound with fresh strips of cloth, then climbed through the window to take Jade's place on the driver's bench. Jade climbed around the carriage, a bow in one hand and a quiver of arrows at her back. She opened the carriage door so that she could brace herself with one foot on the carriage floor. Wind whipped past her, her gaze flicking back and forth in the dark.

"Ella," she called, "hold on to me. I need my hands."

Ella got up nervously and wrapped her arms around Jade's waist. Jade drew the bow smoothly, Ella's ruined dress billowing around her legs. She loosed the arrow.

"There's one," she said. "Hang on tight, sweetheart."

Jade shot arrow after arrow into the darkness while the goblins clinging to the carriage howled and shrieked, sending hapless humans running for their homes. The guards who tried to follow them fell to Jade's arrows, disappearing into the dark as the carriage rolled steadily toward the Brightwood. When they'd finally cleared the city gates, Jade twisted in Ella's arms.

"Thank you," she said, tipping Ella's chin up with a finger. Ella's lips parted softly, and Jade leaned in to kiss her. The wind whirled around them, tossing their hair and teasing the ragged ends of Ella's gown.

Jade broke the kiss with a smile and closed the door. "Keep the boys safe," she said, climbing up the side of the carriage to the roof.

Ella turned slowly and sat down on the carriage floor.

"You're having a busy night," Will said, and winced. "Gods. Can't laugh."

"Be careful," Luc said.

The ride toward the Brightwood felt longer than it probably was. The horses could only gallop for so long before they tired, and when the carriage slowed on the lonely country road, the goblins surrounding the carriage hopped off to keep pace in the high grass. Luc kept thinking that he could hear the call of horns from the royal guards, but with half of them taken out by Kit's poisoned wine, they were probably in a state of chaos. Luc sent a silent prayer to the gods that Alistair and Kit had found a way to escape.

They were well into Westwood when Alara stopped the carriage. She opened the door wide, helping Luc lift Will down to the ground. Will swayed, clinging to Alara for balance, until Luc pulled him into his arms again.

"This is where I leave you," Alara said. Jade handed a mask to Luc, and Ella and Will fumbled to put their masks back on. "I'll try to keep the queen distracted, but she'll learn the truth soon enough. Be careful, and move swiftly. I'll find you again." She placed a hand on Luc's cheek, then climbed back into the carriage.

Will helped strap the mask around Luc's head as they walked through the overgrown weeds and flowers. The wind was gentler now, blowing softly at their backs as though it were pushing them toward the Brightwood. In the distance, the carriage headed toward the gates, a silvery sphere carried forth in the moonlight.

There were no thorns in the woods when they reached the border. Luc hesitated there, his heart thrumming in his chest. If he were still bearing his brass heart, he'd be dead as soon as he stepped under the trees. He turned to look back at Morvane, the country roads disappearing behind long patches of farmland.

Will leaned his head against Luc's shoulder, and Luc turned back to the forest.

He passed under the gently swaying canopy. Nothing happened. His heart kept beating. Will kept breathing, safe in Luc's arms. Soft grass brushed Luc's boots, and in the distance, he could see the lights in the trees of the Brightwood.

"Olven," Will said suddenly, stirring uncomfortably as Luc walked. "I can't forget. I have to tell him I made it back."

"We can't linger." Jade kept her voice soft. "Even stopping for a healer would be a risk."

"But we *will* stop for one," Luc said.

"I promised," Will insisted.

Jade's hard tone softened slightly, though it was hard to see her expression through the mask she wore. "I'll send a messenger," she said. "For now, we keep moving."

The woods gradually opened up before them, and as Luc stepped out into the safety of the Brightwood, his breath hitched. Tiny lights hung in the high boughs overlooking the small village on the border, twinkling like stardust. Even the air smelled different, crisper, cleaner, stirring a memory that Luc could no longer grasp. He stood there in shock, mesmerized.

Will reached up and gently removed Luc's mask. The lights shone brighter in his eyes, and when he smiled, Luc's heart seemed to leap in his chest.

"Now that I have my heart back," Luc said, "I need to tell you something."

Luc leaned down to catch Will's mouth in a kiss. Will slid his fingers through Luc's hair, stroking it gently, and sighed as Luc drew back.

"I love you, Will Fletcher," Luc said. "Truly. With all the strength in the heart you returned to me."

"And I love you, Prince Lucan of the Brightwood," Will said, and kissed him back. "Now let's go home. Wherever home is."

"It's a good thing that I've managed to run off with the best wizard in Morvane, then," Luc said, carrying Will under the glowing boughs of his homeland. "Between the two of us, I'm sure we'll find a way there."

# Epilogue

It was a beautiful summer morning, and Will Fletcher was making horseshoes.

The small smithy was new, tucked away in the corner of Crown Princess Alara's holdings by the coast. The starlit forests that gave the Brightwood its name were a narrow green line on the horizon, and a warm breeze swept in from the sea, swirling into eddies of dust at the door. Heat filled the smithy, dampening Will's hair and making his tunic stick to his skin.

A shadow crossed the doorway, and Will looked up from his work. Olven peered inside, dressed in a loose woolen sweater despite the heat, his feathers rising softly. He'd been staying in Alara's summer villa for three days now, their first true visitor since the night of the festival. The news of Will's injury must have rattled him, because he'd arrived with enough knitted sweaters to outfit an army.

"Horseshoes?" Olven asked. "No enchanted swords? No daggers?"

"Some of the horseshoes are enchanted," Will said, tapping the last horseshoe into shape.

Olven leaned against the doorway. "And you're content with that?"

Will glanced at the window. He could just see the ocean through it, a long stretch of endless blue. He hadn't cast any powerful spells since he'd returned Luc's heart. It wasn't that he was afraid of it. He just didn't see the point in pushing his magic any further than necessary.

Princess Alara hadn't been pleased to hear it. She'd passed through in secret a few weeks after Jade had established Will, Luc, and Ella in Alara's villa. Will had been recovering slowly under Luc's watchful eye, and he'd been surprised to find Alara seeking *him* out instead of her brother.

"We aren't at war yet," Alara had said, sitting awkwardly at the kitchen table with her hands clasped before her. "But you should know that it's coming. The king of Morvane doesn't want to admit what he did to Luc, and my mother doesn't want to admit that her daughters staged a rescue, but the king claims that we killed Faramond and conspired with Telmar to abduct the boy Luc calls Kit."

Will had expected that. The last time Jade had heard from her spies, she'd told Luc that Kit and Alistair were safe, but beyond her reach. Telmar seemed like a good destination for a prince on the run, but blaming the Brightwood was easier.

"I came to you because Luc told me what you did in the palace," Alara had said. "Not just with his heart, but with the elven device."

Will had shifted uncomfortably, looking down at the worn table.

"You do understand that it's supposed to be impossible," Alara had said. "Mages have tried and failed for centuries to destroy elven artifacts, but they're impervious to our magic. With a mage like you on our side to who can enchant a way through the border and break the tools of the god-kings, we can start this war with an advantage."

"We could," Will had said, pushing away from the table, "but we won't."

Alara had gone dangerously quiet. "You are still a human on goblin land, Will. This can change other goblins' perceptions of you for the better."

"I'm not a war mage," Will had said, his voice low but firm. "I'm done being a tool. If you want me to destroy something like that box for you, I have no objections. Those things shouldn't be out in the open for people to use. If you want someone to shoe your horses or fix a door hinge, I'll be here. But I'm no one's war mage."

"It seems a waste."

"Maybe," Will had said. "Maybe."

Now, Will looked at the bucket of horseshoes ready for shaping and smiled at Olven.

"Someone once told me that people will always need horseshoes," he said. "Perhaps he was right."

"He sounds like a clever one," Olven said. "Very wise, very knowledgeable."

"Humble, too," Will said, and Olven clicked his beak in a laugh.

"You'll do very well here," he said. "The sea isn't to my taste, but it agrees with you." His feathers ruffled in amusement. "As does love, it seems."

"Oh, gods," Will said, and Olven clicked his beak again.

"It's true," Olven said. "There is a glow to you that wasn't there before. A warmth. You are still short and disagreeable, yes, but not *as* disagreeable. It is a small victory."

"Thanks, Olven," Will said dryly. "I'll meet you and the others at lunch when I'm done here, all right?"

"Meet your fellow first," Olven said. "He's waiting for you by the river." He walked off, chuckling to himself as Will's face turned even redder than the forge.

He took his time to clean, anxious to keep up the forge that had clearly been a gift from Luc's sisters. Customers from the village were rare, but Jade had spread a rumor that a human from Telmar had settled there with his sister, and he didn't want someone stumbling in to find the place filthy.

Only when he was satisfied did he head out onto the sloping hillside of Alara's villa, breathing in the breeze rising through the wildflowers. Below him, a river twisted slowly toward the marshland by the sea, with cool, clear springs dotted throughout the villa grounds. Will approached the one he and Luc liked best, a small spring surrounded by smooth, flat stones.

Luc was sunning himself on one of the stones when Will arrived. He'd blossomed since they'd left Morvane, his confidence no longer checked by forced humility and subservience, and he smiled wickedly at Will as he reached the spring. His tunic was discarded in the grass, exposing the glass over his chest. His heart beat faster when he met Will's gaze.

"Someone's been working," he said, eyeing Will's bare shoulders and dirty tunic. Will tugged the tunic over his head and let it drop. "Olven stopped by. He had questions about you. Mostly if you've been eating and drinking enough."

"Gods, he'd have me rolling and sloshing around like a barrel if he had his way." Will stepped out of his trousers and eased into the spring with a groan. Luc slipped in after him, claws scraping the stone as he dropped into the water.

"Have I ever mentioned that I like how flushed you get after you've been working?" Luc asked. He pressed Will against the stone. Will's toes only just touched the soft sand at the bottom of the spring, and the cool water swirled around him as Luc pushed his legs apart with a thigh. "Heat touches you so quickly. Sometimes I just stand by the door and watch you."

"I could always teach you, if you're so eager to join me in the smithy." Will gasped as Luc ground his thigh between Will's legs. "You can make nails."

Luc had been anything but idle since they'd fled Morvane. He seemed ready to try anything, picking up new hobbies and skills like a starving man alone at a feast, just as delighted with failure as he was with success. He seemed pleased to have the *chance* to fail, excited by the prospect of choice alone.

"I prefer watching," Luc said, leaning down to kiss him. He slid his sharp claws up Will's back, making him shudder. "The way your muscles tense when you swing the hammer..."

"If you make this a metaphor for your cock, I'm leaving," Will said, smiling into another kiss. "I'm going to live in the forest and never touch a hammer again."

"Even this one?" Luc asked, guiding Will's hand to his cock.

"All right," Will said, twisting around, "I'm off to the forest. Time to eat acorns and speak to squirrels for the rest of my life."

Luc laughed, grasping for Will as he crawled out of the spring. He finally caught him on one of the rocks on the bank, pinning Will beneath him.

"You win," Luc said. "No more metaphors."

"Thank gods," Will said, and wrapped his arms around Luc's shoulders.

They kissed softly in the sunlight, basking in the luxury of no longer needing to hide behind enchanted locks and barred doors. Luc trailed kisses down Will's neck, his stomach, his thighs, parting them to bring Will to a toe-clenching rush of pleasure.

"Gods," Luc said, breathless and dark-eyed with desire. "I still can't believe it sometimes. That we're here. That we did it. That this is *my* heart beating faster every time I see you."

"I know." Will sat up to kiss him again, tasting himself on his lips. He straddled Luc, grinding down against his hard cock. "You'd know the same if you could see mine."

He took one of Luc's hands and pressed it against his chest. Luc splayed his fingers out, feeling for Will's heartbeat, his eyes half-lidded.

Will rode him like that, with Luc's hand over his heart, their gazes fixed on each other as a cool wind swept over the hills from the sea. He moved slowly, quietly, sinking into a heavy warmth that suffused his limbs, Luc's cock filling him as Will's heart beat against Luc's hand. When Luc came, it was with Will's name on his lips, and he lifted his hand to cup Will's face as they kissed.

"I love you," he whispered. Luc never seemed to tire of saying it, repeating it in the quiet of early morning, over dinner, while they climbed down the steep cliffside to the sea. Will could tell that he meant it every time.

They lingered by the spring, wrapped in each other's arms, until they heard voices calling from the villa. Will spotted Ella before she saw them, catching a glimpse of a long white gown fluttering in the breeze. He dressed quickly, slinging on his discarded tunic back-to-front.

"She'll notice that," Luc said, smiling as he helped Will adjust his tunic.

"And she'll quietly judge me for it all afternoon," Will said, also smiling. Ella was still far too meddlesome, but he didn't mind it so much anymore. When Ella waved at them from the top of the hill, Will waved back. He would have never done that in Westwood, hiding from the shadow of Murtagh and his mother.

"You two took your time," Ella said when Will and Luc reached the villa. She gave Will a knowing look. "Did you have a productive morning at the smithy?"

"Don't," Will said. Ella laughed. She laughed a great deal, lately.

Olven was already in the kitchen, plating a massive lunch on the kitchen table. Will was unsurprised to find Jade already lounging in her usual seat. She was always stopping by to check on Luc, drawing him away for long, quiet talks on the hillside. She also happened to stay exclusively in Ella's room.

"You'll spoil us, Olven," Ella said, standing on her tiptoes to kiss him on the cheek.

"I rather think I am permitted to try," Olven said. "Sit. You are being *served* today, young lady, which means no cleaning, no tidying up, and absolutely no *helping.*"

"I will do my best to reject my better nature," Ella said, sitting next to Jade. Will and Luc sat together on the opposite side of the table, Luc with a hand on Will's back. "You know," Ella said, "Jade invited me to stay with her in the South."

Will froze in the middle of accepting a plate from Olven. "She... she did?"

"Don't look so stricken," Ella said. She took a bite of her herb-encrusted potatoes. "I want to stay for a while longer."

"You don't have to deny her on our behalf," Luc said, glancing at Jade warily.

"I'm not," Ella said. She moved her chair so Olven could sit on her other side. "I quite enjoy Jade's company."

"Do you?" Jade asked, smiling into her cup.

Ella blushed a deep pink. "Of course. You're lovely and exciting and a little frightening, and you... you're so very... so very *tall.*" She swirled her fork around her plate idly, staring into it as though searching for the words. "But I only just started to get to know you, Will. *Really* know you," she added, looking up at him. "I'd like for something to actually feel like home before I have to leave it. Does that make sense?"

"I think so," Will said. He looked around the table. They were an odd group, marked by grief and loss, their histories long and complex, yet somehow new again.

"I wouldn't mind you staying for a while," Luc said. "One can never have too many sisters."

"Or brothers," Ella said. She reached across the table, and Will leaned forward to squeeze her hand. "I know it's been fraught, but I'm still glad I met you, Will. And you, Luc, and Jade." She turned to Olven with a smile. "And you've taken such good care of me, and we've only just met."

"Will loves you," Olven said, patting her briskly on the shoulder. "That's enough for me. Now, you will all eat before you faint of malnutrition. Especially you, William."

Will raised his fork in a mock salute. "Yes, sir."

The kitchen fell into its usual din of forks and chatter, punctuated by Olven's clicking laughter. Will let himself sink into it. Theirs was a small family, an unruly mix of goblins and humans, princes, bandits, and commoners, but it was the best family Will had ever known.

Luc slyly lifted Will's hand and kissed it.

"I love you," Will whispered, soft under another one of Olven's rambling stories.

Luc pulled Will's hand to his chest, covering it with his palm. When he spoke, his words came to Will like an incantation, a prayer.

"With all my heart."

The End.

# About the Author

Fae Loxley is a Queer trans man who loves folklore, music, and picking up too many hobbies at once. He grew up in Florida, where he collected increasingly bizarre life experiences before running off to the foothills. He currently lives with his wife and a collection of very strange cats. You can usually find him writing with the worst posture on earth at five in the morning.

www.ingramcontent.com/pod-product-compliance
Lightning Source LLC
LaVergne TN
LVHW090559110826
845146LV00001B/191

* 9 7 9 8 9 9 4 8 6 2 6 1 2 *